Before We Kiss

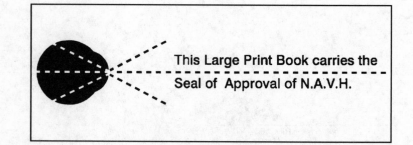

This Large Print Book carries the
Seal of Approval of N.A.V.H.

BEFORE WE KISS

SUSAN MALLERY

WHEELER PUBLISHING
A part of Gale, Cengage Learning

GALE
CENGAGE Learning·

Farmington Hills, Mich • San Francisco • New York • Waterville, Maine
Meriden, Conn • Mason, Ohio • Chicago

GALE
CENGAGE Learning®

LIBRARY OF CONGRESS CATALOGING-IN-PUBLICATION DATA

Mallery, Susan.
    Before we kiss / Susan Mallery.
        pages cm — (A fool's gold romance) (Wheeler Publishing large print hardcover)
    ISBN 978-1-4104-6916-8 (hardback) — ISBN 1-4104-6916-6 (hardcover)
    1. Dysfunctional families—Fiction. 2. Large type books. I. Title.
PS3613.A453B44 2014
813'.6—dc23   2014009420

Published in 2014 by arrangement with Harlequin Books S. A.

Printed in the United States of America
1 2 3 4 5 6 7 18 17 16 15 14

To 2013 Fool's Gold Co-Head
Cheerleader Angela. Knowing you is a
joy. I admire your strength and your
optimism in the face of obstacles. You
brighten every life you touch and the
world is a better place because you are in
it. Thank you for your friendship. This one
is for you. Armadillo.

Being the "mom" of an adorable, spoiled little dog, I know the joy that pets can bring to our lives. Animal welfare is a cause I have long supported. For me that means giving to Seattle Humane. At their 2013 Tuxes and Tails fund-raiser, I offered "Your pet in a romance novel."

In this book you will meet a wonderful little Pomeranian named Caramel. Her owner was one of two auction winners and this is her story.

One of the things that makes writing special is interacting in different ways with people. Some I talk to for research. Some are readers who want to talk characters and story lines, and some are fabulous pet parents. Caramel's dad is a special guy who loves his little girl so much. When he told me about her, she came alive. I hope I have captured her wonderful spirit in this book.

My thanks to him, to Caramel and to the amazing people at Seattle Humane (www .seattlehumane.org). Because every pet deserves a loving family.

CHAPTER ONE

"Returning to the scene of the crime?" Dellina Hopkins asked as she stared at the dark-haired man standing on her porch. She supposed the polite response to his presence was to invite him in. And she would . . . in a minute. But first she was going to make him work for it.

Sam Ridge, all six feet of dark-eyed, arrogant handsomeness, narrowed his gaze. "You're not going to make this easy, are you?" he asked.

Dellina smiled. "No. Would you, if you were me?"

He surprised her by flashing a grin. "No, I wouldn't."

"An honest man." She bumped the door open wider with her hip and stepped back to let him in. "It's a miracle."

He moved into the house. Dellina let the screen door slam into place, but left the thick wooden door open. It was summer in

9

Fool's Gold, and plenty warm. The breeze would be nice. Plus — and this was the part she would never admit to Sam — having the door open meant they weren't totally *alone.* Okay, they were alone, but it didn't feel so intimate. And based on what had happened the last time they'd been together in this house, that was a good thing.

Sam paused in the middle of her living room, as if not sure where to go. His head turned slightly and she had a feeling he was glancing down the hall — toward her bedroom. No doubt remembering what had happened some five months ago.

Dellina wanted to say it hadn't been her fault — that everyone was allowed to be stupid on Valentine's Day. Or in her case, on Valentine's Day night. Only she had known exactly what she was doing and it had been as wonderful and disastrous as anyone could have imagined. Now both she and Sam were going to have to deal with the consequences.

He turned to face her, then motioned to the sofa. "We should probably have a seat."

"Will that make things easier for you?" she asked.

"If I say yes, will you sit?"

"Probably."

"Then yes. It makes things easier."

Dellina settled in one of the club chairs while Sam took the sofa.

He moved with controlled power. It was the former professional athlete thing, she thought, watching him sit down. At the risk of sounding like a groupie, she had firsthand knowledge that the man knew how to use his body. Of course, the last time she'd been in his presence, she hadn't been interested in sitting. Or talking. But then neither had he. They'd practically tumbled over each other in their race to her bedroom. He'd —

Dellina pushed the very visceral memories away. Yes, Sam had been delicious in bed. But then things had gone downhill. She needed to remember what was important. He was here about a job. Not his unrequited lust for her. Based on how he'd been avoiding her for the past several months, when it came to her, he was plenty requited.

But he was also in a bit of a pickle.

The old-fashioned phrase made her want to smile. Yup, Sam needed her. Not in a delicious *take me now* kind of way, but for business. She was a party planner and he wanted to plan a really big business event. He was stuck and she was his way out. Sometimes, not often, but sometimes, circumstances went her way. So after five months of being able to ignore her and that

11

single night, he'd been forced to face her. Was it so very wrong of her to enjoy the moment? She thought perhaps not.

She rested her hands flat on her thighs and looked at him. "How can I help you?"

His dark gaze settled on her face. "Really? You're not going to admit you know what any of this is about?"

She blinked deliberately, then opened her eyes wide. "When you made your appointment to speak with me, you didn't mention a subject." Of course she knew why he was here, but again, a little emotional torture seemed the right kind of payback.

A muscle twitched in his jaw. "All right. We'll play this your way. I'm Sam Ridge. I'm a partner at Score."

She grinned. "I know who you are, Sam. We don't have to pretend that much. Just tell me what you want and we'll move on from there."

He swore under his breath. "You're friends with Taryn. You've done work for her. How long are you going to punish me?"

He was right about Taryn. She and Dellina were friends and had worked together several times. Score, the PR firm in question, had moved to Fool's Gold just after the first of the year. Three of the partners were former NFL players and Taryn was the glue that held the company together.

"I haven't completely decided how long you should be punished," she admitted, wondering if batting her eyes again would be too over-the-top.

He sighed heavily. "Fine. We'll do this your way. Now that we've moved our business here, my partners and I want to have a big party for our clients. We've booked a hotel, but that's as far as the planning has gotten."

"A party," she breathed, and pressed her hand to her chest. "That sounds really nice."

In truth, being a neurosurgeon or the person who used to land the space shuttle probably made the top-ten list of jobs designed to give a person an ulcer. Sam would guess whoever was in charge of the ball dropping in Times Square on New Year's Eve probably had a few sleepless nights. But he would add that being a kicker for an NFL team had its moments of stress. When he'd been with the L.A. Stallions, he'd been responsible for twenty-six wins, including three during play-off games and one Super Bowl victory. He knew what it was like to have everyone watching him, both in person and on TV, and have his job performance critiqued endlessly.

He'd always known the outcome the instant his foot connected with the ball and he was famous for turning away and letting the sounds from the crowd tell him if he was right. He was used to pressure. He'd lived it and breathed it. But he'd never faced down anyone like Dellina Hopkins before, and the worst part about it was, she was right to give him a hard time.

Sam shook his head. "Okay," he said. "I give. I was wrong."

Her brown eyes twinkled. "Wrong about what?"

"That night. Leaving the way I did. It was just . . ." He motioned toward the hallway. "Those dresses and that list. All of it. I'm not looking to get married."

"Neither am I."

"You're the one with a room full of wedding gowns."

Her full lips pressed together. Sam tried not to notice, but her mouth was one of the first things that had caught his attention, back on Valentine's Day.

He'd been staying at Ronan's Lodge for a few weeks, until escrow closed on his new place. He'd gone down to the bar for a drink only to realize it was Valentine's Day and the place was crawling with couples. As he'd recently sworn off women — again —

he'd started to turn around to go back to his room.

But before he could safely escape, he'd spotted Dellina. She'd been with friends. They were laughing and talking. No one had noticed him. She'd been pretty enough, but then she'd smiled and it was like getting kicked in the gut — and he was a man who knew the power of a good kick. He'd sent over a tray of drinks for the table, they'd invited him to join them and an hour later he and Dellina had been having dinner together.

Later, when he'd kissed her, he'd discovered her mouth had been as exciting and intriguing as he'd hoped. She'd invited him home, he'd said yes and the rest had been incredible. Until he'd gotten up in the night and found himself in a nightmare.

He'd spent the past five months avoiding her. Tough to do in a town the size of Fool's Gold. The situation had been complicated by the fact that he'd enjoyed her company and had really wanted to see her again.

Now that his company needed her services, he'd been forced to suck it up. So here he was. Being tortured for sport. Kenny and Jack would point out there was no other reason to torment anyone.

Dellina rose. She was about five-five, with

all the expected curves. When he saw her around — because *wanting* to avoid her and being able to do it were two different things — she was usually in dresses or suits. Today she had on jeans and a frilly sleeveless thing that shouldn't have been sexy and yet was. Looking at her bare arms made him remember the rest of her bare, which was what had led to the problem between them in the first place.

Damn, he should never have gotten out of bed today. Or moved to Fool's Gold. Or joined Score for that matter. Or been born.

"Stand up," she said.

He did.

She walked up to him and held out her hand. "We're starting over. I'm Dellina Hopkins. I own a party planning business."

He didn't know which tack she was taking now, but figured he didn't have a lot of choice in the matter. Time was ticking and he was desperate.

"Sam Ridge. My company is a PR firm."

They shook hands. The second her fingers closed around his he felt heat. His gaze immediately settled on her full lips and he remembered he hadn't had nearly enough time with them. Or any of her. It was just once she'd gotten naked, he hadn't been sure which part of her to enjoy first. Then

16

the nightmare had started.

She withdrew her hand and dropped it to her side.

"Well, Sam, like many small businesses, mine is based in my home. This house I rent has three bedrooms. I sleep in one and I work out of one and that leaves a spare bedroom. Follow me, please."

She led the way down the hall. He hesitated. He had a good idea where they were going and it was not a place any man would want to revisit. What it came down to was how much he needed her. And he needed her a lot.

She paused outside a closed bedroom door. *The* closed bedroom door.

"So my friend Isabel owns a store in town called Paper Moon," Dellina told him. "She sells wedding gowns. Last fall she decided to expand the business to include other kinds of clothing. She leased the space next door and started remodeling. As you can imagine, it was a big project. Because of the construction, she lost some of her storage space. Now, the average wedding gown is a pretty special item. So when one stores them, one can't simply leave them anywhere. They need to be safe and temperature controlled."

The pieces were starting to fall into place.

Sam remembered getting up after making love with Dellina. He'd still been shell-shocked by the heat they'd generated and very much looking forward to a second act. Only on the way back from the bathroom, he'd made a wrong turn. Instead of walking back into her bedroom, he'd found himself staring at what looked like rows and rows of wedding gowns.

Worse, on the wall had been a dry-erase board with a header that read Ten Ways to Get Him to Propose.

He had, understandably, freaked. He'd found his way back to her room, pulled on his clothes and fled. From then until now, he hadn't spoken a word to Dellina. He'd avoided her, he'd avoided anything to do with her and he'd never allowed himself to think about that night. Because if he did, he would find himself wanting her again. And with his luck with women, it was important to stay with those who were completely sane.

Which it appeared Dellina just might be.

She opened the door. He instinctively stiffened and saw they were still there. Racks holding covered white gowns. Like plastic aliens, hanging and shrouded, waiting to be returned to the mother ship.

"Isabel pays me to store her dresses," Dellina said. "I would do it for free, but she insists on a small monthly payment. These are not my dresses."

"Okay." He tried to adjust his collar only to realize that his shirt wasn't buttoned all the way and any pressure he felt was the result of being an idiot.

He cleared his throat. "So, ah, that clears up the problem with the wedding dresses. What about that?"

He pointed to the dry-erase board. It still stated Ten Ways to Get Him to Propose, but there weren't any suggestions by the numbers.

Dellina sighed and sagged back against the wall. "It's Fayrene."

He raised his eyebrows.

"My younger sister," she clarified. "Fayrene met Ryan last spring. They fell in love, but she didn't want to get married because she wanted to focus on her career. Ryan was fine with that and they agreed to wait four years."

"So what's the problem?"

"She's changed her mind and wants him to propose now."

He waited, knowing there had to be more.

"Ryan isn't getting the message." Dellina rubbed her temples. "Probably because she hasn't told him. Fayrene doesn't want to *tell*

19

Ryan she's changed her mind. That wouldn't be romantic. She wants him to guess on his own."

"That's not going to happen," Sam told her. "If Ryan loves Fayrene, he's going to respect her wishes no matter how much he wants to get married sooner. This isn't a winning strategy."

"Thanks for your insight. I happen to agree with everything you've said, but unless you want to take that up with Fayrene, you're telling the wrong person. My point is, the list isn't about me."

Dellina faced him. "Look, Sam, I know you have no reason to believe me, but I don't bring home guys I just met. Ever. Last Valentine's Day was the first time I'd done anything like that."

She kept talking but he stopped listening long enough to revel in the fact that she'd picked him for her first one-night stand. Okay, it wasn't up there with curing a disease, but still, nice to know. He returned his attention to her.

". . . and when you took off, I couldn't figure out what had happened. Then I remembered this room and I knew you'd freaked."

"Understandably," he added.

"Yes. It is a bit off-putting. But you could

have asked me what was going on."

He thought about the other women who had been in his life. His family. If Dellina knew about all that, she wouldn't be expecting a rational response. But she didn't know any of it and he preferred it that way.

"You're right," he told her. "I should have asked. I reacted. It was late and we'd had sex and this room scared the hell out of me."

She smiled. "You run fast."

"I've had training."

Her smile widened, drawing his attention to her mouth. "You've done a good job avoiding me. Fool's Gold isn't that big."

"I noticed. You're in a lot of places. You didn't make it easy."

"I didn't want to," she admitted.

"Then you must have been happy to find out about the party."

Her expression turned impish. "A little."

Because getting the party together had fallen onto him. Normally he would have simply hired someone. But the only party planner in town was Dellina. So he'd put off dealing with her as long as he could.

"Now that you've had your fun at my expense," he told her, "there's still a problem to solve."

"Right. Score is putting on a party for its best clients. Three days of fun and frolic."

"Frolic? Did you really just say that?"

She pushed off the wall and walked across the hall. "You know I did. Come on. Let's go talk about how much extra you're going to have to pay me to pull this all together in four weeks."

Dellina was more relaxed having Sam around than she would have thought. Now that they'd dealt with the past and the awkwardness of that night, they could get down to business.

He followed her into her office. Unfortunately she hadn't been prepared for visitors so there were stacks of papers everywhere. She wanted to point out that usually she went to clients' offices or the venue, but knew that one of the key rules of business was not to apologize unnecessarily. There was plenty of time for that if she actually messed up.

She reached for a pile of papers on a chair at the same time Sam did. His hand settled on top of hers. Instinctively, she looked at him and saw his gaze locked with hers. Probably because of the roaring heat, not to mention sparks, flaring from that single point of contact. Unless only she was feeling the attraction, in which case he was probably wondering what on earth was

22

wrong with her.

She pulled back, as did he, and the pile of papers thudded to the floor.

Dellina stared at the mess. "Okay," she said, circling around the desk. "Leave them. They can't fall any farther."

Her office was in the smallest of the three bedrooms. It was maybe ten-by-ten, with her big desk in the middle. There were a couple of chairs, two file cabinets, corkboard on one wall, a window and a long table, which she mostly used to stack yet more piles. One of these days she really had to come up with a filing system.

She sat down and reached for a folder. She colored-coded her projects and the Score party was going to be crimson. One of the L.A. Stallions colors. Something that made her smile even if no one else noticed.

"About the party," she began, and picked up a pad of paper. "What are you looking for?"

"Taryn must have told you something."

"She did, but I want to make sure I understand what you're expecting. So you tell me." She smiled. "Don't worry. I won't get bored if it's a repeat."

"How reassuring." He leaned back in his chair. "We're inviting twenty couples for a total of forty adults. Between them they'll be bringing twelve children. Ages six to thirteen."

She began to write.

"Our clients include sports celebrities, a company that manufactures rum and a jet time-share."

She looked up. "A what?"

"A jet time-share. Private jets?"

"I know what they are."

"With a time-share, you buy hours rather than having to own a whole plane. There's an annual membership fee. You can buy a hundred hours, two hundred. Whatever you need."

She supposed that owning only part of a jet was better than having to pay for the entire thing. If one were in the position to worry about that sort of thing. She didn't fly much, but when she did, she looked for a bargain online.

"Another client is an international head-hunter." He paused, as if waiting for a question.

"I know what that is," she told him. "They fill executive positions for large companies."

"Very good."

There was going to be a lot of money in the room, she thought as she took more notes. Not a big surprise. The owners of Score were rich, successful guys. Or in

24

Taryn's case, a rich, successful woman. They would attract like clients. She wondered why they'd chosen to settle in Fool's Gold. A quiet, family oriented town with an obsession with festivals. According to Taryn, the guys had been the ones to push for the move. Which made Dellina wonder if they had been trying to get *to* something or *away* from something.

Her gaze returned to Sam. He was just over six feet, with broad shoulders and a lean, muscled build. As a kicker, he wouldn't need to be huge. Jack and Kenny were physically bigger. While she preferred Sam's physique, she would ignore his hunky maleness and the recent sparkage and remember this job was a big deal for her. She was going to dazzle the partners and come away with both a healthier checkbook balance and a kick-ass recommendation.

"The party starts Friday afternoon and goes until Sunday afternoon," he said. "We've got a block of rooms up at the ski lodge."

"How many rooms?" she asked. "Also, what about meeting rooms and other facilities?"

"I have that information back at the office. I'll email it to you."

"Great. I'll need to see copies of the

contracts, as well. So I can review what they're expecting and what you're expecting."

His mouth tightened. "I reserved some rooms," he told her. "There's no contract."

She made a few more notes and told herself not to judge. She was the party professional, not him. "I'll take care of that." She'd learned to get everything in writing. That way the only surprises were good ones. "You'll need activities, meals and goodie bags. Do you want a separate track for the kids? I'm guessing the parents would enjoy alone time, at least part of it."

"Sure."

"Lectures? Musical entertainment? Do you want sitters for the kids?"

"I have no idea."

Which meant he and the other partners hadn't discussed anything past "Hey, let's have a party." The good news was there wasn't a lot to undo. The bad news was the tight time frame.

"We have just over four weeks to pull this all together," she said, turning her attention to him, which was hardly difficult duty. Sam's features were chiseled, his dark eyes intense. He looked like a model for one of those moody fragrances for guys. And sitting oh-so-close. Not that she was going to

26

react. They were working together now. In business. Which meant what had happened between them before was interesting but not relevant.

"I'm finishing up another project this week, then you can have me full-time until the weekend of the party," she told him.

One eyebrow rose slightly as he nodded. "We're going to need all your attention on the event."

"How much do you want to be a part of the decision making?"

"Run everything by me. We can set up regular meetings or you can simply drop by Score. I'll make myself available."

"We'll do both," she said, writing more on her growing to-do list. "Okay — contracts for the rooms and figuring out a schedule will be my top priorities. I bill by the hour. There will be deposits on some items, but because of the tight time frame, others will have to be paid for outright. I prefer to run all the invoices through my office so I know what you were charged."

"Not a problem. When you come by the offices, I'll give you an up-front retainer. This party is going to cost a lot. I don't want you to stretch your cash flow on our account."

"Thank you," she said, thinking he'd been

just as thoughtful during their lone intimate encounter. He'd . . .

No, she told herself firmly. That was not going to happen again. Nor was she going to get lost in remembering how he'd touched her or kissed her or . . .

"I should have enough to get started on all this," she said, putting down her pen. "Let's meet in a couple of days and I'll have more details worked out."

"Sounds like a plan."

They both rose and she walked him to the front door. For a second she wondered what would have happened between them if he hadn't gone into the wrong bedroom that night. If he'd made his way back to her.

Probably no difference at all, she told herself firmly as they said goodbye. He was a big-time ex-jock and she was a small-town girl. She doubted a guy like him was looking for something serious, and she wasn't, either. What happened made for a funny story and nothing else. But, she admitted after he'd left, it was sure fun to think about.

CHAPTER TWO

Three hours later Dellina had the rough outline of a plan for the weekend party. She'd already done some preliminary work, but knowing how many people were coming, and the number and ages of the children, made a difference in what she was going to suggest everyone do. She'd made appointments at the resort and arranged for tasting menus.

She glanced at the clock, then stood and left her office. After grabbing her bag, she walked out of the house and started for the center of town.

Fool's Gold was set in the foothills of the Sierra Nevada. The town was at an altitude of about twenty-five hundred feet, which meant there were four definite seasons. Just one of the things she loved about living here. While tourists were the main source of income, there were plenty of small businesses in town, along with a big casino-hotel complex on the outskirts of town and a new outlet mall. To the north was a facility that constructed wind turbines and to the west were lots of vineyards.

Dellina and her sisters had been born and raised here. Dellina had briefly thought about moving to a bigger town but had quickly realized she was a hometown girl at heart. Sure, growing her business would be easier somewhere else, but easy wasn't always right. Her folks had taught her that.

She turned on Fourth and saw the sign for Brew-haha up ahead. Taryn and Larissa had arranged for a coffee date the second she'd told them about her scheduled meeting with Sam. No doubt they wanted details. Dellina was prepared to say everything had gone well. She wasn't going to confess to any tingles. That would be embarrassing for all of them.

As she approached the coffee shop, she saw a tall curvy redhead pacing along the sidewalk. Bailey Voss wore a navy dress and jacket, along with sensible navy heels. A little on the business side for her. Realizing what the professional dress meant, Dellina hurried toward her.

"Is it today?" she asked by way of greeting.

Bailey turned toward her and nodded as

she pressed a hand to her stomach. "In about half an hour. I got ready too early and then . . . I was afraid to stay home, but once I left, I didn't know what to do with myself."

Dellina turned the other woman toward Brew-haha. "Come inside. We'll distract you until it's time."

"Thanks," Bailey said, then bit her lower lip. "Just don't be so entertaining that I forget where I'm supposed to be."

"We'll set an alarm," Dellina promised, and guided the other woman into the store.

Brew-haha was a bright, cheerful place with small tables by the big windows. There were the usual coffee and tea drinks, along with pastries. Dellina spotted Taryn and Larissa right away. They'd already collected their lattes and were seated.

Taryn, one of the partners at Score, was in her mid-thirties. Tall with long dark hair and violet-blue eyes, she dressed as if she was a high-fashion model. Today Taryn had on a fitted jacket over a tight skirt. Her heels were at least four inches high; her bag was a leather-and-snakeskin Hobo. Dellina would guess that the combined cost of the outfit would be about the same as a decent used car.

In contrast Larissa wore a brightly colored

T-shirt and yoga pants. Her long blond hair was pulled back, she wasn't wearing makeup and she had daisies painted on her toes. Taryn spent her days ruling Score with an iron fist while Larissa gave massages and acted as Jack's assistant. It was an interesting dynamic.

Both women looked up and saw her. They waved.

"Look who I found," Dellina said as they approached the table.

Bailey twisted her fingers around the strap of her handbag. "I have my interview with Mayor Marsha in a few minutes."

Taryn pulled out a chair. "Sit here. You can tell me everything that has you nervous and we'll work through it."

Bailey sank down and sighed. "I'm just scared I don't have enough experience."

Dellina walked up to the counter and ordered a latte. "Bailey, you want anything?"

Bailey shook her head. "I'm afraid I'll spill."

Something Dellina could understand. No one wanted to go to an interview wearing a stain. As she waited for her latte, she studied Bailey's subtle makeup and the frown between her eyebrows. Being a single parent wasn't easy. Dellina had lost her folks and become responsible for her sisters at an early age. While that had been devastating, she'd been able to return to Fool's Gold where she knew everyone and there were plenty of people to look out for them.

Bailey and her husband had moved to town a couple of years ago. Neither of them had any family to speak of. There'd been an uncle or great-uncle around but he'd passed only a few months after their arrival. Then Bailey's husband, a soldier, had been killed in Afghanistan. Dellina hoped Bailey got the job with Mayor Marsha so that she could feel financially secure. That would go a long way to healing a broken heart.

She returned to the table with her drink. Bailey turned to her. "You grew up here. Any Mayor Marsha advice?"

"Be yourself," Dellina told her. "If Mayor Marsha didn't already like you, you wouldn't have the interview."

"I hope my skills are good enough," Bailey said. "I took that refresher course at the community college, but I haven't been in the job market for a while."

Taryn smiled at her. "Relax. As much as it pains me to admit it, the wily old woman knows what she's doing."

"You'll do fine," Larissa told her. "And when you get the job, you'll have the inside scoop on the town gossip." She leaned

33

forward and grinned. "I remember when I interviewed for my job at Score. Wow, was I nervous."

Bailey glanced at Taryn. "Yes, I can see why."

Taryn's eyes widened. "Hey, if that was about me, I'm a very gentle interviewer."

Larissa grinned. "She wasn't the problem. I had to talk to Jack. I was so scared because he was this famous, hunky guy. At least you won't have to worry about being tongue-tied because Mayor Marsha is good-looking."

They all laughed.

Dellina smiled at Bailey. "Larissa's right. Once you get the job, you will have the inside track on all the town gossip."

"Delicious," Larissa said.

Taryn looked at her friend. "You don't have time for gossip. You're too busy trying to kill people with poisonous snakes."

Larissa hung her head. "I've apologized about a thousand times for that."

"Give me a thousand more, I'll consider dropping it," Taryn teased.

Dellina didn't know much about Larissa beyond the fact that she had a soft heart and liked to rescue critters of all kinds. Unfortunately it seemed she didn't always think through her plans. A couple of months ago she'd been transporting snakes for a local wildlife organization. The snakes were going to a sanctuary somewhere in the southern part of the state. When the top of the container had come loose, one of the snakes had gotten out and Larissa had immediately stopped the car and jumped out.

Angel, Taryn's now-fiancé, had offered to help. He'd found out a bite too late that the snakes were poisonous and had spent the night in the hospital. Angel was fine and the snakes had made it to their new home, but Taryn was still torturing Larissa about the incident. In this case, Dellina found herself on Taryn's side. Helping animals in need was one thing, but dealing with poisonous creatures should be left to the professionals.

Bailey stood. "I need to go. I want to walk slowly to city hall so I'm not sweaty when I arrive." She pressed her hand to her stomach again. "I hope I can do this."

Taryn rose and hugged her. "You can. You'll be great. Tell me everything that happens."

"I will," Bailey promised, and left.

Taryn watched her go. Pride filled her eyes. For some reason the other woman had taken an interest in Bailey to the point of arranging a clothing exchange with the sole and secret purpose of getting Bailey a new interview dress. Taryn had figured Bailey wouldn't simply accept it as a gift and she sure couldn't afford it herself. So there had been a ladies-only clothing exchange.

Taryn sat down and picked up her latte. Her engagement ring sparkled in the afternoon light. "So," she said slowly. "Start talking."

Larissa grinned. "She's right. We want details. You said hi and he said hi and then?"

Dellina did her best to keep from smiling. "Are you talking about my meeting with Sam? It really wasn't that interesting."

Taryn's gaze narrowed. "If I had something to throw at you, I would do it in a heartbeat."

Dellina laughed. "No throwing. Our meeting was fine. Very professional."

"No sex on the kitchen counter?" Larissa asked.

Dellina shook her head. "No. Sam wouldn't do that."

"But you would?" Taryn asked. "Interesting."

"That's not what I meant and you know it. Sam was pleasant, we cleared up any lingering confusion about our past and talked about the party."

Both women stared at her, as if wanting more. No way she was going to mention the tingles. They were private. And probably foolish. She'd had a night with Sam and it had been great. But they'd both moved on and now they were working together. End of story.

"I was hoping for more," Larissa admitted.

"I think he's good-looking," Dellina told her. "Does that help?"

"Not really. I've never slept with Sam. Was he good?"

Taryn laughed. "Larissa, my sweet, that makes it sound like you've slept with Jack and Kenny."

Larissa's blue eyes widened. "What? No. Of course not. I work with them." She flushed. "Especially Jack. We're friends. Nothing more. Just, you know, good friends." She pressed her lips together as if trying to prevent herself from babbling. "For the record, I have not slept with anyone at Score. I was just wondering about Sam."

Dellina felt a little of Bailey's tummy unease but it had nothing to do with being nervous. For a second she couldn't place the cause.

"Because you're interested in Sam?" Taryn asked, her eyebrows raised.

The second Taryn asked the question out

loud, Dellina realized the cause of her anxiety and it didn't make her happy. Why did she care if Larissa had a thing for Sam? She'd spent one evening with him and had a single conversation since. What did she care if he slept with the entire state of California?

"I'm not interested in Sam," Larissa said with a sigh. "I meant I work with them, they're sexy, handsome men. All of them. Equally. I've heard things in the media and from various women and I wondered if any of it was true." She looked at Taryn. "You slept with Jack and you won't give me any details. Maybe Dellina will be more forthcoming."

"I was married to Jack," Taryn said. "And no, I'm not talking about that part of our relationship."

They both looked at Dellina expectantly.

She held up her hands. "Um, no. I'm not comfortable getting into specifics."

"How about a gross generality?" Larissa offered. "Was he good?"

Dellina felt herself start to smile. "Yeah, he was good."

Larissa squeezed Taryn's hand. "Our little boy is all grown up."

"You're a freak," Taryn told her. "You know that, right?" She turned to Dellina.

"As Sam's business partner, I would encourage you to have sex with Sam. I'm guessing it would improve his mood and I'm for that. As your friend, you probably want to think more than once about getting involved with a man who has that much bad luck with women."

"Arguing each side equally," Dellina murmured. "Impressive."

"Isn't she?" Larissa sat back in her chair. "What is it about sports guys that make them so appealing?"

"Their bodies," Dellina said without hesitating, telling herself she was speaking in generalities and not talking about Sam at all.

"The danger," Taryn added. "Remember during the Olympics when we couldn't stop watching Kipling Gilmore? When he skied down that mountain, it was the sexiest thing ever." She paused and grinned. "Except for Angel, of course."

"Yes, don't leave your fiancé out of it," Larissa murmured. "I'm with you on Kipling. Yum and double yum."

Larissa leaned toward them both. "So I heard from a friend of mine."

Taryn groaned. "Run," she told Dellina. "Run while you still can. Run and never take her calls."

Larissa's mouth turned into a pout. "You don't know what I'm going to say."

"Yes, I do. Some creature needs rescuing. It's going to be weird and inconvenient."

"Mostly to Jack," Larissa reminded her.

Taryn perked up. "That's right." She looked at Dellina. "Jack is forever helping Larissa with her various projects. Whether he wants to or not."

"It's one of his best qualities," Larissa said.

"Why doesn't he just say no?" Dellina asked.

"It's not in his nature," Taryn said. "He's a sucker for Larissa's causes." She picked up her latte again. "All right. What is it now?"

"There might be a lady in Barstow breeding chiweenies."

Larissa paused dramatically. Dellina looked at Taryn. "What's a chiweenie?"

"Hell if I know. And where's Barstow?"

Larissa put her hands on the table. "They're dogs. A Chihuahua-dachshund mix. There's concern she has a puppy mill rather than a breeding program. We're still investigating. But we might need to go in and rescue them."

Taryn's right eye twitched. "Save us all," she murmured. "Fine. Go rescue your chiweenies, but don't ask Dellina for help until after the party. I mean it. She's working on a deadline."

Larissa's eyes widened. "But they're puppies!"

Taryn looked at Dellina. "You see what I put up with?"

Dellina heard the love behind the frustration. Because for Taryn, the people at Score were her family. Dellina knew how important belonging could be. She would do anything for her sisters and her friends. Every now and then she wondered what it would be like to have a Mr. Right in her world. Then she told herself she was doing just fine and that a man would simply get in the way of that.

Sam arrived at Score a little before six in the morning. He stored his change of clothes in his locker, then headed outside.

While the days were warm in summer, the nights were still cool, as were the early mornings. The sun had just started to climb over the mountains when he walked onto the basketball court across the street from the company offices.

When he and Kenny and Jack had first come to Fool's Gold for a charity event, they hadn't been looking to leave Los Angeles. But something about the town had appealed to them. They'd come back individually over the next few weeks and had ultimately decided to relocate. When Taryn had gone looking for a building, they'd requested a space for a half basketball court. Ever the overachiever, she'd found one where they could put in a full court. Which meant three mornings a week there were pickup games with the guys in town.

Now Sam stepped through the gate in the high fence and walked toward the people already there. He, Jack and Kenny made up the Score contingent. From CDS, the local bodyguard school, were Justice, Angel, Ford and Consuelo, the only woman who joined them. Gideon, who owned the local radio station and his twin brother, Gabriel, showed up most mornings. Usually someone else came to play. One of the Stryker brothers, Josh Golden or Raoul Moreno.

They played to thirty points and generally followed NCAA rules. Teams were decided by drawing poker chips from a bag and whichever team Consuelo *wasn't* on was skins. Given the choice, Sam preferred having the petite brunette on his side. She was small but fast, and she played dirty.

"Hey," he said as he approached. As he greeted everyone, he did a quick head count and realized they were down one player.

Clay Stryker had arrived just after Sam, which meant one of the regulars was absent.

"It's Angel," Consuelo said with disgust. "I'm sure he's still in bed with Taryn."

Not anything Sam wanted to hear. Taryn was too much like a sister for him to be thinking about her having sex with anyone. When it came to personal information, he didn't want to know.

Just then a man on a Harley rounded the corner and parked. A couple of the guys whistled loudly.

"Who's finally getting some," Ford yelled. "Did your woman not want you to go?"

"Can I help it if I'm a god in bed?" Angel asked as he pulled off his helmet.

Sam grinned.

The first few mornings after the court had been finished, there had only been the three guys from Score. Later in the week, the team from CDS had shown up. The game had grown from there. Sam wasn't sure, but he would bet Taryn had something to do with it. There were more greetings, then everyone drew from the cloth bag and divided into teams.

Sam saw he and Consuelo had different colors. He grimaced as he pulled off his shirt. He would have to be careful around her. She thought nothing of throwing an elbow. If it went high, the man she was guarding ended up with a black eye. If it went low, he generally walked like a cowboy for the rest of the day. Neither was appealing.

"Let's go," Jack said, clapping his hands together.

Kenny rolled his eyes. "Once a quarterback," he muttered to Sam.

Sam chuckled.

The ball was tossed into the air and they were moving.

Sam ducked around Justice and reached for the ball. He moved downcourt only to sense more than see someone coming up beside him. He turned, shifted his weight and jumped up to shoot. The ball spun through the air and fell gracefully into the net.

"Way to go, Sam."

The high-pitched yell had him looking over his shoulder and then swearing under his breath.

"They're ba-ack," Ford said as he ran past.

Most mornings two old ladies showed up with lawn chairs and mugs of coffee. They sat and watched until the game was over, cheering both sides and often suggesting that shirts weren't the only thing that should come off.

He had no problem with that. It was that one of the old ladies seemed especially interested in him and that was kind of weird. He'd run into her a few weeks ago at one of the town festivals and he would swear she'd pinched his ass.

Justice scored for the other team, then Jack stepped out of bounds to take the ball. Sam got into place and caught it, then passed it to a teammate. As they all moved up the court, he thought that if someone was going to go after his ass, he would pick Dellina. They'd only been together that one time, but it had been memorable. The way she'd kissed him, he thought as he turned and reached for the ball. Her mouth had made him —

He came to a stop involuntarily as his face made contact with something hard and sharp. Pain exploded by his eye, but before he even started swearing, he passed the ball to Clay. Only then did he reach up to touch the rapidly swelling lump that was going to not only leave a mark but give him a black eye. He turned to Consuelo.

"Seriously? You had to do that?"

"You weren't paying attention. You know I hate that." She sounded more defensive than contrite. Then she pointed to his face. "Your nose is bleeding, too."

45

He rubbed his chin. Sure enough, his hand came away with blood on it.

"Man down," Jack yelled, walking toward him.

"I'm standing," Sam told him even as he headed off the court. Dripping blood would make the court slick. And he should probably get some ice on his eye.

"I'm not going to say I'm sorry," Consuelo yelled after him.

He smiled. No, she wouldn't, and he liked that about her.

Sam walked across the street. It was still before seven but when he entered the offices of Score he found Taryn in the foyer. She took one look at him and shook her head.

"No," she said firmly. "I'm not patching you up. And don't bleed on the carpet." She walked to the phone at the reception desk and picked up the receiver. A second later she said, "Sam got injured." She paused and looked at him. "Black eye and bloody nose." Another pause. "Yes, they *are* idiots."

She hung up. "Larissa will meet you in the locker room." She pulled a box of tissues from the reception desk and thrust it at him. "Use these. I swear, if you drip on our carpet . . ." she began.

He took the box and pulled out a handful.

"You'll what?"

"Be very angry."

"Ooooh. I'm trembling."

She glared at him, then stalked off. Considering she was wearing four-inch heels, the pace was impressive.

Twenty minutes later Larissa removed the ice pack to check the swelling. "You're going to have a black eye," she murmured. Her touch was light as she brushed her fingers over his cheek. "You want to go see a doctor?"

"No."

"Typical. Use the ice packs for ten minutes on, ten minutes off. Don't press hard."

"I know how to do this," he reminded her.

"You know what would be better than knowing how to treat a black eye? Not getting hit in the first place."

He nodded. "Point taken."

She started putting away her first aid supplies. "It's not usually you who gets distracted. What happened?"

He'd been thinking about Dellina's mouth. Not that he would share that with Larissa. "It was one of those things."

"Poor Sam." She picked up her kit, then paused. "I've been talking to one of my rescue groups about —"

He was already halfway out the door.

47

"Good luck with that."

"You didn't hear what we want to rescue."

"I know."

Fayrene Hopkins was a big fan of having a plan. She knew exactly where she wanted her business to be by her twenty-eighth birthday. She understood the market in her town, the opportunities and had even been saving to buy a small apartment building. Because in addition to having her own company, she was going to start buying up real estate in Fool's Gold. She had friends, family, a wonderful man who loved her and a plan. What she didn't have was an engagement ring and not having it was killing her.

It wasn't the ring itself, she admitted. It was what the ring represented. Commitment. Because as much as Ryan swore he loved her, he seemed in no hurry to pop the question. Fayrene was ready to get married and get on with the next phase of their relationship.

She sat on the stool in her sister's spare bedroom. Dellina was on the phone, dealing with a client issue. Which left Fayrene alone with a dozen or so beautiful wedding gowns. Some were samples, others had been ordered for soon-to-be brides. Brides engaged to men who were willing to cough up a ring and set the date.

Fayrene sighed heavily. She knew in her heart she had no one to blame but herself. When she and Ryan had first met, she hadn't been looking for love. She'd been interested in building her business. She was young and sometimes that meant she wasn't taken seriously. She knew that for the other businesses in town to be willing to use her services and trust her to get the job done, she had to be willing to do more than was expected. Falling in love would only be a distraction.

Only Ryan had been so . . . nice, she thought wistfully. Sweet and funny. They'd met at Hendrix Construction. He'd been there as an engineer while she'd been filling in for the receptionist. She'd also been pet-sitting a pregnant cat who had chosen that morning to go into labor.

While she'd been running around like a crazy person, Ryan had calmed her down, checked on the cat and kept it all together. She'd been impressed. She'd tried to keep her distance from him, but she'd been unable to resist his charms. And when he'd kissed her . . . well, she'd been totally lost.

Now, as she picked up one of the dresses and held it against her, she supposed Ryan's greatest virtue was that he was doing exactly what she'd asked. Waiting. When they'd admitted their love, she'd been scared about losing her chance at her business dream. Getting married would have been too much of a distraction. So they'd agreed to wait four years. One of which had passed, which left three more to go.

Only she didn't want to wait anymore and she couldn't figure out how to get that information to Ryan without telling him directly.

She held the dress in front of her again. From what she could see through the protective plastic, it was a beautiful strapless gown with layers of —

"Leave that dress alone!" Dellina walked into the room and put her hands on her hips. "Fayrene, that's either a special order or a sample. You can't mess with the merchandise."

"If it's a sample, I can."

"Then go to Paper Moon and try it on in the store like a normal person."

Fayrene returned the dress to the rack and sighed. "I'm not normal. I'm an idiot. Ana Raquel was smart. She realized she loved Greg and got engaged immediately. They moved in together."

"They also eloped."

Fayrene wrinkled her nose. "I wouldn't

50

want that. I want a big wedding." With all her friends there. She wanted to walk down the aisle and see Ryan at the other end. She wanted a church ceremony and a backyard reception.

"Fayrene, I love you like a sister," Dellina began.

"I *am* your sister."

"I know. You're a smart businessperson, but when it comes to love — specifically with Ryan — you're making this way too hard. Tell him how you feel."

Fayrene shook her head. "The guy is supposed to propose."

"That's unbelievably old-fashioned."

"I don't care. When I'm telling my daughter a bedtime story and she asks me how Daddy proposed, I don't want to tell her he didn't. That I had to ask."

It was more than that, she thought sadly. She wanted Ryan so swept away by love that he couldn't help himself. That he didn't care what she wanted. That being with her was the most important thing in the world and he would ask her to marry him no matter what. Only that didn't seem to be happening.

"Maybe he doesn't love me anymore," she said with a sigh.

Dellina leaned against the door frame.

"Kill me now."

"Before your big party?"

Her sister straightened. "You're right. The party is huge and I'm going to do such a good job that people will be talking about it for weeks. You still up for being my head babysitter?"

"You bet. I'm looking forward to it." As a rule, Fayrene liked kids. She would also like the big, fat check she would earn for just three days of relatively easy work.

"Good. By the way, you don't happen to know how long it takes to play a round of golf, do you?"

"I don't know. I've never played. Four hours, maybe."

"That's what I'm thinking. I'll do some research online and then talk to someone at the golf course. I'm planning the events for the weekend. I have to present the schedule to Sam tomorrow." She tilted her head. "Don't take this wrong, but what are you doing here?"

Sulking, Fayrene thought. "I was hoping we could brainstorm more ways to get Ryan to propose," she said, pointing to the dry-erase board.

Dellina walked toward her and put her hands on Fayrene's shoulders. "You're my sister. I love you very much. I would step in front of a bus for you."

"But?"

"But you're going about this all wrong. Tell him how you feel. And if you won't, comfort yourself with the knowledge that Ryan will propose."

Fayrene groaned. "In three years."

"Which is exactly when you told him to."

CHAPTER THREE

Dellina arrived at the office of Score five minutes before her appointment with Sam. While she knew where the offices were, she'd never been in them before. Now as she walked through the glass doors, she took in the open foyer with the two-story ceiling. A big reception desk stood in the center. There were stairs to the left and an elevator beyond that. But what really caught her attention were the nearly life-size pictures on the wall.

Sam, Kenny and Jack stared down at her from all angles. There were photos of the guys in uniform, in shorts and T-shirts, standing around and working out. There was one of Jack about to throw a football, another of Kenny jumping to catch. One showed Sam in that last nanosecond before he kicked the ball.

She turned slowly, taking in the various poses and expressions. In the back, by the

54

stairs, was one picture showing all four partners together. In her heels, Taryn was the same height as Sam. Jack was an inch or so taller with Kenny a couple of inches taller than him. The guys were in suits and ties and Taryn had on a long-sleeved black dress that showed every skinny inch of her body. Dellina immediately sucked in her stomach.

A middle-aged woman walked toward her. "May I help you?"

"Dellina Hopkins. I have an appointment with Sam."

The woman smiled. "Yes, of course. This way, Ms. Hopkins."

"Dellina, please."

She was led down the hallway. Signed jerseys and trophies lined the walls. The receptionist stopped in front of a partially open wooden door.

"Thank you," Dellina said before she stepped inside.

She found herself in a large office. One end had a big desk with a computer. There were windows, a long leather sofa and, at the far end, a small conference table.

The square footage probably came close to that of her house, she thought with amusement. Ah, to be a rich, famous football player, she thought. Talk about serious perks.

A door by the conference table opened and Sam walked into the room. Her girl parts cheered, her breath seemed to catch and she wondered if it was just her or if the sun was shining just a little brighter now. He smiled when he saw her.

"Right on time."

She was about to ask if there was a private restroom or if he and the other guys had secret passages back and forth between their offices when she took a look at his face. His left eye was slightly puffy and there was a deep violet and red bruise from the bridge of his nose to his cheekbone.

"What happened?" she asked, instinctively stepping toward him.

"You should see the other guy."

"You got in a fight?"

The smile returned. "No. I played basketball and got in the way of Consuelo's elbow."

"Consuelo did that to you?" Dellina cleared her throat and lowered the pitch of her voice. "On purpose?"

"That second question is harder to answer. She would tell you it was my own damn fault and she would probably be right."

"You have a black eye."

"That seems to be the consensus."

She was only a few feet from him. For a second she thought about moving closer and lightly touching his skin. While the idea was tempting, she couldn't figure out an excuse. It wasn't as if she had magical healing powers. While being around Sam made her think of tangled sheets and soul-stirring kisses, the information wasn't relevant for their current discussion. Or any discussion. Because what had happened that night had been an anomaly. Given the choice between the job and man, she would take the job.

But being with the man had been very, very nice.

He pointed to the conference table. "Have a seat. We can go over what you've brought."

She sat down and set her tote on the chair next to her. Sam sat on her other side and pulled a stack of papers toward himself. She saw plugs for hooking up a computer and suspected a screen lowered on one of the walls.

"Fancy," she said, pointing to the connections.

"I have finance meetings in here," he said. "With the accountants. We keep them small because no one else wants to attend."

"Your partners want to know their checks cleared and little else?"

"Something like that."

She pulled out her stack of folders. "I get that. Just once I'd like to have a phone call with my bookkeeper that doesn't have her trying very hard not to sigh in my ear. Every time I think I've got stuff the way she wants . . ."

Dellina trailed off, thinking that admitting a shortcoming like that probably wasn't a good idea.

Sam leaned back in his chair. "Don't worry. I'm not hiring you for your genius with numbers. I want you to make sure our guests have a good time."

"Much more my area of expertise." She passed him the top folder. "The preliminary schedule of events."

He handed her a couple of sheets of paper. "The guest list, including who has kids and their ages."

Sam flipped open the folder. The top two pages contained the calendar for the weekend. He scanned the lists. Per his request, the party began at four on Friday and went until two-thirty on Sunday.

"As you can see," Dellina said, leaning toward him and pointing, "we're keeping both kids and parents busy. The only places where the children need to be kept separate are the welcome wine tasting and dinner at Henri's. I have a private room reserved for the event. Not only won't it hold extra people, the kids would be a distraction."

"I agree," he told her.

"The other possible need for separation could be the lecture, but as I haven't lined up anyone yet, I don't know. Regardless, I'm running a full second track for the children. I suggest we go item by item through both schedules."

He nodded.

Dellina shifted her chair closer. Her wavy brown hair slipped off her shoulder and brushed against his arm. He was wearing long sleeves and couldn't really feel the contact, but he could imagine it. His fantasy for round two of their lone night together had been her on top. Only things hadn't gotten that far.

"The wine tasting is the first item," she said. "It will be held on the patio by the restaurant. I want to feature local wineries. Condor Valley Winery is right here in the valley, so they'll be the star. I have an in with the owners. My sister Ana Raquel is married to the nephew of the winemaker. He'll give a short talk on wine making, and the hotel wants to provide the appetizers. After the tasting we'll head into the restaurant for a full sit-down dinner. You and I will figure out the menu. Their wine cellar is impressive, so we have a lot to choose from."

She pointed to the second sheet. "While this is going on, the kids will be learning how to make various mocktails and appetizers. Ana Raquel and her husband are professional chefs. They'll be teaching the class. It seems like an easy way for everyone to get to know one another. There will be an informal dinner. During which we'll have a local band playing."

"You have a band suitable for children?"

She grinned. "A high school band, but still fun."

His gaze dropped to her mouth. Her lips were full and shiny from some gloss. He wondered if it would have a flavor and how much trouble he would be in if he tried to find out.

"There's a group in Sacramento that puts on plays for children. I want to hire them to do a kid-friendly play. It's a little pricey but will be a great end to the evening. The fun part is the kids learn lines and participate as well as watch."

It was a lot, but as she said, memorable. Better for the parents to know their children were entertained and tired at the end of the day.

"Is the play going to cost more than ten thousand dollars?" he asked.

Her eyes widened. "Hardly."

"Then it's fine."

"Sheesh. We have different definitions of expensive," she murmured.

He was sure that was true. "What about babysitters?"

"There will be at least two adults with the kids at all times along with several teenage sitters to keep an eye on things. I'll have references for everyone working two weeks before the party so parents can check them out if they want."

"Impressive," he told her.

She smiled. "I live to dazzle. Okay, Saturday morning. We'll have a stretching class for those who are in the mood, followed by breakfast on the terrace. Then we split up. Adults go to CDS for a fun obstacle course while the kids go bike riding with Josh Golden."

"Josh agreed to this?" Sam asked.

Dellina nodded. "I wouldn't have put it on the schedule if he hadn't. He does a lot of Saturday morning rides with different people. If you're visiting town, you can sign up for it through your hotel. They start on

61

the track at his school, and then when everyone is comfortable they head out to the bike path that circles the city."

She angled toward him. "I've talked to Angel and CDS has several corporate obstacle courses for us to choose from. They have balance beams and things with tires."

He held in a smile. "Things with tires?"

"You know what I mean. You jump in and out of tires. It's supposed to be fun."

"You don't sound convinced."

"I don't see the point, but that doesn't matter. This isn't about me. You and Jack and Kenny are the stars. Your guests will be expecting a lot of physical activities and this will be a fun one."

She wore a lightweight sweater over black pants. Low-heeled shoes that Taryn would turn her nose up at but Sam thought were cute. Dellina was professional and obviously good at her job. She also smelled good and he couldn't stop wanting to pull her close and violate several state statutes on sexual harassment.

"After that," she continued, "we meet up with the kids and head into town. It's the weekend of the Summer Festival. We'll have lunch together, then split up to explore. There will be a tour of the town for anyone interested. We shuttle back to the hotel at

62

three-thirty and then there's the lecture for the adults and the children get to hang out with Max and his therapy dogs."

She pulled a brochure out of another folder and passed it to him. "Normally Montana does the community outreach with the dogs, but she's seriously pregnant and taking it easy. K9Rx Therapy Dogs does what it sounds like."

"I know what therapy dogs are."

"Then you get the fun the kids will have with friendly, adoring dogs. Angel will bring his Acorns by to talk about their recent project with therapy puppies."

Acorns? Sam started to ask what or who they were. Then he remembered Taryn's involvement with a group of girls. They were like scouts, only local. There had been activities and a project involving puppies. More interesting was take-no-prisoners Taryn now spent her days staring at her engagement ring and sighing like a school-girl.

Love did strange things to people. Once he'd wanted that for himself. Not the acting like a fool part, but the rest of it. The connection. The family.

Dellina continued, "We finish the evening with a barbecue on the terrace. Kids with their parents, although there will be sitters available if Mom and Dad want to stay up late." She drew a breath. "Sunday morning we have brunch together. Then there's golf for those interested, a spa day here at the hotel for the ladies and the kids get on a bus to head to Castle Ranch."

"Horseback riding?" he asked.

"Horses and goats and an elephant."

He shook his head. "I'm not paying for an elephant."

"You don't have to." Her smile was smug. "There's one at the ranch."

"An elephant?"

"Yes."

"In Fool's Gold?"

"Of course. Her name is Priscilla. She lives on the ranch. She has a pony named Reno as a companion."

Sam wondered if the elbow to his face had bruised more than his eye. "You're sure?"

"You can't make up something like that."

She had a point there.

"Elephant rides, it is."

"Then we all meet back at the hotel and the weekend is over."

He studied the papers. "You did great. Our clients will be talking about this for a long time."

"That's the goal."

"The lecture is still a problem."

"I know." She sighed. "It has to be special. I'm figuring it out."

"This is where you tell me the short time frame doesn't help."

Her mouth twitched. "Why state the obvious? You were in an emotional crisis. We all have to deal with the aftermath."

"I wasn't in an emotional crisis."

"What would you call it?"

"Hell."

She laughed. "Fair enough. The combination of the list and wedding dresses were probably off-putting."

"That's one name for it."

She tilted her head. "You could have talked to me."

"Not after seeing all that."

"You assumed the worst."

"It wasn't much of a stretch," he told her.

"I guess. But you should trust people more."

"Not likely." He studied her. "You, on the other hand, are too trusting."

"I'm okay with that. I want to assume the world is a nice place. To think otherwise is too sad."

An innocent, he thought, not sure if he admired her or wanted to warn her against all that could happen.

"It's because I grew up here," she added

65

with a shrug. "You've lived here now. You know what it's like."

"True. A Fool's Gold native would have a tough time being cynical. So what was it like? Four perfect seasons and a warm, loving community?"

She laughed. "You're right about the community. I'm not sure I'd agree the seasons are perfect, but it was nice." Her humor faded.

"What?" he asked. "Something ruin Pleasantville for you? What was it? A lost dog? A bad prom?"

"Prom wasn't great." She shrugged. "It wasn't all sunshine and roses. Bad things happen everywhere, even here. My parents passed away."

Sam reached for her hand, then drew back. "I'm sorry. I didn't mean to be a jerk."

"You weren't."

"I assumed nothing bad had ever happened to you."

"I'm not sure anyone gets through life without some kind of pain."

"How old were you?"

"Seventeen. My sisters were nearly fourteen. My parents took their first vacation by themselves." She looked away. "At the last minute my mom wanted to cancel, but I said we'd be fine."

This time Sam did take her fingers in his. "It wasn't your fault. You couldn't have known what was going to happen. There's no way she knew, either."

"Which all sounds very logical." She returned her attention to him and didn't pull free of his touch. "But back then I felt so responsible." She swallowed. "It was a freak thing. They were on a boat in the Caribbean and there was a storm. It took a couple of days to find their bodies."

Sam couldn't imagine what that must have been like. His parents made him crazy — especially his mother — but at least he knew they were around. Ready to torment him at a moment's notice.

He continued to rub her hand. Her skin was warm and soft, but this wasn't about him.

"It was awful," she continued. "Honestly, I can't remember much about that time. There was a funeral and then our aunt and uncle came to get us."

"You moved away?"

She nodded. "There was no other family. We'd met them before — the aunt and uncle. But that was different than going to live with them. We were in a different state and different schools. Fayrene and Ana Raquel had each other, so that helped. But

I didn't feel like I had anyone else."

Sam remembered being seventeen and wishing for nothing more than to be left alone. His sisters and parents were always *there* hovering, checking on him. It wasn't pleasant or fun. In retrospect, he'd been damned lucky.

"I finished high school and turned eighteen. Then I petitioned the courts to get custody of my sisters." She laced her fingers with his. "My parents had left enough money to take care of us, assuming we were careful. There was insurance on the mortgage, so the house was paid for. The town helped. Julia Gionni moved in with us for the first two months. Denise Hendrix taught me how to balance a checkbook and pay bills, that sort of thing. We managed."

Without thinking, he stood and pulled her to her feet. He drew her close and wrapped his arms around her.

"I'm sorry you had to go through all that," he said.

She put her hands on his chest and stared into his eyes. "You do realize it was a decade ago, right?"

"Still, a lot for you to deal with."

She was smiling, which made his attention drop to her mouth. Instantly, he remembered what it was like to kiss her. To feel her lips against his. He'd kissed a lot of women in his life, but there was something about Dellina. The feel of her, the way she tasted. The heat.

Last Valentine's Day, when they'd walked out of the hotel together, he hadn't thought about much more than how he wanted to see her again. Then he'd kissed her. The second her lips had moved against his, he'd known he was lost. He'd wanted her — in his bed. Or her bed. Or up against a wall somewhere. The need had hit him like a linebacker, nearly dropping him to his knees. From that second until he'd walked into the hell room at her place, he'd been operating on need.

Now he wondered how much trouble he would be in if he tried to kiss her again. There were a thousand reasons not to — most of which revolved around the weekend they had to plan. But the reasons to do it were powerful and starting to win.

She moved her hands to his upper chest and gently pushed him back.

"I appreciate the sympathy and support," she said as she sidestepped him. "But your reaction means I told you way too much. Both my sisters are doing great. They're successful and happy."

The message was clear, he thought. Back

off. He'd crossed a line with her. The realization was made all the more uncomfortable because he was the guy who prized his own boundaries.

"Except for Fayrene and Ryan," he said, hoping to restore equilibrium to their conversation.

She sank back in her chair and smiled. "There is that. The quest to find a way to get her boyfriend to read her mind. I suspect if something like that existed, it would have been discovered long before now."

He returned to his seat. "Telling him isn't possible?"

"Apparently not. She wants him to propose."

"You could tell him."

Dellina smiled. "I could, and believe me, I've thought about. But every time I start to have the conversation with him, a voice in my head says Fayrene needs to figure this out on her own." She glanced down. "I know this is going to sound weird, but it's almost like my mom is there, giving me advice. So I listen."

"Not weird," he said. "Nice."

Her smile widened. "Thanks. Because I don't want you to think I'm really hearing voices. At least, not scary ones." She looked at her notes. "Let me put together a list of

70

everything we're going to need to check out. Menus at Henri's, of course. The various hotel venues, Castle Ranch, the obstacle course. Obviously the festival will happen without us checking on it, but everything else that can be tested, tasted and reviewed will be."

"Do I get to ride the elephant?"

"I'm confident that can be arranged."

Sam made a joke about Priscilla. Dellina was pretty sure she'd responded appropriately, although she wasn't positive. She was still shaking, still fighting the fiery need that burned low in her belly.

When Sam had pulled her to her feet and held her, she'd nearly melted from the inside out. His hands on her body had reminded her of what had happened between them before. She'd actually had the thought that if they pulled the blinds at the big windows looking into his office, they could pick up where they'd left off right there.

Which was beyond insane. She wasn't that girl. She was cautious and responsible. She didn't bring strange men home and she didn't have sex in people's offices. Except when it came to Sam.

She drew in a breath and nodded at what

she hoped was the appropriate place. She could do this, she told herself firmly. She could act normal and be a professional businesswoman. There was a lot at stake with this party. No way she was going to let her hormones and girl parts ruin a great opportunity.

So she'd pushed him away when what she really wanted to do was drag him closer and let him show her a good time. How strange that he was the one to rock her world . . . sexually at least. Couldn't she have the hots for a nice, regular kind of guy? Like a plumber or one of Ryan's friends? Did she have to go all slutty for a former football star with a fan club and who knows how many exes in his past?

". . . talk about the lecture," he said.

"We should," she murmured, not sure what he'd been saying. Obviously something about the lecture.

He frowned. "You'll pull some ideas together?"

"Of course. I'll find people who are available and there will be a range of topics. We'll narrow it down."

"So, in two days?"

"Yes," she said, figuring he was talking about their next planning session. "Let's meet at my place. I'll have charts and graphs for you."

He grinned. "My favorite."

"As long as there are numbers, too?"

"You know it."

He waited while she collected her paper-work and then walked her to the front of the building. When they'd said goodbye, she walked outside and drew in a deep breath.

Talk about embarrassing, she thought as she headed for her car. When she got home, she was going to give herself a stern talking-to. Then she'd have some ice cream. Because there were very few problems chocolate chip cookie dough couldn't solve, at least temporarily.

Kipling Gilmore glanced toward the win-dows. Snow came down steadily, promising a good day of skiing tomorrow. So far he hadn't done much more than mess around on the slopes and get back into fighting shape in the gym. But the rest of his team would arrive by the end of the week and then the training would get serious.

He used a towel to wipe the sweat from his face, then slowed the treadmill to a walk. Music pounded from the speakers in the hotel gym, but he kept his earbuds tucked in place. Not that his music was any better. The earbuds were his way of keeping the world at bay. At least while he worked out.

The post-Olympic whirlwind had finally slowed. Not that he was complaining. If the price of two gold medals was a round of media events, red carpet appearances and lavish parties all over the world, well, he was man enough to be willing to pay. Although he had tired of finding strange women in his hotel room. Fortunately the management at his hotel in New Zealand were determined to protect his privacy.

He stepped off the treadmill and headed for the exit. He would be back later for a second workout. Weights this time. What he did on skis required more than coordination and luck; it required strength, and he'd gotten lazy since the Olympics.

"Hi, Kipling."

The greeting came from a sultry blonde in the hallway. Her skintight workout clothes showed that either Mother Nature had been extremely generous or her plastic surgeon had been willing to go larger than suited her frame.

Two years ago he would have paused to talk. Three years ago he would have been backing her into the closest private room and letting her have her fifteen minutes of fame. Now he simply nodded and walked on.

As he waited for the elevator, he checked his cell phone. He hadn't heard from Shelby in a couple of days and that bothered him. His half sister had recently moved home to care for her dying mother. An admirable decision, but one that worried him. Mostly because it put her in close proximity to their mutual father.

Nigel Gilmore looked and sounded like a British diplomat. But he was also a brute with a temper. He was a man who enjoyed hitting women. Kipling had been saved by both his gender and his quickness. Early on, he'd learned how to duck. But Shelby and her mother weren't so lucky. Kipling didn't understand why some women stayed with men who beat them. He'd protected Shelby as best he could. His leap to the top of the pack had meant endorsement deals and money to pay for Shelby's college. They'd vowed to never go back home.

But that had changed a few months ago when Shelby's mother had been diagnosed with stage four ovarian cancer. She was in the last stages of her life and Shelby had wanted to be with her. Unfortunately that meant facing Nigel.

He didn't like that he was half a world away from the small Colorado town where he'd grown up. He liked it even less that

Shelby was there on her own.

He stepped into the elevator when it arrived, then exited on his floor. As he walked down the hall, he saw the window at the end. Snow continued to fall. Tomorrow would be a good day, he told himself. He would be back on the mountain searching for the ultimate goal — going faster than anyone ever had.

CHAPTER FOUR

Fayrene stuffed her keys into her jeans pocket and headed for the front door. She was going to swing by Dellina's to have yet another heart-to-heart with her older sister. She needed a plan to get Ryan to propose and Dellina was the best planner she knew. But before she could reach the door, someone rang the bell. She pulled it open a second later.

Mayor Marsha stood in the hallway of her triplex. Fayrene rented the bottom floor, mostly because it had a tiny yard. She liked seeing grass and flowers when she looked out her kitchen window. The upstairs units had a better view of the town, but she liked where she was.

Fayrene looked at the older woman. Of course she knew the mayor — everyone who lived in town did. But the other woman had never once come to her apartment.

"Hello," Fayrene said cautiously. "May I

help you?"

"I hope so," Mayor Marsha told her, then smiled. "I understand you have a pet-sitting service."

It was only then Fayrene noticed that Mayor Marsha was holding a leash in one hand. And at the end of the leash was a fluffy, adorable Pomeranian.

Fayrene immediately dropped to her knees. "Who is this?" she asked in a soft voice.

"Caramel."

"Hi, pretty girl," Fayrene said softly as she stroked the dog's head.

Caramel's button eyes widened as her face seemed to relax into an adorable doggy grin.

Mayor Marsha picked up a tote bag and handed it to Fayrene. "There's a folder with instructions inside. Caramel is very friendly. She prefers people to dogs. She likes squeaky toys, bacon, Thai food and tummy rubs. It's probably best if you don't leave her home alone. She likes to be involved in what's going on."

Fayrene stood. Somehow she found herself holding the bright pink leash, along with the tote. Caramel gave a little spin.

"I didn't know you had a dog." She'd never seen the mayor with one before. Or heard her talk about one.

"This is a several-week commitment," Mayor Marsha told her. "Will that be all right?"

"Sure. I have a few temp jobs right now, but there's no reason she can't go with me."

Mayor Marsha gave her a few instructions about feeding Caramel, then mentioned the name of her vet. Before Fayrene could figure out what was happening, she found herself alone in her building's hallway, facing a fluffy Pomeranian.

"Okay, then," she said slowly. "I guess it's you and me."

Caramel gave another spin, as if expressing excitement.

Fayrene stepped back and pushed open the door to her apartment. "Want to come in?"

Caramel walked into the apartment. She waited while Fayrene unclipped her leash, then set off to explore her new home. Fayrene unpacked her dog food and set out a bowl of water. She found Caramel on her bed, curled up in a nest of decorative pillows.

"Not the type to sleep on the floor?" she asked.

Caramel wagged her tail a little, as if to ask why anyone would choose the floor when there was a perfectly comfortable bed for the taking.

Sam arrived at Dellina's place right on time. He'd walked, because Fool's Gold was the kind of place where people walked instead of taking their cars. As he'd made his way to her house, he'd passed plenty of residents and a few tourists. The latter had mostly ignored him, but he'd seen the townspeople giving him the once-over.

He wasn't sure if he was supposed to acknowledge them or just keep moving. In Los Angeles, he'd managed to stay anonymous — which was what he preferred. Of course in Fool's Gold no one seemed to care about his former career, so maybe it didn't matter if people knew he was walking on the street.

Dellina opened her door before he could knock and grabbed him by the arm.

"You are going to be so impressed," she said as she pulled him into the house. "I've been working my butt off and do I have a lot to show for it."

Her enthusiasm made him smile as he followed her down the narrow hallway. They stepped into her office where charts and lists covered the walls. Which seemed safer than the infamous dry-erase board with Fayrene's ongoing list of how to get Ryan to propose. But now that he knew the logic behind the brainstorming, he wasn't worried. It turned out that Dellina had been exactly what she'd seemed that lone Valentine's night. A sweet, sexy, funny woman who took him places he wanted to go again. She wasn't married, a stalker or even secretly a man. All pluses in his book.

The only thing standing between him asking her out was the party they had to pull off and the knowledge that with his bad luck, however good things started, they were going to finish in disaster.

Dellina walked to the sheets tacked to the wall. She had on worn jeans and a T-shirt and was barefoot. While he liked seeing her in business attire, he had to say there was something appealing about worn jeans. The soft, faded denim molded to her curves in a way designed to make him think about —

"Here are the cost estimates," she said, pointing to one of the lists on the wall. "It's not complete and it will change, but it gives us a starting place."

He reluctantly raised his gaze to where she pointed. "That's why they're called estimates."

She flashed him a smile. "You're such a numbers guy."

"I've been called worse."

She pointed at another list. "Our tasting schedule."

She went on about food and maybe even wine, but he was busy thinking about another kind of tasting. One that involved his mouth and her body and lots of moaning.

In an effort to distract himself, he glanced at a list of what looked like craft projects. The word *birdhouses* had several question marks next to it.

"For the kids?" he asked.

She shrugged. "I can't decide. A birdhouse can be built in a single day. The glue doesn't take long to dry. We could finish them in the morning and then paint them that afternoon and the next morning."

"Interesting."

"Now the lecture series," she said, pointing to the chair by the desk.

He sank onto the seat. She settled across from him and handed him pages she'd printed out on her computer.

"I think these are the most interesting so far. This man is an astrophysicist. He talks about the origins of the universe in terms laypeople can understand. He's supposed to be funny and relatable."

"Our clients aren't the science types," he told her.

"Well, *I* think he'd be really interesting,

but I thought you might say that." She handed him a second sheet. "What about a race car driver? He's very successful on the Formula 1 circuit. I looked him up online and he has a few really funny videos."

The car guy had more appeal, but Sam wasn't feeling it. "How many women are interested in cars?" he asked. "Even racing? Taryn's going to say it's not anything she wants to listen to."

Dellina sighed. "I can hear her tirade already," she admitted. "Darn. I thought this was it."

Sam raised his eyebrows. "Darn?"

She smiled again. "I don't swear in front of clients."

"A good policy."

She stood up suddenly and hurried to the wall where she scribbled a few words. He studied the list and saw it was items she had to research or questions she needed to get answered. Like "Does Castle Ranch have a first aid kit?" and "Confirm none of the children have food or sunscreen allergies." She was thorough, he thought, wondering why he'd resisted hiring her for so long. Sure their night together had ended badly, but she was good at her job and he respected that.

The sound of someone knocking on the

front door was followed by a female voice calling, "It's me."

Dellina turned. "My sister Fayrene," she said.

A petite blonde walked into the office. She was pretty, with hazel eyes, but what caught his attention was the small fluffy dog who walked next to her.

Dellina turned. "Hi," she said, then nodded to Sam. "I have a client meeting."

He rose. "Sam Ridge."

Fayrene's eyebrows rose. "One of the football players. Nice. Fayrene Hopkins. This is Caramel. She's a Pomeranian."

Dellina finished writing and faced her sister. Her gaze dropped to the small dog. "She's adorable. Pet-sitting?"

"Yes. Oddly enough, Mayor Marsha brought her to me."

"I didn't know she had a dog."

"Me, either."

Dellina crossed to the small animal and let Caramel sniff her fingers. "You're too cute for words," she told the dog. "Can I pick her up?"

"Sure. She's superfriendly and really well behaved."

"Hey, pretty face," Dellina said in a low voice. "You want me to pick you up?"

Caramel gave a little half jump as Dellina

reached for her. Dellina snuggled her close, then laughed when the dog licked her chin.

Sam eyed the fluff ball and wondered how much she would shed on his clothes. Although he had to admit, Caramel looked pretty cute. More teddy bear than dog. And she seemed to have a decent personality.

He'd never had pets growing up. His house had been wild enough with three kids and his not-quite-normal parents. A dog or cat wouldn't have stood a chance.

Dellina's cell rang. She pulled it out of her pocket and glanced at the screen. "I have to take this. It's about another lecture possibility. I'll be right back." She handed Caramel back to Fayrene and ducked out of the room.

Fayrene looked at him.

Sam saw that the sisters had some similarities. The same shape to their faces and the set of their shoulders. Although Dellina was a few inches taller, which he liked. He remembered what he'd been told.

Fayrene took her sister's chair and smiled at him. "So, you're a man."

Sam immediately glanced toward the exit. No conversation that started like that was going to go well, he thought grimly. Maybe he and Dellina could wrap up the rest of the details over the phone.

He cleared his throat. "Yes."

Caramel wiggled free of Fayrene and jumped into his lap. Before he knew what was happening, she'd planted her tiny back feet on his thighs, her front feet on his chest and was staring at him expectantly.

"What?" he asked as he stared into round dark eyes.

"I think she wants you to hold her," Fayrene said. "I've only had her a couple of hours so I don't know everything she likes."

Sam didn't want to hold the dog, but he also wasn't sure about her staring. He reached for her, not clear on how to pick her up. As his hands closed around her, he realized she was a lot smaller than she'd seemed. She was mostly fur. Her body was small, her bones slight. Jeez, he could crush her if he wasn't careful.

But before he could figure out how to hand her back to Fayrene, Caramel had wiggled and shifted until somehow she was on her back, gazing up at him. Her expression held contentment and absolute trust. She relaxed against his arm, nestling her head in the crook of his elbow. He stroked her chest, then rubbed her little belly. She sighed and closed her eyes.

"She likes you," Fayrene told him.

News that was both gratifying and terrifying.

"You're one of Dellina's clients, right?" Fayrene asked.

He nodded. "She's planning an event for my company."

"Great. And there have been a lot of women in your life?"

Sam's head snapped up. "Excuse me?"

Fayrene grinned. "Groupies. Girls in hotel rooms. You know what I mean. You're experienced when it comes to women."

Sam shifted uncomfortably. What the hell was she asking?

"It's about my boyfriend," Fayrene told him.

"The mysterious Ryan." He relaxed and thought of the dry-erase board with the Ten Ways to Get Him to Propose header. "There's an obvious solution."

"To what?"

"The proposal."

Fayrene's hazel eyes widened. "Okay. What is it?"

"Tell him you want to get married."

Her mouth twisted in disappointment. "Like that is *ever* going to happen. I can't just say I've changed my mind and want us to get married now."

"Why not?"

Her gaze turned pitying. "Because he's the guy. He's supposed to propose. I want the romantic moment. If Ryan really loved me, he would know things were different. Or he wouldn't be able to wait for me. He'd insist."

Sam thought attitudes like that were one of the reasons the divorce rates were so high. "Unrealistic expectations and too much idealized fantasy about what it *should* be," he muttered. "If Ryan loves you, he'll respect you. Did you two agree to wait for a few years before getting married?"

"Yes."

"Then every single day he doesn't mention getting married, he's showing you he loves you and wants what you want."

"But I don't want that anymore."

"He's a man, not a mind reader. He's doing exactly what you asked him to do. Changing the rules now isn't fair to either of you. This is the man you want to spend the rest of your life with. If you can't be honest about how you feel, how do you expect your relationship to last?"

Fayrene's eyes narrowed. "You're no help at all," she told him, then stood and scooped up Caramel. The little dog settled easily in her arms.

"Tell him the truth," Sam called after her.

Fayrene didn't answer and seconds later the front door slammed.

Dellina returned to her office. "Did my sister leave?"

"Yes. I don't think she was happy."

Dellina didn't look overly concerned as she settled back in her seat. "What did you say?"

"That if she wants to change the rules with Ryan, she needs to tell him directly."

"Excellent advice."

"Thank you."

"Not that she'll listen."

"I got that."

Dellina arrived at Jo's a few minutes before she was scheduled to meet her friends. As she walked into the bar, she saw Taryn and Larissa were already at a big table, along with Consuelo Ly. Taryn, as usual, wore something fabulous. This time a gray plaid sleeveless dress with a slim belt of the same material and some kind of foldy-draping across the front. The style was deceptively simple, but Dellina had a feeling the designer was a name everyone knew and that the dress had cost more than a vacation to Hawaii.

By contrast Larissa was in apple-green capris with a matching polka-dot T-shirt. Her hair was pulled back in a ponytail and Dellina was sure she hadn't bothered with makeup that morning.

Consuelo defied all fashion convention in her work uniform of cargo pants and a khaki-colored tank. All she needed was a bit of camouflage paint on her face to look like she'd stepped out of an action movie.

From Dellina's point of view, they were all versions of exotic. Taryn with her upscale taste and glossy beauty. Larissa was the classic blonde bombshell with an athletic twist, while Consuelo was both stunning and powerful — combined in a petite package. By comparison, Dellina felt average. She had brown hair and brown eyes. She was sort of pretty, but nothing like them. She guessed she looked like what she was — a small-town girl. In a word — *boring.*

For the most part she was content with that, but every now and then she wondered what it would be like to be glamorous and sexy.

"Hi," she said as she approached the table. She set down the ceramic container she held. "I hope this is what you were thinking of. Rakisha from Plants for the Planet swears it's going to last."

Taryn and Consuelo both stared at the dish garden Dellina had picked up on her way over to lunch. They'd all agreed to get Bailey a small gift to celebrate her new job with the mayor. Larissa touched a couple of leaves.

"Nice," she said. "There's *dracaena, spathiphyllum* and *syngonium.* Pretty and it will last even if she's not great with taking care of it."

Taryn winced. "You frighten me."

"I know about plants. Big whoop."

"It's one thing to recognize them. It's another to know their Latin names."

Dellina grinned as she took a seat. Her friends were nothing if not entertaining.

Larissa pointed to Taryn's dress. "Who designed that?"

"Oscar de la Renta."

Larissa turned to Consuelo. "And who made your pants?"

Consuelo glared at her. "Hell if I know. I get them at a surplus store or online. They're pants."

Dellina leaned back in her chair. "I wish Jo served popcorn because this is like live theater."

Larissa grinned at her, then turned back to Taryn. "We all know stuff."

"I got that. But my stuff makes sense. Yours is weird." She looked at Consuelo. "I know better than to diss anything you know."

"Good." Consuelo started to say something else, then looked up. "Bailey's here."

They all rose and clapped as Bailey approached the table. The other woman blushed nearly as red as her hair as she drew near.

"Stop, please," she pleaded. "You don't have to make a fuss."

"We're making a fuss," Taryn told her. "You got a great new job. A fuss is required."

They all hugged Bailey, then took their seats. Bailey thanked them for the plant. Jo walked over and stopped at their table.

"Congratulations on the new job," she said. "Lunch is on the house." She paused. "For Bailey. The rest of you can still pay."

"Of course we can," Taryn said with a grin. "All right. I think this calls for champagne all around."

Bailey's mouth parted. "It's lunchtime."

"I know," Taryn told her. "That's the point. A single glass won't hurt your work performance. This is a big deal. We're all happy for you."

"I like how you roll," Dellina said.

"You'll like her even more when I tell you she called ahead, so my best bottle is already chilled," Jo said. "Back in a flash."

"Champagne at lunch," Bailey whispered. "I haven't had any champagne since my wedding. Thank you all. You've been so nice to me."

Consuelo waved away the praise. "Yeah, yeah, we're amazing. How's the new job?"

Bailey started talking about how much she had to learn, not only about working with Mayor Marsha but about the town government.

Dellina was more interested in the women at the table. For all Taryn's toughness and attitude, she'd been the one to preorder champagne. And while Consuelo couldn't handle a simple compliment or a thank-you, she would cheerfully strangle anyone who tried to hurt Bailey or her daughter. Larissa was the one Dellina knew the least, but from what she could tell, the other woman was caring and had no trouble poking fun at Taryn. A fun combination.

Jo returned with the champagne. She expertly popped the cork, then poured them each a glass.

"To new beginnings," Taryn said to Bailey. "May you always be happy."

Everyone joined in the toast, then they sipped. Dellina took a drink. The champagne was light and fizzy. She glanced at the bottle and saw the label read Dom Pérignon. Which was so Taryn, she thought with a grin. Well, everyone should have it at least once in their life!

She set down her glass. "Did you know Mayor Marsha had a dog?" she asked Bailey.

"No. She's never said anything. Why?"

"She left her dog with Fayrene. I remember somebody mentioning a trip."

"Me, too," Taryn said. "Then everyone freaked out, as if Mayor Marsha wasn't allowed to travel. Can't the woman take a vacation without causing a scandal?"

"I think it's because Mayor Marsha doesn't go away much," Dellina said. "I don't remember it ever happening when I was growing up, although she must have left town sometime."

"Where's she going?" Larissa asked.

"New Zealand."

"That's far," Dellina said, wondering how long the flight had to be. Twelve hours? Longer? "What's there?"

"The *Lord of the Rings* tour," Taryn said with a grin. "Maybe our mayor is a fan."

"The what?" Consuelo asked. "Because of the book?"

Larissa patted her arm. "The movie. Remember from a few years back? It was a big deal. They filmed it there and I guess they left the sets in place. You can tour it all. See the hobbit village."

Consuelo shook her head. "No way our mayor is going all the way to New Zealand to look at a bunch of fake hobbit houses. Maybe she's going to watch Kipling Gilmore ski."

Dellina stared at her. "You know where he's skiing right now?"

Consuelo lifted a shoulder. "I read it in *Sports Illustrated* the other day. He's there for summer skiing. Which they don't call it there, because it's their winter."

"Someone has a bit of a crush," Dellina murmured.

Consuelo's lips twitched. "I like watching him. You were looking, too, during the Olympics."

"I have to say I'm more comfortable with the idea of our mayor being a ski groupie than looking at hobbit houses on her vacation," Taryn announced. "Which is, on the surface, kind of strange. I'm going to have to think on that." She turned to Dellina. "Speaking of fun things like vacations and handsome men, are you torturing Sam about the party?"

Dellina laughed. "Which category does that question fall into?" She held up her hand. "Never mind. I don't want to know. For the record, I'm only working with him.

There's no torture. It's all very professional."

A little too professional, Dellina thought. Because he was one good-looking guy. Nice, too. Quiet, but she liked that about him. Flashy didn't suit her — not that Sam was making any offers.

Jo came by and took their orders. When she left, Dellina helped Bailey set the plant on a chair in the corner.

"Rakisha said her niece and grand-niece were coming to help with the business," Dellina said as they returned to the table.

"Who?" Consuelo asked.

"The owner of Plants for the Planet," Taryn said. "I've met her. She's got to be a hundred and three."

"Not that old, but probably into her eighties," Dellina told them. "We were all afraid she would be selling the business." There had been a scandal a few years back, she thought. Something about a man. But she didn't mention that to her friends. No need to spread rumors.

"I'm glad she has family to help out," Larissa said. "I love how the businesses are run in Fool's Gold. I'd hate to see any of them go corporate."

"The good of the many over the profits of the few," Taryn murmured. "How I adore your tree-hugging nature."

Larissa grinned. "Mock me all you want. I have a thousand causes I can talk about."

"Yes," Taryn said. "And all supported by Jack. The things that man does for you. It defies logic."

Lunch passed quickly. There was plenty of conversation and laughter. Dellina walked out with Taryn, who stopped her on the sidewalk.

"The party is really moving forward?" Taryn asked. "While I like to torture Sam for sport, the truth is we all want to please our clients. So if you need anything, let me know."

"Thanks, but it's coming together really well. So far the only stumbling block is the evening lecture. I can't find the right topic or person. What are both men and women interested in?"

Taryn raised her eyebrows. "Is that a real question?"

Dellina laughed. "I can't hire someone to talk about sex."

"I don't see why not. You'd have everyone's attention." An SUV pulled up at the curb. Taryn waved at the driver. "That's my ride."

Because Angel had come to pick her up, Dellina thought, glancing at her friend's five-inch heels. No way anyone could walk across town in those.

Love, she thought as she strolled toward the center of town. It did crazy things to people. She had neither a man nor five-inch heels. Not that she wanted the latter. Or had time for the former. Serious relationships weren't on her to-do list. But a couple of nights with a certain former NFL kicker would be nice.

Dellina walked past Brew-haha. She thought briefly about popping inside and getting coffee, but then was seduced by the thought of a piece of fudge. On her way, she could check out what was new at Morgan's Books. If she couldn't have sex with the guy she wanted, she could buy a romance and read about someone else doing it with an equally hunky guy — however fictional he might be.

She turned left on Frank Lane. At The Christmas Attic, she paused to wave to Noelle, who was behind the counter, helping a couple of tourists. Her friend waved back. Dellina continued to Morgan's Books, only to come to a stop in front of the display.

"It can't be that easy," she murmured, every fiber of her being hoping it could be just that simple.

In the front window was a display for an

upcoming book signing. Lark Heuston, a *New York Times* bestselling author, was going to be signing at Morgan's store the Thursday before the Score party. Which meant she would be in town. Just as exciting was the title of her new book. *Using Tantric Sex to Strengthen Your Marriage.* Talk about an unexpected gift. Because Taryn was right. Sex was the one thing men and women could agree upon, she thought happily.

The subject matter was appealing and informational, she thought as she headed for the door and stepped into the store. All she had to do was get the contact information from Morgan and then call Ms. Heuston to see if she would like to spend a couple of extra days in Fool's Gold and give an easy ninety-minute lecture. Maybe they could even set up a book signing. Authors liked that sort of thing, didn't they?

Dellina practically bounced with excitement as she hurried toward Morgan and began to explain what she needed.

CHAPTER FIVE

The Gold Rush Ski Lodge and Resort had a ridiculously long name but an amazing location. It was located only a few miles from the town, but most of that distance was straight up — putting the resort's ski slopes well above four thousand feet. While Fool's Gold itself generally only saw thirty or forty inches of snow a year, the ski slopes saw on average ten times that amount.

Dellina parked and got out of her car. She was meeting Sam here so they could go over logistics. Everything from the menu at Henri's — the resort's five-star restaurant — to various accommodations. Both were equally important. But while she could totally get into food sampling, she was less sure about looking at bedrooms with Sam. Because the last time they'd been in a hotel together had been Valentine's Day and look how that had ended.

Dellina walked toward the hotel. She'd

always been a big believer in telling the truth — at least to herself. If Sam was offering, she would be mighty tempted to say yes. So it was probably good that he wasn't.

She saw a sleek black Mercedes convertible by the valet station and had a feeling that meant Sam was already here. She had used the regular self-park lot, like a normal person. She was still smiling at the comparison when she walked into the resort.

The Gold Rush Ski Lodge and Resort was part Victorian mansion, part chalet. There was wood everywhere, high ceilings and lots of attentive staff. The place would make a good impression on the most discerning of clients, she thought as she headed toward the tall dark-haired man standing by a window.

Even from the back, Sam was impressive. He had broad shoulders and long legs. He stood with an easy grace — still and yet poised for movement. Probably the result of all that athletic training. His suit pants had been tailored by an expert and showed off his narrow hips and muscular butt before falling in a straight line over his thighs.

He must have left his suit jacket in his car because he didn't have it with him. He'd rolled up his sleeves to his elbows and she figured there was a fifty-fifty chance he had on a tie.

All in all, an impressive man, she thought.

She moved closer. He must have sensed her because he turned and spotted her, then smiled.

"A nice place," he said as he walked toward her. "Good choice."

"Thanks, but you're the one who picked it," she reminded him, wondering how unhealthy it was for her heart to suddenly thunder so hard in her chest. Could the organ be bruised by all the flopping around and banging against bone?

She wanted him to be impressed by her and was tempted to mention her conversation with Lark Heuston's agent. The author was coming to Fool's Gold and seemed very interested in staying for the lecture. But until things were confirmed, Dellina wanted to keep the happy news to herself.

A pretty woman in her forties walked over. "Dellina," she said with a smile. "Great to see you." She held out her hand to Sam. "I'm Jody LaCroux, the events manager here at the hotel. You must be Sam Ridge."

They shook hands. Jody motioned for them to head down the hall. "We're very excited about the weekend you and Dellina have planned for your company, Mr. Ridge."

"Sam, please," he told her.

Jody had short blond hair and brown eyes. She wore a no-nonsense suit with a knee-length skirt, and sensible flat shoes. Dellina happened to know that when not overseeing weddings and banquets, Jody skied in the winter and ran marathons the rest of the year. She probably couldn't kick Sam's butt, yet she could sure outrun him.

"Nice to meet you, Sam." Jody smiled at Dellina. "You I know."

Dellina laughed. "When my sisters and I moved back to Fool's Gold, Jody spent a couple of Saturdays helping me work out a schedule for taking care of my sisters, the household and staying up with my classes at community college."

"I'm good with organization," Jody said. "I just never thought a degree in hotel management would come in handy in the community. I was happy to help."

She walked past the larger of the ballrooms and led them down the hallway to the smaller meeting rooms.

"Based on the number of couples and children you'll be hosting on-site, I think this part of the hotel will be best." She walked into a room that had an entire wall of windows, along with big doors that opened onto a patio and then a walled garden beyond. There were plenty of plants, but also a grassy area.

"For the children," Jody said with a wave of her hand. "Dellina, I'm thinking Friday night and Saturday afternoon. For Friday, we'd set up the mocktail and appetizer stations in the room. The kids will eat next door while the band sets up and we'll return here. It's big enough for them to move around, the walls keep them contained. There are restrooms right through there, so they never have to go out into the hallways."

"Good security," Dellina said as she took notes. "On Saturday, you're right. This is perfect for the meet-and-greet with the therapy dogs." She glanced at Sam. "You agree?"

He nodded. "I like the space."

They saw the patio where the adult wine tasting would be held, then went back toward the elevators.

"We have your guests together in a block," Jody told them as they waited for the elevator. "There will be another large party. A wedding. But your guests will have the entire top floor." Jody glanced at her notes. "Taryn Crawford put in a request for the presidential suite."

Sam grimaced. "Of course she did."

Dellina raised her eyebrows. "Is that a problem?"

"No. I'm sure she and Angel will enjoy it."

Jody met Dellina's gaze and smiled but didn't comment. They got on the elevator.

The top floor had high ceilings and beautiful moldings. The theme of woodwork and old-world charm continued. Jody showed them a large executive suite where a hospitality station with refreshments and light snacks would be manned from nine in the morning until midnight. Then she opened one of the rooms their guests would use.

She stepped back and motioned for them to go in. Dellina thought Sam would go first. He was the client. He hesitated, as if expecting her to lead the way. She took a step at the same time he did and they bumped into each other.

Heat engulfed her. His upper arm grazed her right breast and the contact sent a ribbon of need curling through to her lower belly. Her hand swung back and came perilously close to his groin. She jumped, he pulled back and they were both back in the hallway.

Sam cleared his throat. "You first," he said, his voice a little thick.

Dellina did as he suggested, hoping Jody was too busy taking notes to notice the awkwardness.

They stepped into a large bedroom. There was a sofa against one wall and French doors leading to a large balcony.

Jody followed them inside. "The rooms are all similar to this," she said. "We have enough adjoining rooms for the parents who have older children. For those with smaller kids, we can provide a rollaway." She consulted her list again. "You won't need any cribs, right?"

"The youngest is six," Dellina told her. "No cribs. And the oldest is thirteen, so I don't know if anyone will want adjoining rooms. That seems kind of young to be alone in a hotel room. Sam?"

He looked at her. "You're asking the wrong guy. We have the option, if the clients want adjoining rooms."

"Of course," Jody told him. "There are thirty rooms on this floor, plus the presidential suite. I'm holding a handful of rooms on the floor below for emergencies." She smiled. "Also for Dellina, the yet-to-be-named lecturer and Fayrene, who will be in charge of the children."

Sam turned to Dellina. "Smart," he said with a grin. "Not only will it take her mind off Ryan, she's someone you can trust to show up and do a good job."

"You're forgetting I can also boss her

around."

Jody grinned. "Is this where we have a conversation about your management style?" she asked.

"Not necessary. Fayrene can take it."

Jody walked them through the rest of the room. She pointed out the views, the large closets and all the amenities in the marble-and-glass bathrooms.

"A tub big enough for two," she said, and tapped a switch on the wall. "With jets. More fun for the couples who aren't bringing children."

Dellina nodded, thinking it was really weird how the room had suddenly gotten hot. And the bed was huge. Even from the bathroom it seemed to dominate the space. Although she couldn't say if it was better or worse than the giant tub complete with pulsing jets. Somehow an image of her and Sam in the tub lodged in her brain and she couldn't think about anything else . . . except maybe tumbling onto the bed while he —

"Great room," she said cheerfully, and made a beeline for the door.

Once in the hallway, she was able to breathe again. What was wrong with her? Sure Sam was a great-looking guy, and yes, the sex had been fabulous, but still. She was a professional. This was work and her biggest job of the year. No way she was going to allow herself to be distracted by hormones and huskiness.

Sam followed her into the hall and Jody made sure the room was locked.

"Food next?" Jody asked as if she hadn't noticed anything was wrong. Dellina hoped it was true.

They went back to the main floor and into the elegant dining room. The resort's five-star restaurant had been written up in both national and international publications. They'd received awards for everything from their menu to their wine list.

"Dellina sent me some suggestions for preliminary menus," Jody said as they sat at a round table. She opened a folder and then pulled out several sheets that she passed around. "Any vegetarian or vegan diets?"

Dellina turned to Sam. "Not that I know of."

"I'll find out," Sam said, a muscle twitching in his cheek. "For now, let's assume there aren't."

"Good." Jody rose. "Let me go tell the chef we're ready."

Dellina waited until they were alone to turn to him. "Why do you hate vegans?" she asked. "You got scrunchy-faced when

Jody asked about them."

"I don't hate vegans. I have problems with people who are picky eaters to get attention."

"Ex-girlfriend?"

"We don't need to talk about it."

Which meant yes. Dellina knew Sam had been married before. She wasn't much of a tabloid reader and didn't have time for entertainment-industry-based TV shows, but even she had heard something about it. Although she couldn't remember the specifics. And given his combination of sports-based career choice, income and physical appearance, she would guess there were always a lot of women around him. Which meant the picky eater could have been anyone.

She thought briefly that she could ask Taryn only to realize she couldn't be sure the other woman would know. After all, Sam was a man who liked his privacy. For all she knew, he was in a relationship right now.

Oh, God. Was he? Why hadn't she asked sooner? Here she'd been feeling all quivery when she was near him and he might be on the verge of proposing to someone.

"I think there's another executive suite on the top floor," she said, not looking at him. "If you want something nice for you and your guest."

His dark gaze settled on her face. "Guest?"

"Date? Girlfriend? Significant other? Whatever you want to call the woman you might be bringing to the event."

"I'm not bringing anyone. Taryn is the only one of us with a date."

She kept her gaze firmly on her notes and even pretended to write something. "Okay, then. A boring, standard room for you."

"What about you?"

Her head came up and her eyes locked with his. "Are you asking about my love life?"

"No." He turned away. "It's not my business. I apologize."

She remembered he was the guy who had never admitted he knew her, let alone that they'd shared a night together. A man who obviously didn't talk about personal stuff very much.

"You're allowed to ask," she told him. "And no, I won't be sharing my room. This is business, and even if it wasn't, I'm not seeing anyone."

Which fell into the category of TMI, she thought, although she didn't regret making things clear between them. Crazy, but there she was. Ridiculously happy that neither she nor Sam was seeing anyone else.

■ ■ ■ ■

CDS — or what the locals called the body-guard school — was located just east of town. Sam knew all the guys who worked there. They played basketball together several mornings a week. But he'd never been to their offices, or the obstacle course and trail run on the edge of their property.

Now he parked and walked inside. Dellina was already there, talking to Angel. For a second Sam allowed himself the pleasure of simply looking at her. She wore sweat-pants with a T-shirt. Her long hair had been pulled back into a ponytail. Her ever-present tote was overflowing with papers and folders and she had a clipboard in her hands.

The more-casual Dellina was just as appealing as the dressed-for-business version. She was efficient, friendly, and when she moved her mouth it was all he could do to keep himself from dragging her into the closest private space and kissing her for the next three days.

She got to him. He could admit it — mostly because he wasn't going to do anything about his reaction to her. For one thing, they worked together. No way he was wading into that kind of a mess. For another, he *liked* her. So why would he want to ruin that by getting involved? Every relationship he'd ever been in had ended with disaster. Even his one-night stands had created some problem or drama. He had the world's worst luck with women. He'd accepted that and could live with it. Mostly. There were times when he thought about what nearly everyone wanted — a traditional family. But that wasn't going to happen.

She looked up, saw him and smiled. The second her lips curved, he felt the kick to his gut. Breathing seemed impossible, his blood heated and sensory memories from their lone night together filled his brain.

"I'm nervous," she said by way of greeting. "I've never been overly coordinated." She turned back to Angel. "You're not doing much to make me feel better."

Angel grinned. "Scaring civilians is the best part of my day, dollface. I can't help it."

"You can but you don't want to. There's a difference." She walked over to Sam and showed him the clipboard. "Okay, this is the route we're considering. It's challenging, but not impossible. Or so Angel swears."

"Would I lie?" the former sniper asked.

"That remains to be seen," Dellina told him.

Sam told himself to stay still and keep breathing while he figured out what was wrong. A growing sense of anger and urgency seemed to be swelling inside of him. He wanted to hit something — specifically Angel. Except he generally liked Angel. So what was wrong?

Before he could decide, Ford joined them. The other man shook hands with Sam, then greeted Dellina.

"I told Angel to go easy on you," Ford told Sam. "You've got corporate types in for the weekend. We're not in boot camp. Plus, I know you, Kenny and Jack are pretty washed up."

Sam narrowed his gaze. "What did you say?"

Ford shrugged. "It's not like you have a real job anymore. Or ever. Kicking a football? They paid you for that?"

Dellina's mouth twitched. "Boys, can we stay focused on the task at hand, please? We need to try the obstacle course. Then the three of you can decide who is more manly."

"That would be me," they all said at once.

Dellina laughed.

They went outside. Angel explained the basics of the course. There was an area with

113

cones for sprints, followed by a balance station. Beyond that was a pull-up bar, several tires, a large pipe to crawl through and then a wall to scale.

Sam studied it all, then nodded. This was going to be fun. He was about to ask Ford to time him so he could beat his best run the next time through when he saw Dellina biting on her lower lip. The action was momentarily distracting until he realized she wasn't trying to be sexy.

"What's wrong?" he asked.

"That's pretty challenging," she said. "How fit are your guests?"

"The range will vary." He'd never met any of the spouses.

"Let's do a walk-through," Ford said. "We'll talk modifications as we go."

They walked to the starting line. Angel explained how the cones could be moved to lengthen or shorten the distance of the sprint. Sam took the distance at a run while Dellina walked through and made notes. At the balance beam, he crossed over easily. She handed Angel her clipboard, then walked across much more slowly, both arms out from her sides.

"Okay, both of those are a go," she said, retrieving her clipboard and making notes. "If I can do it, anyone can do it."

"Next up, chin-ups," Angel told her.

"Oh, joy."

Dellina tried to remember a time when she'd felt more out of shape. Some of it was the obstacle course itself and some of it was being around three very fit guys.

They had all been in professions that required physical prowess for success. In the case of Angel and Ford, being in good shape meant the difference between living and dying. The biggest exercise challenge Dellina usually faced was how fast to walk to her destination.

While Sam hadn't had his life on the line, he, too, had been expected to be in perfect condition. And he still was, she thought, glancing at his broad, muscled back as he completed yet another pull-up.

She managed to get through the line of tires without tripping, then watched Sam easily scale the wall. He grabbed the rope, walked up quickly and then sailed over the top. She groaned and walked around.

Angel shook his head. "You disappoint me," he told her. "You didn't even try."

"I'm clear on my limitations. You'll have to live with the disappointment." She looked back at the course. "This is great. Can you get me the contracts today?"

Ford nodded. "Not a problem. I'll get them out to you ASAP. Want to walk the trail?"

Sam had done a second circuit of the course. He cleared the wall with just as much ease and grace as he had the first time. She sighed.

"Sure. Let's add hiking to the mix." She briefly wondered how sore she would be tomorrow and decided to expand the Sunday morning mani-pedi event to include massages. Just in case.

Angel showed them the start of the trail. "It's marked and goes in a big circle. If you get lost, there's cell service."

The tone of his voice clearly implied that only wusses would dare to call for help.

"We'll be fine," Sam told him.

Dellina was less sure about that but was also confident Sam would keep her safe from any creepy nature thing lurking in the foliage.

"Want to know the fastest time for completing the route?" Angel asked.

"No," Dellina told him.

"Sure," Sam said eagerly.

She faced the former kicker. "We're walking the trail so we can know what to tell *your* guests. Maybe you can break records next time."

"Oh. Right." He shrugged. "We'll walk it."

"Fair enough." Angel started to turn away. "By the way, I hold the record."

Ford grinned. "You are so lying and I'm going to tell Consuelo. Someone's getting his ass kicked."

Angel glared at his friend. "Fine. I'm off her top time by a tenth of a second. She faked me out at the end."

"Always with the excuses," Ford said. He started back for the main building. "Consuelo, guess what I found out."

Angel took off after him.

Dellina watched them. "Is it like that with you and Jack and Kenny?" she asked.

"I have no idea what you're talking about."

She smiled. "Right, because I believe that."

She dug her ever-present notepad out of her tote and made a few notes about the obstacle course. "Larissa isn't actually licensed in the state of California, is she? I kind of remember Taryn telling me that."

"She has the training," Sam said. "But I don't know if she sat for her boards or not. Why?"

"I'm thinking the Sunday afternoon spa experience should include massages. She would be good to have on hand."

"Include the information in what you send

the guests and have them sign waivers. If you tell them she's our private masseuse, they won't care about a license."

Dellina nodded. He had a point. She would check on the legality of it all and then make her decision. Besides, they would need more than one masseuse, anyway.

She and Sam headed toward the trail. Only a few feet from the CDS warehouse was a grove of trees that stretched toward the mountains. Soon, she found herself in dense growth and all signs of civilization quickly faded.

The air was cool and quiet. If not for the gravel path, she would have assumed they were lost. A couple of dozen feet later, gravel became dirt, but she was pleased to see that the well-worn track was as easy to follow as Angel had promised.

"This is nice," she said as they walked next to each other. She did her best to focus on her work and not notice that every now and then Sam's arm brushed against hers. He was warm and sexy and she found herself anticipating the little tingles that shot through her with each second of contact.

"We should get one of these by the office," he said.

She laughed. "You're not in the middle of town, but you're still surrounded by other buildings. How do you propose getting a forest on your property? Isn't the basketball court enough?"

"This is better," he said as he glanced around.

Boys with toys, she thought fondly. "You must have been quite the athletic kid," she told him. "I was more of a reader. Fayrene and Ana Raquel were into soccer and dance. I liked taking art classes." She paused as he looked at her. "What? You're the one who doesn't talk about personal things. Does that mean I can't?"

"I like hearing about your family."

There was something in his tone, she thought. A question? A concern? She wasn't sure.

She stopped and faced him. He was taller than her. His dark eyes were unreadable in the twilight of the forest. She could smell earth and leaves and flowers, but none of them were as appealing as the man standing in front of her.

Oh, to not be working with him, she thought. Just for five minutes so she could inappropriately throw herself at him. Not that she would. That had never been her style. But a girl could dream.

"It's normal to share information," he told her. "I get that. You tell me something personal and I respond in kind."

She risked putting her hand on his forearm. "Except you don't roll that way. You want to keep things private and I'm okay with that."

"I don't roll that way?" he repeated. "Did you just say that?"

She grinned. "Maybe."

He moved toward her. For a second she thought he was going to . . . Well, she wasn't sure what, but a kiss would be nice. Or a declaration that being near to her drove him so crazy he couldn't control himself. Hmm, what would an uncontrolled Sam be like? she wondered wistfully. Amazing, for sure.

He raised his arms. For a second she thought he was going to pull her close. Her heart started to beat fast and flutter a little and her throat got tight. His hands were headed straight for her shoulders. Okay, not exactly a traditional hug position but she was open to experimenting. If he —

Sam dropped his hands to her shoulders, turned her around so she was facing the trail, then gave her a little push.

She held in a sigh.

"I wasn't athletic as a kid," he told her as they walked down the trail. "I was sick."

She stopped and faced him again. "Sick how?"

"Asthma. It was pretty bad when I was little. I outgrew it, but my parents were protective." He grimaced. "Especially my mom. My dad had played professional basketball and Mom was an equestrian. One of my sisters played volleyball professionally and the other had planned on playing women's basketball until she was discovered by an agency and became a model."

It was probably as much information as she could have gotten off of Wikipedia, but still. This was Sam telling her personal stuff. She had a thousand questions — about his parents and his sisters — but she could only focus on one fact.

"I'm sorry you were sick. It must have been tough for you."

He shifted uncomfortably and reached for her again. This time she knew what he wanted and started walking again. He fell into step beside her.

"It wasn't fun," he admitted. "I was the youngest and the smallest. I hated always being left behind. Once I started to get better, I wanted to play sports, but everyone was worried. When I insisted on going out for football, my mother practically chained me to my bed."

"She might have thought you were over-compensating."

He shot her a sideways glance. "You're not the first one to suggest that."

She grinned. "Then I'm in good company." She paused as the path curved. As Angel had promised, it was easy to see where to go.

"You compromised on the kicking." She could see how that would be less stressful on his body. Almost no direct hits. Kicking was more about skill than brawn.

"I practiced until I was good, then tried out for the team without anyone in the family knowing. When I made it, my dad signed the paperwork. Mom and my sisters didn't know until the first game."

Dellina thought about how she would have felt if they were talking about her son. "I'm amazed your dad is still standing."

"She wasn't happy, but she got over it."

"And the rest is history," she said. "Now you're in a profession that's safer. She must like that."

"She does."

"You were married before."

The words popped out before she could stop them. Because while bringing up other personal information with anyone else was no big deal, it was with Sam.

"Not that we have to discuss that," she added softly.

He didn't speak for a second. "I was. It didn't work out."

"I'm sorry." The statement was automatic, because in truth, she wasn't sorry. Married Sam wouldn't be interesting at all.

"It happens. She wrote a tell-all after the divorce."

For the third time, she came to a stop. This time when she faced him, she had her hands on her hips. "There is no way. Seriously? A tell-all? About you? That's horrible." She drew in a breath. "You know that's not normal, right? It's one thing to be mad at your ex, but that's what girlfriends are for. You complain to them. Maybe send a hostile email. But a tell-all?"

"I have really bad luck with women."

"Including finding the only one in town who has dozens of wedding dresses stored in her house?"

"Yup."

She smiled. "Except I turned out to be not so bad."

"That's true."

He raised his arms. She dropped hers to her sides.

"I know, I know," she began. "We need to keep moving."

"No, we don't," he told her right before he pulled her close and kissed her.

She was so not expecting to be pulled against him, nor was she anticipating the feel of his warm, firm mouth against hers. All the previous anticipation heightened her senses and made every point of contact, every bit of pressure, even more tingle-worthy.

He kissed her lightly at first, then with more intensity. His mouth lingered, as if he liked touching hers.

His hands rested on her hips. The light contact made her want to squirm closer. As it was, she was already nestled against his broad, hard chest. And thinking about that made her wonder if other things were hard and if he was interested in . . .

His tongue touched her lower lip. Electricity surged, blood heated and her breasts swelled until they were uncomfortable. She parted her lips for him. At the same time she wrapped her arms around his neck and gave herself over to the kiss.

He tasted sweet and hot, and the slow, leisurely way he began to explore her mouth had her melting from the inside out. He circled her tongue and teased the tip with his before retreating just enough to make her want to whimper. Then he was back with deeper thrusts and intense attention.

Her chest was tight, as if breathing had

become difficult. She wanted him with an intensity that reminded her the last time she'd made love had been several months before and it had been with the very man kissing her now. Before that . . . well, she couldn't remember how long it had been.

She was about to tell him that the leaves were probably very comfortable when Sam drew back.

"I'm sorry," he told her. "That was unprofessional."

For a brief second, she thought he was talking about his performance, which to her mind had been completely spectacular. But then she realized he meant the fact that they worked together and still had the big party to prepare. Desire and arousal battled with her love of her career and common sense. Internally she stomped her foot and threw a hissy fit. On the outside, she nodded sagely.

"We're equally to blame," she said, her voice as normal as she could make it. "It was one of those things. No big deal."

"It won't happen again."

Instead of asking "Why not?" she nodded again, turned and started walking more quickly. She ignored the humming sensation inside of her and the gnawing need that made her want to whimper. She was a strong, self-actualized woman. And if things got really ugly, she had a massage shower-head back home.

Sam stood outside of Dellina's small house. She'd left him a message, saying it was important. So here he was. Except she hadn't asked him to come over. He'd made that decision on his own. He could have called, and that was why he was standing on her porch instead of ringing the bell.

He wanted to see her. The kiss had been a rookie mistake. He knew better, but there had been something about the way she'd been standing there, looking all sexy and pretty and charming. He'd reacted. He knew the dangers of getting involved and he'd kissed her, anyway. Because there was something about Dellina. Something that made him make bad choices.

He raised his arm and pushed the bell. He was going to tell her that, he decided. Admit he had a problem where she was concerned and say he was going to back off. Let her handle the party without him being involved at all. He trusted her to get it right. That would be better for both of them.

Her front door flew open and she stood in front of him. The second she saw him, she started grinning and dancing in place.

"I did it!" she told him. "I totally and

completely did it." She motioned for him to step inside, then closed the door behind him and twirled in place.

Her long wavy brown hair fanned out behind her. She was barefoot, in jeans and a T-shirt. She radiated happiness and excitement and it was contagious. Or maybe it was just being around her, because all he wanted to do was join in the dance and then kiss her until they both forgot why he was there.

She came to a stop in front of him and grinned. "I found the perfect person for the lecture. She's a bestselling author and a teacher and both men and women are going to love her."

She motioned for him to follow her, then led the way to her office. On the way, he noticed the spare room was now empty of all wedding gowns. Even the racks were gone. A futon had been pushed against one wall and there was a floor lamp. The dry-erase board was still in place. He saw Fayrene's current suggestions for getting Ryan to propose included "Pretend to be pregnant" and "Learn to make pot roast."

He stepped inside and wrote "no" by the former and "yes" by the latter. Dellina watched from the doorway.

"Offering commentary?" she asked with a grin.

"I don't usually give advice but in this case I'm feeling confident."

They went into her office. She reached into her large bag and pulled out a book.

"Sex," she told him happily.

All the reasons not to disappeared as he started to say yes. So what if it would lead to disaster? This was Dellina and he'd wanted her from the first second he'd seen her. Having her once hadn't been nearly —

His gaze dropped to the book in her hand. It was like being plunged into a frozen lake. At first there was nothing, then icy cold claimed his body and he couldn't do more than stare at the familiar cover and let the horror overtake him.

"Lark Heuston said yes," Dellina told him proudly. "She was already coming here for a signing and she's agreed to stay through the weekend. She said the timing was perfect because she has family in the area. She's going to do the lecture and maybe a demonstration. Sam? Are you okay?"

He tried to speak and couldn't. A demonstration. He swore silently, knowing exactly what that meant. Or worse, guessing. Because whatever he imagined, reality would be so much worse.

He cleared his throat. "You do realize that when Lark Heuston says demonstration she means exactly that. Having sex onstage. Or possibly showing a video of it." Because the book in question was about using tantric sex to strengthen a marriage and the author was nothing if not thorough. "She's done a series of instructional videos."

He could barely say it and he sure didn't want to think about it.

"She wouldn't really get naked and do it in front of people," Dellina told him.

"I sure hope not, but she has in the past."

"You know her?".

He nodded.

Why? Why now? Why here? Why couldn't she leave him alone? He tried to tell himself that knowing she was coming would mean he could prepare. Based on what Dellina had just told him, the original plan had been for her presence to be a surprise.

"She's bringing her husband," Dellina was saying. "They're well into their sixties, I think. I can't imagine them having sex in front of us."

"I can," he said grimly.

"How do you know her?"

"She's my mother."

CHAPTER SIX

Sam didn't remember walking back to Score, but suddenly he was there, pushing through the front door. He must have left Dellina's and gone through town. It was all a blur of her pointing out that he and Lark had different last names. He'd explained how his mother had used her maiden name with her work and that yes, he'd seen several of her lectures and workshops. They were etched into his brain, just one more in a series of hideous memories from his childhood.

He loved his entire family, including his mother, but growing up with them had taught him that not every intimate detail needed to be shared. He hadn't wanted to know that his parents had enjoyed a new sexual technique the night before or that his sisters had their periods. He hadn't wanted to talk about his own sexual development or, back when he'd been a teenager, have

130

his mother ask him, over breakfast, if he'd masturbated yet that day. He'd just wanted to be normal and have parents who understood that some topics shouldn't be discussed.

Now, shocked and more than a little disoriented, he stood in the foyer of the Score building and waited for the world to right itself. Then he would figure out a plan. Because there was no way he could get through a visit from his mother without a plan.

Kenny strolled into view, took one look at him and hurried to his side.

"What happened? Were you in a car accident? Man, you look terrible."

Sam swallowed and forced himself to speak. "My parents are coming to town."

Kenny started laughing that huge laugh of his, which echoed up both stories of the foyer. Seconds later Jack had joined them.

"What?" Jack demanded. "What'd I miss?"

"Lark and Reggie are coming to town," Kenny told him, then slapped Sam on the back. "What brings them here?"

Jack shoved Sam into one of the visitor chairs. "Give the man some room," he told his friend. "Sam's relationship with his parents is complicated. Respect that."

The sharp, steady sound of high heels on

131

tile warned him that Taryn had joined the party.

"What's going on?" she asked. "Why are you three congregating out here?"

"Lark and Reggie are coming to town," Kenny told her.

Taryn sat next to Sam and took his hand in hers. "Talk to me," she told him. "What's going on? Obviously you just found out. Breathe and we'll get through this."

Sam did as she instructed. He stared into her violet-blue eyes and felt more in control. "She has a new book out."

Taryn nodded. "I know. She sent me a copy. It's interesting."

He winced. That was one way to describe what she did. "She set up a signing here in town and she's staying for the Score weekend. Dellina arranged for her to do the lecture."

Taryn's mouth twitched. Sam wasn't sure if she was holding in a smile or trying not to recoil.

"That will be fun," was all she said.

Kenny chuckled. "Think she and Reggie will have sex onstage?"

"No," Jack said firmly. "She wouldn't do that to us."

Sam hoped he was right but thought maybe his friend was being optimistic.

"She might show a video," Kenny said. "She gave me the whole set one Christmas. I tried to watch them, but it was too scary. I mean, I like sex as much as the next guy, but watching people I know do it was just too . . ."

"Tell me about it." Jack looked at Sam. "You okay?"

"No." Sam dropped his head to his hands. This could not be happening.

Taryn patted his back. "Look at it this way. She was coming to town for a signing. There was no way she was going to leave without seeing you. At least you can be prepared."

He nodded. "I was going to come up with a plan."

"There you go. Forewarned and all that. You'll get through it. I know your folks are difficult for you. But they're sweet people. I still remember when your mom explained to me how to do deep-throated fella —"

He rose and faced them all.

"Stop. Just stop. Don't talk about my parents, don't reminisce and, for God's sake, don't encourage them. Do I make myself clear?"

Before any of them could answer, he stalked away.

■ ■ ■ ■

Fayrene put the first dish in the oven and checked the timer. Ryan was setting out the appetizers and their guests were due any second. Everything was going according to plan.

After racking her brain for a solution to the "Ryan" problem, she'd finally come up with the perfect answer. She was going to show Ryan how amazing married life could be. So she'd invited Pia and Raoul over for dinner. They'd been married a few years now, had four kids, including three-year-old twins and a six-month-old little boy. More important, they were wildly in love with each other. Her plan was for Ryan to see that and realize what he was missing.

Ryan didn't know the other couple very well, but Fayrene had worked for both of them. They were lovely people. Maybe ten years older, but so together in their relationship.

Tiny nails made a clicking sound on the kitchen floor. Fayrene smiled as Caramel rounded the corner and hurried toward her.

"Hey, fluffball," Fayrene murmured, reaching for the small dog. Caramel, ever the polite little girl, gave a tiny push off the

134

floor as she was picked up. "You know, I think I can handle the four pounds plus fur."

Caramel stared adoringly into her face, then leaned in and kissed her chin.

"Thank you," Fayrene said, holding her close. She'd only had the Pomeranian a few days, but somehow Caramel had melded with her life effortlessly. "I'm going to miss you when Mayor Marsha takes you back. You know that, don't you?"

Fayrene always connected with the pets she took care of, but something about this one was different. A problem she would deal with later, she told herself as she set the dog on the floor and together they walked out into the living room.

"Impressive, huh?" Ryan said with a grin.

She nodded in agreement. He'd not only straightened up the room, he'd set up a drinks station on a bookshelf and put the appetizers on the coffee table. For a second she let her gaze settle on his handsome face. Sometimes, when she looked at him, she thought her heart would crack from being so full of love for him.

She crossed the room and put her hands on his shoulders, then rose on tiptoe and kissed him. He kissed her back. About three seconds later, she felt Caramel's little feet on her leg as the Pomeranian stood on her back legs as if asking, "What about me?"

"You're important, too," Ryan said, sweeping the little dog up in his arms. Caramel immediately rolled onto her back and gazed lovingly into his eyes.

"She's got you twisted around her little finger," Fayrene told him with a grin.

"Yeah? I'm not the only one."

The doorbell rang. Ryan walked to open it, Caramel tucked under one arm.

The next few minutes were a flurry of greetings. Raoul, a former Cowboys quarterback, stayed close to Pia, his attractive wife. They were warm and friendly, saying nice things about the small apartment. When they were seated on the sofa, Caramel hopped onto the cushions, then stepped onto Raoul's muscled thighs and studied him.

Pia smiled. "Pretty girls are always attracted to him."

Raoul petted the dog. "Yeah, but this time I want to like her back."

"What can I get you to drink?" Fayrene asked.

"Do you have wine?" Pia asked. "I haven't had wine since I found out I was pregnant and tonight's the night." She covered her mouth briefly, as if holding in a yawn. "Just one, though. Ryder's started teething and that means I've been up a lot at night."

Ryan went to get the bottle of wine from the bookcase. "What about you, Raoul?"

"A beer if you have it."

Ryan grinned. "I do. It's from a local microbrewery."

"Good man."

Pia accepted the glass of wine and kicked off her shoes, then tucked her legs up under her. She took a sip and sighed.

"This is so nice," she said to Fayrene. "Thank you for inviting us. These days we rarely get out. We could, of course. There are plenty of people willing to babysit. It's just with the twins turning three and Ryder, it's difficult."

Raoul put his arm around her. "Plus you're shepherding Peter to a lot of things these days." He glanced at them. "He's thirteen now. Seriously into baseball and cycling."

Ryan returned from the kitchen with a beer in each hand. He gave one to Raoul. Fayrene took her glass of wine and sat down opposite the sofa. Ryan settled on the floor at her feet. Caramel abandoned their company to crawl on Ryan's lap and curl up as she frequently did.

"Four kids is a lot," Ryan said.

"But wonderful," Fayrene added, thinking

they needed to be talking about how great it was to be married and have a family. "They must bring you a lot of happiness."

"They do," Pia said with another yawn. "The age difference is challenging. Mostly because it's in Peter's nature to help and I don't want his childhood to be about taking care of the twins or his baby brother." She looked at Raoul. "He's a great kid. We got so lucky with him."

"With all our kids," her husband said, then kissed her forehead.

Fayrene knew that Peter was adopted and that the twins weren't theirs biologically, either. Ryder was the first child they had together.

Raoul turned to Ryan. "You work for Ethan," he said. "I've been hearing about the modifications you're making on the wind turbine designs. Innovative thinking."

"Thanks. I like my work."

The two couples talked about what was going on in Fool's Gold these days.

"I'm hearing that the town is annexing more of the surrounding areas," Pia said, then covered another yawn. "Someone told me that the Nicholson ranch will be within city limits now. At least the acreage with the house on it. I remember Zane Nicholson from high school. He was in my class." She smiled at her husband. "He was very popular with the ladies, just like you."

"As long as I don't have competition with him now."

Pia smiled. "You don't." She set her glass on the coffee table and leaned against her husband. "How's your business, Fayrene?" she asked.

"I'm busy."

"That's good," Pia murmured. "The wine was nice. Did I mention I haven't had wine in over a year?"

As she spoke her eyes drifted closed. Fayrene waited for her to say something else, only to realize that her guest had fallen asleep. Pia's breathing deepened and her body relaxed. Raoul glanced down and grinned.

"It's the kids," he murmured. "Keeping her up too many nights." He paused awkwardly. "I'm sorry but I think we're going to have to take a rain check on our dinner. I really should get her home and in bed."

Fayrene involuntarily glanced at the clock. It was six. Barely evening. She looked at Ryan, who seemed just as startled.

"Come on, sleepyhead," Raoul said gently, shifting Pia into a sitting position. "Let's get you home."

"What? Did I fall asleep?" Pia flushed.

"I'm so sorry. It's just everything going on. You know — three kids under four — it's challenging." She shook her head. "I'm fine. Really. Can I have a cup of coffee? Then I'm sure I can stay awake through dinner."

"You don't have to," Fayrene told her. "You should go home and sleep."

Pia hesitated, then stood. Raoul did the same and put his arm around her.

"If you don't mind, we'd love to take a rain check on dinner." She yawned again, then leaned against her husband. "Thanks for understanding."

Ryan held Caramel as he and Fayrene ushered out their guests. When the door had closed, Fayrene leaned against the wall. So much for showing Ryan how wonderful marriage could be. It was barely six in the evening and the Moreno family was in for the night.

Ryan handed her Caramel, then put his arm around her. "So," he said with a grin. "What's for dinner?"

Dellina stretched out on the chaise and sipped her margarita. The sun was warm and she was with friends. Talk about a great way to spend an afternoon. Besides, she was with the right group to get information.

They were in Taryn's beautiful walled

140

garden. Taryn was next to her in another chair while Larissa was on Dellina's other side. A couple of big umbrellas shaded them and there was a light breeze. Taryn had promised Angel would be by later with snacks. As Dellina hadn't had an afternoon off, let alone a day, in about three weeks, she was going to soak up every second of this before she had to throw herself back into the Score party.

The good news was everything was coming together. The bad news was, she didn't know if she should be worried about having Lark Heuston lecture or not.

"You two have met Sam's mother," Dellina began. "He's totally freaked about her coming to the event. Should I be concerned?"

Taryn leaned forward to look past her toward Larissa. "You want to go first or should I?"

"You go," Larissa told her. "You know her better than me."

Taryn leaned back in her chair. "I love her breathing techniques. I use them all the time."

"Me, too," Larissa said. "They help me relax."

"I use them for sex," Taryn murmured, then sipped her drink.

141

Dellina opened her mouth, realized she had nothing to say, then closed it.

"The thing is," Taryn continued, "Reggie and Lark are really sweet people. They love their kids and are generous to everyone they meet. They just don't have regular privacy boundaries. They're open, affectionate people."

"Who share everything," Larissa added.

"They do," Taryn said. "I've met Sam's sisters and they're just like his folks. Sweet and funny, but they'll tell you anything. Sometimes it's okay and sometimes it's a little weird."

Larissa nodded. "Like the time Lark wanted to show me this technique where you press down on your clitoris as you rub to increase intensity during orgasm."

Dellina had been swallowing. She started to choke. "Show as in *show*?" she asked when she could talk again.

"Oh, yeah," Taryn said. "I asked her to describe it instead, then went home and practiced." She grinned. "It works and now Angel is an expert."

Dellina felt her cheeks begin to burn. "I don't think I could do that. Watch or be shown."

"Sam would agree with you," Taryn said. "His family makes him insane."

Dellina could relate. She was also worried about the weekend, although everything about this conversation was surreal. "I'm going to have to talk to Lark and explain we need to keep things at a steady PG-13. Do you think she'll listen?"

"Sure," Larissa told her. "After I said I was uncomfortable with a real, live demonstration, she only described things. She respects other people's boundaries."

"Except Sam's," Taryn added. "I'm not concerned. She knows this is our business and our clients. I'll talk to her before anything gets started. Not that I can calm Sam down. Poor guy."

They talked about the opening of Isabel's boutique and how fast the year was racing by.

"I'm looking forward to the Summer Festival," Larissa said. "I just love how this town celebrates."

"You should see us at Christmas," Dellina told her. "It's magical."

Larissa sighed happily. "I'll bet it's romantic here, that time of year. Not that I have anyone to be romantic with."

Taryn wrinkled her nose. "Save me from too much sappiness."

"Not one for twinkle lights?" Dellina asked, her voice teasing.

"Not really. But maybe it will be different. With Angel."

Her voice changed as she spoke his name. It softened and deepened and made Dellina feel a little left out. She couldn't remember the last time she'd been in love — probably because she never had been. There had been guys, but no one that special.

Larissa stood. "I'm going to get a refill. Anyone want one?"

"I'm good," Dellina told her. She had to work later and too much tequila would make that impossible.

Taryn sat up. "I'll stick with what I have."

Larissa walked into the house. Taryn swung her legs toward Dellina and pulled off her sunglasses.

"I want to talk to you," the other woman said, her blue-violet eyes intense.

"Sure. About the party? I'm open to suggestions."

"God, no. You're doing great with all that. I don't want to be involved. I'm worried about Sam."

"Okay," Dellina said slowly, not sure what Taryn meant.

"Don't break his heart."

Dellina felt her mouth drop open. "Excuse me? Break his heart? That's not possible. We're working together." She conveniently

144

ignored the recent kiss. "Sam isn't going to fall for me."

"I'm not so sure about that. Sam tries to withdraw from the world as much as he can. Especially when it comes to relationships. He's had horrible luck with the women in his life. But the thing is, he's basically a pretty traditional guy. He wants to be married and have a couple of kids. He wants a happy ending." Taryn paused. "In the emotional sense, I mean."

"I get that. Look, you don't have to worry about me. I'm not looking for Mr. Right. I've raised my sisters. I don't need to do that again. Sam knows that. Even if he is looking for more, he's not going to find it with me."

"You're sure he knows that?"

"We had a very clear discussion before we started working together. But like I said — it's not an issue. I'm not his type."

"Maybe," Taryn said. "We'll see."

Dellina shook her head. There was no "seeing" involved. They were friends. Sure, she liked Sam and thought he was sexy, but he was some famous football guy. He would never be interested in a regular woman like her. He would want a supermodel or a . . . Well, she wasn't sure what, but not her.

"If you should be worried about anyone's

heart, it's mine," she grumbled.

Taryn grinned. "Duly noted." Her smile faded. "In the meantime, read this."

She pulled a book out of the large tote next to her on the patio. Dellina was half expecting an older release from Sam's mother. Instead she stared into the blue eyes of a beautiful woman smiling back at her from the front cover.

The title said it all. *Getting the Man You Want: Tales from My Marriage to NFL Star Sam Ridge.*

"Sam's ex really did write a book," Dellina breathed.

"With pictures and everything. You know how Sam guards his privacy. This would have devastated any man, but for Sam it was worse."

Dellina started to hand it back. Taryn shook her head. "Keep it. Read it. Learn from her mistakes. Just don't break Sam's heart."

Sam turned onto Forest Highway as he headed out of town. Dellina sat next to him in his car, her clipboard in hand.

"I'm thinking the drive out to Castle Ranch will be a good time for a little history on the area," she was saying. "We can tell them about the first known residents.

The Máa-zib tribe, then a few lines about the Spanish settlers. I'm not sure we need to go into the history of the ranch itself." She paused and looked at him. "Do you think that would be interesting?"

He'd already turned on Mother Bear Road and was quickly approaching the ranch. "Is there time for much more information?"

She glanced around. "Not really. It's a quick trip. Have you been here before?"

"No."

He slowed at the sign and turned onto a paved driveway. He could see a large house that seemed to be in the middle of major renovation, along with a big barn. There was another house in the distance and some kind of fenced-in structure that was smaller than the barn, but obviously not a residence.

He parked by a pickup and a Mercedes, then turned off the engine. Dellina was already climbing out of the car.

The woman had energy, he thought, following her. As always, she'd dressed appropriately. A T-shirt and jeans over boots. And real boots — not the kind Taryn wore with ridiculous heels and exotic skins. Dellina was more casual. More approachable. Sexier.

He shook off the last thought and moved

next to her.

"Horses," she said, pointing. "They only have a few that they board. Mostly the horses are at Shane and Annabelle's place. That's a few miles away. On the other side is where Charlie and Clay live. Clay owns the Haycation Village."

"Haycation?"

"People come for a week to experience ranch and farm life. A simpler time, only with Wi-Fi. Rafe, Clay and Shane are brothers. Rafe is a developer. Heidi raises goats. She makes cheese and soap." Dellina pointed to the largest fenced-in area. "The brothers' mother is the animal rescue person. That's her elephant, Priscilla, along with her pony, Reno."

He nearly confirmed that the "her" who had the pony was the human in the sentence, but stopped himself. It sounded familiar and, of course, this was Fool's Gold and it was far more likely that Priscilla had the pony.

A pretty blonde with pigtails approached. She greeted Dellina with a hug, then introduced herself as Heidi Stryker.

"Come on," Heidi said. "I've got several ideas for our Sunday morning with your kids. You can pick and choose the ones you think will be best."

They walked to the main house. Once inside he saw the kitchen had already been remodeled. It was big and open, with lots of counter space and an eat-in area. Heidi got them iced tea, then joined them at the table. She passed out several sheets of paper.

"We have options," she said. "Given the range of ages, I thought that was important. Shane can be available for a basic roping lesson." She smiled. "It's pretty fun. We set up a sawhorse with a little toy cow head on one end and a fake tail on the other. We'll also have several gentle horses available for riding. Shane teaches kids how to ride all the time. He's really patient."

Sam studied the list. "Cheese and soap-making?"

Heidi nodded. "I can do a demo only or we can get the kids involved. The problem is that soap has to cure or dry for several days. So while they could work on it, they can't take that batch home with them."

Dellina was busy making notes. She glanced up long enough to ask, "Cheese making is going to be the same, right? They can't take home what they start."

"Right."

"We'll talk about it and get back to you," Dellina said.

They went over the lunch menu next. Sam

thought the choices were fine. Dellina asked a lot of questions and had some suggestions, which was why he'd hired her.

He liked her quiet efficiency and how she thought through the details. Now that he'd been spending time with her, he couldn't figure out why he'd gotten so spooked that night. No normal woman kept that many wedding dresses in her house without a good reason. Even the crazy ones would only have a couple.

He should have stayed to ask, he thought. He should have taken a breath and figured out what was happening. Because then he wouldn't have disappeared into the night and he and Dellina would have . . .

Would have what? he asked himself. Kept seeing each other? To what end? Hadn't he been down that road enough?

"This is going to be the best part of the party," Dellina said as she and Sam headed back to town. "The kids are going to love the ranch. It will be a great time for them and their parents are going to appreciate that they not only had fun but are nice and tired."

"Is that the voice of experience?" he asked, his voice teasing. "Your sisters were teenagers when you had to take care of them. Hardly an age where you want them tired."

She laughed. "Okay, that's true, although I'll admit it was nice when they came home exhausted and simply went to bed. There was less worry." She shook her head. "That's not fair. Both Ana Raquel and Fayrene worked really hard to be responsible and not give me reason to worry. We'd all suffered a horrible loss and we pulled together."

He lightly touched the back of her hand with his fingers. "I didn't mean to bring up bad memories."

"You didn't."

She leaned back in the comfortable leather seat. Sam's Mercedes sure was nice, she thought idly. It was like him. Steady and dependable. There might be those who were more interested in something like a Ferrari, but she thought he and his car were just right.

"It's not just my sisters," she said. "It's how the town pulled together for us. Like with Heidi. She grew up in the carnival."

Sam glanced at her, then turned his attention back to the road. "Traveling around the country with a carnival?"

"That's her. She said she always dreamed of a house that was attached to city plumb-

151

ing and couldn't be moved. She bought Castle Ranch and moved here with her grandmother. He fell in love, she fell in love, her husband's brothers and sister fell in love. Now they all live here. It's the town. Something happens when people settle here."

She started to say more, then caught sight of Sam's pinched expression. She chuckled.

"Go ahead," she told him. "Resist. I can see you want to. But it won't help."

"We'll see."

"You're saying it's a little too perfect?"

"I'm saying you've idealized reality."

"A cynic. We like that. It makes convincing you all the more satisfying." She glanced down at her ever-present list. They were getting closer and closer to the event and she was starting to feel the pressure. In the next couple of days, she was going to have to start finalizing everything.

"We have to discuss goodie bags," she told him. "I have samples at my place and I have to make the final orders. As it is, everything will be shipping overnight."

"Say when and I'll be there."

Now that sounded nice, she thought, knowing what he meant and how she would *like* him to mean it. She was debating pushing at the limits of their business relationship just a little when her cell rang. She pulled it out of her pocket and glanced at the screen. "Fayrene," she told Sam before pushing the talk button. "Hey, what's going on?"

"There's a fire at the storage center." Fayrene's voice was frantic. "It's the rabbits."

Dellina went cold. "No," she breathed. "Where are you?"

"On my way. I can't get ahold of Ryan. He's flown out to an installation site and won't be back for a couple of days." Her voice was thick with tears. "The rabbits."

"I know," Dellina told her. "We'll get there in time."

CHAPTER SEVEN

Sam followed Dellina's frantic instructions as they headed into town. She was pale and shaking. All he'd been able to get out of her was, "It's the rabbits." A sentence that didn't make sense. What rabbits? He'd never seen rabbits in town.

The closer they got, the more traffic clogged the streets. Dellina tapped impatiently on her armrest, then shook her head. "I'm getting out."

He barely had time to slow the car before she jumped out and started running along the sidewalk. He swore, then pulled into the first parking space he found and sprinted after her.

As he did, he was aware of dozens of people running in the same direction. He also noticed the smell of smoke in the air. Seconds later he heard sirens. All of which made sense. What didn't was a handful of people walking in the opposite direction with what looked like piles of white fur in their arms. Then there were two guys with giant rabbit heads tucked under each arm.

Sam caught up with Dellina at the corner. He grabbed her arm. "What's going on?"

Her eyes were wide, her expression frantic. "There's a fire at the storage place that stores all the rabbit costumes." He must have looked blank because she added, "Every Easter families dress up in them and there's a parade. It's a tradition."

Tears filled her brown eyes. "I used to walk in the parade with my parents and my sisters. We can't let anything happen to the costumes. Do you have any idea how many memories are in those costumes? They last for years. We have to hurry. We have to help!"

Then she took off again. Sam stood on the sidewalk as the street filled with people carrying costumes. Armfuls, including the heads and giant rabbit feet. It was strange and funny and maybe a little moving.

He saw a woman in her late forties staggering with a pile of costumes that nearly went over her head. He jogged toward her and took the costumes from her arms. She wiped away the tears trickling down her cheeks.

"Thank you," she said, her voice thick

with emotion. "The fire is under control, but the smoke could damage everything. If you could just carry those to the park."

"Sure."

He held the costumes easily as the woman went off to help someone else.

He followed the moving crowd and found himself in Pyrite Park by the lake. Several deputies were there along with city officials. Order had been restored and people were laying costumes out on the grass so they could air out.

Sam put his down where directed, then stepped back to study the odd site of a couple of hundred rabbit costumes lying on dark green grass on a summer afternoon. Several people were checking tags and matching large heads with bodies. Others were doing the same with the feet. The scene was both funny and slightly horrific. Like a shot from a movie.

Sam helped several more people with their piles of costumes. He spotted Dellina and walked over to her. She stood with her arms wrapped around her body, looking shell-shocked.

He wanted to tell her they were just costumes and could be replaced. But he knew they were much more than that. Somehow these ridiculous bits of fake fur and plastic had become important — a part of a tradition. So instead of speaking, he pulled her into his embrace and held her close.

She leaned against him, pressing her cheek to his shoulder.

"It's so awful," she whispered.

"They're all safe now. After they air out, they'll be fine."

"I know. It could have been much worse, but still . . ."

He kissed her forehead, then led her back to his car. "You live in a really weird little town," he told her.

She managed a laugh. "I do and I love it. One day you'll love it, too."

Not enough to rush into a burning building and rescue rabbit costumes, he thought. Although God knew, he'd been wrong before.

Sam got back to the office an hour later. He headed directly for the locker room where he always kept a change of clothes. After stripping out of the ones that smelled like smoke and singed fake fur, he grabbed a towel from the stack and headed for the showers.

Score had been remodeled to the partners' exact specifications. The offices were large, the colors neutral and the locker room was a combination of pro-sports-team efficient and five-star-hotel fancy. The big showers were kept stocked with high-quality products, the water was extrahot and there was plenty of room for the guys to congregate if they wanted.

So it was no surprise to step out of his shower and find Kenny and Jack lounging on the benches by the lockers. Sam finished drying off and walked to his locker.

"There was a fire," Kenny said conversationally. "We've been getting calls. There are rabbits in danger. What do you know about this? Should we be worried?"

"Is Larissa involved?" Jack asked. "She has to be. Rabbits are just like her. Is she rescuing them? Am I going to have fifty rabbits in my house?"

Because whatever Larissa was involved with, she dragged Jack along. Sam found their relationship interesting. He knew they weren't romantically involved. Larissa was the partners' private masseuse, but she was Jack's personal assistant. She also allowed him to stay emotionally detached while she got in the thick of things for him.

He'd often wondered how she kept her distance, emotionally. Every now and then he thought he saw something in her eyes, but then it was gone. He figured if Jack wasn't worried, he wouldn't be, either.

"There weren't any rabbits," he started, only to be interrupted by Taryn walking into the locker room.

He'd already pulled on briefs, but didn't bother covering up. Taryn had seen it all before, with all of them. Sometimes, just to mess with her, they insisted on holding meetings in the steam room. Not that she cared about them all being naked. Instead she objected to what the moist heat did to her hair.

"Someone set fire to a bunch of rabbits?" she asked as she approached. "And you saved them?"

Sam pulled on a pair of jeans. "Rabbit costumes," he corrected. "There were rabbit costumes. Hundreds of them."

His three partners stared at him blankly.

"Hey, I can't explain it, either," he told them. "They have a parade every Easter and people dress up like rabbits."

Taryn frowned. "Bunnies," she murmured. "I read about it in the Acorn handbook. It's a tradition. Our girls will be in the parade next year."

A couple of months ago Taryn had agreed to help Angel with a special project. Fool's Gold had its own version of scouting called

Future Warriors of the Máa-zib. The youngest were Acorns. Even now, Sam couldn't imagine Taryn sitting around with a bunch of little girls, but from what he'd heard, she'd been very popular with the Acorn set.

Kenny grinned. "So you're going to dress up in a slightly crispy rabbit costume?"

Taryn wrinkled her nose. "Of course not. I'll order one custom-made. Are they all right? The rabbits?"

"De-smoking out in Pyrite Park." Sam shrugged into a fresh shirt. "The weather looks good. They'll be fine."

Taryn sighed. "My hero."

Kipling Gilmore flew down the mountain. Probably not his smartest move after so long away, but part of his need for speed *was* because of time spent partying and promoting and generally enjoying the end of a season that had included two Olympic gold medals.

Now he leaned forward and let gravity and aerodynamics increase his speed. He cleared his mind of conscious thought, allowing his body to react. The adjustments were automatic. Tightening, leaning, reaching for every advantage. In his game, failure was measured in hundredths of a second.

Serious training would start in a couple of

days. Kipling was ready. He'd given up the late nights and the drinking. And the women. Now he would focus. The cold felt good, as did his body. His time in the gym paid off in quick responses. He was in control.

But he wasn't alone on the mountain. His goggles impeded his peripheral vision just enough that he wasn't sure what the blur was that raced across the side of the mountain. He was far enough away that it wasn't a problem, but the guy on his left involuntarily jerked — and at sixty miles an hour, that could be deadly.

Kipling shifted out of the way, but it wasn't enough. One second he was flying and the next he was falling.

For several heartbeats there was only silence and the world spinning and spinning. He knew he was in trouble, but he didn't have time to consciously react. Trees came up hard and fast and when he hit there was a blinding light, followed by nothing at all.

Dellina had known the panic would come. It was inevitable with a project this big. The trick was to hold it off for as long as possible. To stay in the moment and be focused on her list. Because in the end, good planning would save her.

Only she'd woken up that morning with what felt like a giant clock ticking in her head. They were less than two weeks away from the weekend and she didn't have finalized menus or a completed schedule or goodie bags. She had to get the decisions made so she could lock it in with her vendors. Why didn't Sam understand that?

She sucked in a breath and crossed to her front door. She pulled it open, glared at the handsome man standing on her front porch, then announced, "You're not making this any easier."

Sam's eyebrows drew together. "What are you talking about?"

"I'm panicking. We have to make some decisions. There isn't enough time."

"What has you freaked out specifically?"

"Everything. Pretend it's tax season."

His frown deepened, then cleared. "Finance," he told her. "Not accounting. I don't do tax season."

"Okay, whatever. I need you to make decisions."

He stepped into her place. "Absolutely. Where do you want to start?"

"Goodie bags."

She led the way to her small dining alcove. There she'd set up all the samples. There were bottles of lotion, scarves, barbecue tools, Lark's book, an NFL computer game and a print of all three of the guys from Score. She picked up the print.

"You'd all sign the copies of this," she said. "I wasn't sure about leaving Taryn out, but she's not a famous former NFL player."

"She'll be fine with it."

She went through the items she'd chosen for the kids, then stood back as he walked around the table.

"We need more splash," he announced

It was really good there wasn't a decorative sword on the table, because she probably would have attacked him with it. As it was, she drew in a breath and spoke slowly.

"Can you define *splash*? I'm assuming you don't mean an inflatable pool of some kind."

Sam flashed her a grin that had her girl bits sighing. "You're really stressed."

"Thanks for the news flash. Yes, I am. Now do you have specifics in mind?" She held up her hand. "If you tell me you'll know it when you see it, I'm going to have a very large man sit on you until you whimper like a little girl."

The grin stayed in place. "You don't know anyone who could do that."

She crossed her arms over her chest and

raised her eyebrows. "Have you met Kenny Scott? Because I'm pretty sure he could crush you like a bug."

Sam's good humor stayed in place. "Point taken. I'll be specific. Mind if I use your computer?"

She thought about the state of her office and decided she wanted the information more than she cared what he thought about her lack of filing system. She motioned for him to follow her, then walked down the hall and into the spare bedroom.

There were the usual piles times five hundred. Invoices were scattered across her desk. As she really needed to keep track of those, she collected them and put them in her "superimportant" box.

"We'll be talking about those later," she told him. "When I get them figured out."

"Billing issues from vendors?" he asked.

"Yes. I can't get my books and estimates to balance with theirs. But not a problem for today. Find me something splashy."

He sat in her chair and started typing. She blinked a couple of times when his first destination turned out to be Tiffany & Co. Before she could even ask what he was thinking, he'd brought up a picture of diamond earrings that made her think with that kind of cash she could get a new car.

"These are nice," he said.

"Yes, they are."

"Order them with gift receipts so if any of the women don't like them, they can return them."

She thought about the scarves she'd chosen and realized she should have had a clearer understanding of his budget.

Sam's next internet stop was for handheld games for the kids, then fancy compass watches for the guys. In a matter of minutes, he spent more than the GDP of several small nations. She pulled up an extra chair and sat down.

Sam was generous, which shouldn't have been news. Dellina might not admit it to him, but she'd been busy reading the book Taryn had given her. The one written by Sam's ex-wife, Simone. In it she'd shared a lot of personal information — the kind that would make Sam cringe. But what came out in the pages was that Sam was a great guy. Dellina was left with the impression that Simone had been a fool to let him go. She had a feeling she wasn't the only one who had thought that after finishing the book.

He ordered a few more things, then turned to her. "Done. What else can I help with?"

She motioned to the menus posted on the walls. "Let's talk about those."

"It's what I live for."

She smiled. "You're in a happy mood. Is it the shopping? I thought guys hated shopping."

"I don't like stores, but I enjoy the internet. I get to conquer from a distance. It's satisfying." He stood and crossed to the menus she'd posted on the walls.

She joined him. "Okay, Friday night dinner." She pointed out the drawing that was to represent the table in the private room. "I added your parents to the guest list," she began.

Sam sighed. "Did you have to?"

"I thought I should. Would you rather they weren't there?"

"Yes, but you're right. They'll show up whether we invite them or not."

While she understood he didn't want to think about either of his parents attending the weekend, she couldn't wait to meet them. Taryn and Larissa had tried to scare her, but she knew better. Still, it would be interesting to meet some of Sam's family.

She pointed out the names on the paper. "Kenny and Jack aren't bringing dates. Larissa doesn't want to come to the dinner. Taryn's bringing Angel. So this should be the final count."

"You're missing one."

She frowned. "I am? No, I'm not. I've been over this like fifteen times."

He shook his head. "You're not on the list."

"But I'm not attending the party."

"You're going to be there all weekend, aren't you?"

"Sure, but coordinating things. I'm working behind the scenes."

"You should be at the dinner."

"It's for your company and your clients. I'm not part of either. It would be like me planning a wedding and then sitting at one of the tables."

"What's wrong with that?"

She laughed. "It's not how it works. I'll be there making sure your weekend runs smoothly. But that's all."

He looked back at the list. "It's a stupid rule."

"Many of them are."

"I wouldn't bring a date." He was still staring at the names and the tiny drawing of the table, then he turned his attention back to her. "We kissed."

"You and me?"

"Is there anyone else in the room?"

She met his dark gaze and couldn't decide if she wanted to move closer or step away. Which wasn't exactly true. She knew exactly what she *wanted* to do. The question was more about which action was smart.

"I wouldn't have kissed you if I was seeing someone else."

"Good to know," she whispered. "I feel the same way."

"So there's no mystery guy?"

She smiled. "I told you that before. Not only because that's not my style but because this is Fool's Gold and we don't have secrets here."

"I didn't know about the rabbits."

"That doesn't make them a secret."

She didn't feel as if she was moving, but it seemed that she and Sam were standing a little closer than they had been. And he wasn't bothering to look at her lists anymore. All of his considerable attention was focused on her.

The intensity of his gaze made her shiver — but not because she was cold. Just the opposite. The room had gotten warm and she was having a little trouble catching her breath. He didn't help the situation when he reached out his hand and cupped her cheek. Her eyes fluttered closed, which was why she had no warning when he leaned in and kissed her.

The feel of his mouth on hers stole away the last of her breath and made her knees go weak. Generally Dellina fought being a cliché, but this time she didn't mind very much. Not when Sam's warm mouth claimed her with a combination of need and passion that had her sliding her hands up his chest and surrendering to the inevitable.

Good thing because he hauled her against him, wrapped both arms around her, tilted his head and thrust his tongue into her mouth.

She met him stroke for stroke, losing herself in the wanting that flooded her. Her body burned with both arousal and hunger. She wanted to touch him everywhere, but more important, she wanted him touching her. She wanted skin on skin. Only his fingers or mouth could make her stop aching so much. Except in that one place. There she needed more than his mouth or his hands.

He kissed her deeply, claiming as he offered. She let her fingers roam across his shoulders and down his arms. He stroked the length of her back. For a second, she thought . . . hoped . . . he would slide around and cup her breasts. Or more. Instead he kept kissing her, brushing his tongue against hers until it was all she could do not to beg.

Before she could, he drew back slightly

and rained soft kisses on her cheeks, her chin and then on her lips. He tucked her hair behind her ears, then kissed the tip of her nose.

"You'll be at the dinner," he told her. "Do I make myself clear?"

She nodded because speaking was impossible.

"This can't happen again," he said. "We're working together. But that doesn't mean I don't want you."

And with that declaration, he left. She stared after him, then sank into her chair and tried to catch her breath. Sam Ridge was not an easy man to know. But he sure knew how to make an exit. She might not date very much but she'd been around enough to know that was not a quality an intelligent woman sought in a man.

CHAPTER EIGHT

Fayrene absently rubbed Caramel's back as she studied the list her sister had given her. The schedule with the kids wasn't overly aggressive, she thought. There were plenty of activities to entertain them. She was there to provide supervision. After all, Dellina had hired several teenage girls who had recent babysitting experience to help. Now to get Ryan involved.

Because having him help with the kids was part of her plan. The dinner with Pia and Raoul had turned into a disaster. No way he could see the wonder of a loving family when the wife in the relationship couldn't stay awake past six o'clock. But that was in the past. The party would be exactly what they needed.

She glanced at Ryan, who sat on the sofa, watching a baseball game. He looked up at her and smiled, then muted the sound and patted the couch cushion next to him.

"Game not that interesting?" she asked as she carried Caramel with her and plopped next to him. The dog immediately jumped onto his lap and stood on her tiny hind feet to kiss his chin. Then she flopped down in his lap and went to sleep. Fayrene cuddled close.

"The game's okay," Ryan said as he kissed her. "You're better."

She leaned against him. "You're sweet to me."

"I love you."

"I love you, too." She glanced back at the table. "I've been over the schedule for the kids' events. It looks doable."

"You know I'm happy to help. Just tell me when to be where."

"You don't mind being around a bunch of children?"

He chuckled. "Nope. It'll be good practice for us."

Fayrene told herself to stay relaxed. That she couldn't read too much into what he was saying. Although if he *did* propose, that would solve all of her problems.

"Good for us how?" she asked innocently.

He grinned and kissed her on the mouth. "For when we're married. Although we're not going to have as many as will be at the party. How many is that?"

"Twelve."

"Right. I'm thinking more like two or three."

"Do you want boys or girls?" she asked, willing herself to stay calm.

"Both. Either. I don't care." He kissed her again, then picked up the remote. "Not that we're going to talk about this anymore."

Disappointment flared. "We're not?"

"Nope. You made it clear you want to wait for us to get married and I promised I was fine with that." The humor faded as he looked at her. "I mean it, Fayrene. What you want is important to me. I know you said talking about our future too much is like pressuring you. So let's drop the subject and watch the game. Caramel is a Dodgers fan."

Fayrene told herself not to stamp her feet in frustration. That Ryan was a great guy and only doing what she asked. She should be happy about that.

Only she wasn't.

"I don't think she is," she managed to say. "I think she's more into the American League."

Ryan laughed, then reached down and rubbed the dog's tummy. "Is that true, little girl?"

Caramel wiggled to get on her back and

then closed her eyes and sighed with contentment.

Dellina arrived at Sam's office armed with folders and lists, but also with the determination that the two of them were going to have a serious talk. Last time she'd been overwhelmed by the offices themselves — the pictures, the obvious success and power flaunted. Now she barely saw the larger-than-life photos, although she was still going to have to worry about being dazzled by the man. But at least the *number* of her problems had been cut in half.

"I know the way back," she told the receptionist, and walked purposefully toward Sam's office. As she wasn't stopped at any point, she must have been given the all clear by Sam or maybe Taryn.

She paused briefly outside his partially open office door, drew in a breath for courage, then knocked once and went inside.

Sam sat at his desk. He wore a long-sleeved white shirt with a tie. The tie was loose and the sleeves rolled up. He looked mussed and a little distracted, as if he'd been wrestling with a weighty problem. She had the brief thought that it would have been so much more fun for both of them if he'd been wrestling with her.

174

Before she could scold herself for getting off topic so quickly, even if it was just in her head, he glanced up and saw her. In that nanosecond before the walls came down, she saw the flash of desire. It was hot and bright and made her feel all quivery inside. Even after it was hidden, she knew what she'd seen. A little of her annoyance faded. They were still going to have to talk about what happened, but maybe she could be less shrill.

He rose. "Dellina. Did we have a meeting scheduled?"

"No, I stopped by. Do you have a minute?"

The question was offered out of politeness because she wasn't leaving until they got their problem if not fixed, then at least managed.

"Of course," he told her as he stood. He glanced at the tote bag she held. "Why don't we use the conference table?"

Better than the sofa, she thought. Less sexy. With a table between them, she would have a chance to remember she was here about business. That she and Sam had a weekend party to get through and that whatever was going on between them would have to be dealt with after that.

They sat down across from each other.

She did her best to ignore how the slightly disheveled look made him seem more approachable and therefore more appealing.

"You're like Mr. Darcy," she said without thinking.

His eyebrows drew together. "Excuse me?"

She did her best not to grin. Now that she'd had the thought, she couldn't escape it. "Proud, remote, difficult to read." She paused. "It's not a bad thing. Most women like Mr. Darcy. He's a Jane Austen character. From *Pride and Prejudice.*"

"I'm familiar with the work," he said drily.

"You've read it?"

"And seen the movie. Yes."

She desperately wanted to ask why. The movie made sense. Lots of guys were dragged to various versions by girlfriends, sisters and wives. But reading the book was a whole different story.

Interesting. But not why she'd stopped by.

She thought about pulling out papers to pretend they had official party business. But that felt too much like cheating. So she squared her shoulders, looked him in the eye and said, "You can't do that again. Kiss me, make cryptic comments and then walk out. It's not right. We have to work together. I need our relationship to be completely professional."

Because after another night of tossing and turning, she'd figured out that she was under enough stress without having to worry about defining how things were with Sam.

"If there's something you want to pursue between us, it needs to be put on hold until after we're done with the party. Getting involved would be a distraction."

"You're right."

She blinked. "Okay. About?"

"All of it." His gaze never left hers. "I apologize for kissing you. I won't say I'm sorry, because I'm not, but I was wrong. I put you in a difficult situation. We have a professional relationship, as you say. It's important to focus on the job at hand. I don't suppose telling you I've been tempted beyond reason will get me anything."

His voice wasn't even the slightest bit teasing and he wasn't smiling, but Dellina wasn't sure he was sincere, either.

"This job is important to me," she said.

"I understand that. I promise, nothing will happen between us again."

She waited, hoping he would add "until after the party," only he didn't.

"Thank you," she murmured, wanting to say that she'd really enjoyed the kiss. It was more the timing that was a problem for her. Only now that seemed inappropriate, as if she were complaining and leading him on in the same breath. Which was pretty much what he did to her when he kissed her and then left her hanging. But she was going to take the high road.

Sex complicated everything, she thought with a sigh.

She pulled several files from her tote and spread them out in front of her. "It's Friday. The party is a week from today. All the swag has been ordered and will be at my place by Wednesday. I already have the bags so I'll have plenty of time to load everything. My final walk-through at the hotel is Monday morning. I'm finalizing everything with Heidi tomorrow. Josh is already confirmed for the bike ride, as is the entertainment for the kids. The transportation is in place to CDS for the adult obstacle course, the trip to the town festival, the golf game and the visit to the ranch."

She went over everything else on the schedule and explained what was done and what still had to be completed. With panic setting in, she wasn't sleeping well, and that meant plenty of time to clean up her lists.

Sam was quiet until she'd finished. "You're good," he said. "Thank you for all of this. The party is going to be a success and you're the reason. I should have come to you sooner."

"Yes, you should have but you were afraid. To be honest, I get why. That night was weird."

One of his dark eyebrows rose. "Weird?"

She smiled. "After. The dresses, the dry-erase board. A little strange. You were scared and it's okay. I would have been freaked out, too. Now it would be different. You know me so you'd ask a few questions." She held up her hand. "I'm not implying anything." Or hinting. Or even wishing — although if she put some thought into it, wishing would be easy.

"I get what you're saying. We are the victims of bad timing. My mother would say there was a message in that."

Dellina tried not to smile. "The sexual demonstrations everyone keeps warning me about aren't enough? She gets messages from the great beyond?"

Sam grinned. "Not exactly but she's a big believer in paying attention to the little things. I don't suppose she's canceled."

"Sorry, no. She's confirmed."

"With me, too. I had a call from my dad last night."

She leaned toward him. "They're your

179

parents. Taryn and Larissa have tried to scare me by telling stories, but seriously, they're, what, in their sixties? How bad can it be?"

"You'll meet them soon enough. You can decide for yourself." He relaxed. "I appreciate your attitude in all this. You could have constantly reminded me the scramble for the party was my fault."

"Not my style."

"I like your style." He studied her for a second. "Why isn't there a Mr. Dellina?"

She laughed. "I'm not sure I'd be okay with a guy who wanted to call himself that. And I don't know if I want the whole serious boyfriend thing."

"Why not?"

"It's just . . . I don't know. I raised my sisters so I have a sense of been there, done that. I'm not sure I want a family."

He continued to watch her.

She shifted some more in her seat, not sure how they'd ended up talking about her instead of the party or even him.

"I do realize not every dating relationship results in a permanent arrangement or children," she continued. "There was a guy a few years ago. I thought he was great and we were happy, but then he cheated. I broke things off as soon as I found out."

"And?"

How had he guessed there was more to the story? "She got pregnant and they got married. About a year later he showed up, wanting to know if I was interested in seeing him again."

"He'd gotten a divorce?"

"No," she said quietly. "He hadn't. Which makes him a jerk, but what really bothered me was that he thought I was the kind of person who would be interested in that kind of relationship. I didn't like what it said about my character."

Sam grimaced. "It doesn't say anything, Dellina. You're right — the guy's a jerk and he was only thinking of himself. He'd screwed up, he missed you and he was hoping you were as lousy as he was. You told him no."

"Are you asking or telling?"

"I'm telling. I know you and you'd never do that."

"You're right. I felt disgusted just talking to him. They moved away a couple of years ago. Since then, I've been busy growing my business. Plus this is a small town. It can be challenging to have a private life. I know from experience it's hard to see the ex on a daily basis."

"At least I didn't have that," he said. "You

know I'm divorced."

She hesitated. "Taryn gave me Simone's book. I probably shouldn't have read it but . . ."

A muscle tightened by his jaw but otherwise he didn't react. "It's like a train wreck," he told her. "Impossible to ignore. Then you know about our relationship."

"I know what she said about your marriage. I suspect much of it isn't exactly true. At best, there are a lot of ways to put a spin on some things."

Simone had discussed everything from her courtship with Sam to how he performed in bed. She'd detailed his frustration when he'd missed a kick, how everything was always about the team. Dellina suspected she'd wanted her ex to come off as a self-absorbed, spoiled athlete.

"For what it's worth," she added, "you come off really well in the book."

"I've read it and you're exaggerating."

"I'm not. She makes it clear you care about doing the best you can in your work and your relationships. You have concerns about privacy, but why wouldn't you? From what you've told me, your family wasn't good with boundaries and there's the whole being a sports legend."

He gave her a smile. "Now you're mocking me. I was good. I wasn't a legend."

"So modest. It's refreshing."

"Not modest. Realistic." The smile faded. "I tried to keep Simone from publishing the book, but I couldn't get an injunction. Because I was a national figure, I was considered fair game. The only good news is the judge took her advance and royalties into consideration during the settlement hearings. Simone has to send me fifty percent of every check she gets."

"Does that help?"

He shrugged. "I send it to charity. I don't want her money. I want her not to have published the book. But if she hadn't been that kind of woman, things might have gone better between us."

"Do you miss her?"

"Hell, no. She was a mistake. I was young and she knew what buttons to push."

"You have buttons?" She picked up a pen and held it over a sheet of paper. "What might they be?"

"Sorry, no. You're going to have to figure that out on your own. Besides, it was a long time ago." Now it was his turn to hesitate before speaking. "I told you I was sick as a kid."

She nodded.

"I was also small for my age. Basically

183

invisible. I started kicking in tenth grade and I was good, but no girl wants to date some guy three inches shorter than her."

She tried to reconcile that image with the tall, sexy, muscular man sitting across from her and couldn't.

"There must have been a transformation at some point," she said.

"The summer before my senior year. I grew about six inches. During my senior year I added a couple more and then I started to fill out. Add that to a stellar college football career and it all changed. At least for other people. But I was still the same guy. So when Simone came along, I was ripe for the taking."

"I can't imagine you vulnerable."

"Everyone is," he told her. "It's just a matter of finding out how."

She supposed that was true. Now Sam was a successful, worldly businessman, but in college, everything would have been different. He'd gone from the cliché of a ninety-pound weakling to a football god in a matter of a couple of years.

"I hope you don't hold yourself responsible for what happened between you two," she said.

"Most days I don't." He rose. "Come on. I'll walk you out."

She grinned. "That's subtle. You can just say you don't want to talk about yourself anymore."

"I don't want to talk about myself anymore."

"Then we won't."

She collected her folders and followed him to the front of the building. Once there, he lightly touched her arm.

"Let me know if you need anything," he told her. "I'm keeping my schedule open from Wednesday on. I can run errands, stuff bags, check on the liquor delivery. Just say the word."

"I might take you up on that."

"I hope you do."

She smiled and walked out. On her way back to her place she thought about how nice Sam was and how Simone had obviously been an idiot. Why choose a single book over a guy like Sam? If she were looking for something permanent —

Not that she was, she reminded herself. But for once, her "been there, done that" argument didn't spring to mind. She admitted, if only to herself and if only for that one time, that there were other reasons she didn't want to get involved. That they mostly had to do with how devastated she'd been at the unexpected loss of her parents.

That between their deaths and her life experiences so far, she'd learned caring came at a price. One she mostly wasn't willing to pay.

Sam tapped the screen on the treadmill. He was already jogging and the increase in speed pushed him to a run. Not the smartest thing for his knees, but he would worry about pain and swelling later. Right now he needed to clear his head.

Sweat poured off him. A baseball game played on the big TV on the wall opposite the cardio equipment. He hadn't bothered with the sound. Because paying attention to who was playing and the score was impossible. Right now, all he could think about was Dellina and how much he wanted her.

He didn't know what it was about her that got to him. She was pretty, but he knew women who were incredibly attractive who didn't interest him in the least. It wasn't her sense of humor, although he liked it. Or how smart she was. Again, he knew lots of intelligent women. So what was it? Why her?

Maybe it was the combination — that indefinable essence. Like in kicking. You could know everything and have talent, but if you didn't have that gut instinct that told you exactly how to kick the ball, then you weren't going to be great. And Dellina was great.

She'd been right to call him on his shit. Kissing her like that, then saying it couldn't go further because they were working together was wrong. He was better than that and she deserved a whole lot more. It was just that when he was around her, he wanted her. Up against a wall, in a bed, the beach, the mountains — he didn't think it would much matter. As long as they were naked and she was climaxing five seconds before he lost it.

The combination of the image and his running made it impossible to breathe. He gave in to the inevitable and slowed the treadmill back to a jog. After picking up the towel, he wiped the sweat from his face.

Kenny walked into the cardio room and raised his eyebrows. "We played basketball this morning."

"So?"

"Why are you running?" His friend grinned. "Afraid you're getting fat?"

Sam threw the towel at him and turned off the treadmill. His friend ducked and let the towel sail over his head.

"You're not that old," Kenny said cheerfully. "You've got another couple years until it all goes to hell."

"Thanks for the support."

"Anytime." Kenny studied him. "What's up?"

Sam had met both Jack and Kenny in college. Together they'd become an undefeatable triad. Jack could throw farther and faster than any other quarterback in their division and Kenny had both speed and magic hands. When that wasn't enough, Sam got them out of trouble with a perfect three-point field goal.

Over a million kids played high school football. Statistically one in about seventeen would make it to college ball. And from that pool, about one in fifty was drafted. The odds of making it, let alone making it big, were infinitesimal. But he and his friends had.

After college they'd all been drafted. Jack had gone in the first round and Kenny in the second, to different teams. Nobody wasted an early round pick on a kicker — not since 2000 and look how that had ended. He'd gone in the fourth round for more money than he'd ever hoped.

Four years later, they'd all ended back up together, playing for the L.A. Stallions. They'd won the Super Bowl and been on top of the world. Then Kenny had taken that hit and had to sit out nearly half a season, and Sam had decided it was time to reevaluate. The two of them were ready to retire. Jack had still been on top, but he'd joined them in leaving and had brought them to Score.

Now Sam looked at his friend and wondered what regrets Kenny carried. He could guess at a lot of them but doubted any of them were about his career.

"What has your panties in a bunch?" Kenny asked. "You only run when you have something on your mind."

"I don't want to talk about it."

Kenny grinned. "Tell me something I don't know." He held open the door. "Come on. I'll buy you a beer."

Sam followed Kenny upstairs. They walked down the long hallway and through double doors into a room about half the size of an airplane hangar. There were a half dozen or so black leather sofas, a giant television, a big bar and beer on tap. It was a place to relax, to hang out. To escape. Because even now, there were times when the world closed in. When fame was too much and the guys needed to unwind, they came here. No one bothered them.

They'd had a room like this back in L.A. They'd tried to ban Taryn, but she'd retaliated by having their cable cut off, in the middle of a play-off game. They'd never messed with her again.

Kenny walked behind the bar and poured them each a beer. Sam pulled a large towel from a stack on a shelf and tossed it across the sofa, then sat down. Kenny took a seat opposite and leaned back against the leather.

"Folks?" he asked.

Sam shook his head.

"Then it's a woman."

Sam grimaced. "I know better."

"We all do. Except Jack, who is careful to never get involved."

Sam drank his beer. Kenny was right. Jack was good at making it look as if he cared without getting emotionally engaged. His brief marriage to Taryn had been because of her pregnancy, not emotions. Before and after her, there had been a string of beauties who weren't interested in much more than saying they'd slept with Jack McGarry. While Jack was involved with several charities, it was always from a distance. If something personal was needed, he sent Larissa.

Sam turned to Kenny. "You still think about what happened?"

"Every day," his friend said flatly. "Every damned day."

"Sorry."

190

Kenny shrugged. "It happened. I was an idiot. The signs were all there, but I didn't want to see them."

Which made his situation sound less horrific than it was.

"You talk to her at all?" Sam asked.

Kenny shook his head. "Never."

Sam knew better than to ask if his friend ever spoke to the child he'd thought of as his own. The answer would be no. And that was the hell of it.

"You sleeping with Dellina?" Kenny asked.

Sam nearly spit his beer. "No."

"Why not? She's pretty. Sexy. She likes you."

Sam forced himself to sit quietly when what he really wanted to do was jump up and demand, "How do you know? Did she say anything? What have you heard?"

Which was what Kenny wanted. Sam stretched out his legs in front of him and did his best to look casual. "How much are you prepared to lose when we play golf this weekend?"

"I'm kicking your ass," Kenny told him. "Don't think I didn't notice the change in topic."

Sam smiled. "I have no idea what you're talking about."

"I hate you," Dellina said forcefully. "I don't use that word lightly, just so you know. And I mean it. I really, really hate you."

Her cursor blinked as if unaffected by her declaration, which was so not a surprise. Stupid computer, she thought glumly. And stupid, stupid program. Why wasn't it working?

She glanced down at the printout in her hand, then back at the screen and sighed heavily. The job with Score was a big one. She was billing lots of hours and invoicing them for everything she bought. Sam paid her promptly. So why wasn't she coming out ahead financially?

A party like this one should have provided her with lots of extra income. But when she ran her statements, she wasn't much further ahead than she'd been two months ago. She would cover costs and walk away with a little extra, but nothing like she'd thought. And nowhere near the amount she'd been hoping for.

She tossed the papers back on the desk and turned from the screen. She would figure this all out after the party, she promised herself. When she didn't have fifty million things going on. Then she could find out why, after working so hard, she was steadily losing money and facing the real possibility of having to shut her doors.

CHAPTER NINE

In Los Angeles, Sam had lived in a condo. The building had been secure with plenty of staff to keep the world at bay. In Fool's Gold that hadn't been an option, so he'd bought a house. The place was bigger than he needed, but it was on the golf course, which he enjoyed, with large rooms and high ceilings. He'd liked all the extra space. The downside of having more rooms was having more bedrooms. And the downside of that was he had no reason to tell his parents they couldn't stay with him when they came to town. Which was why he was pacing back and forth in his foyer, all the while wondering how long it would take him to drive to Mexico.

He heard a car pull up and opened the front door. Fortunately it was only Jack and Taryn. Kenny pulled up behind them. He noticed how they now blocked the driveway, which would make it harder to escape.

Harder, he thought, but not impossible.

It was late afternoon and they'd all come from the office. Taryn wore one of her usual tight dresses that probably cost more than he'd spent on his favorite suit. But she looked good, he thought. Happy. Her relationship with Angel was good for her and —

He swore under his breath. Dear God, it was already happening. Just the knowledge that his parents were only a few miles away was changing him into a woman! He had to get out of here now.

"Don't even think about it," Taryn said as she walked up the front walkway. "You aren't leaving. You're going to stay and greet your parents like the mature, full-functioning adult that you are. You're going to listen to their stories and be grateful you have a loving family, no matter how much they annoy and frighten you."

Her violet-blue gaze was steady. She spoke quietly, as if only for him to hear. And he got the message. Because Taryn's home life had been shit. She didn't say much but he'd figured out enough to know that things had gone badly for her. That when she'd met Jack, she'd managed to put herself through college and graduate with honors, but she'd also been broke and practically living in her car.

In the scheme of things, he had it easy. His big complaint was that his family loved him too much. And his parents had sex on the brain. Poor, poor him.

"Good point," he said, pulling her close and hugging her. She wrapped her arms around him and hung on. The contact was comforting. And siblinglike. There were no thrills when holding Taryn. No need for more, no burning hunger.

He stepped back and grinned. Probably for the best, he thought. Angel could so take them all. It wasn't that the other man was stronger; it was that he knew how to fight dirty and wouldn't hesitate to do whatever it took to win. Jack, Kenny and Sam had been raised with the idea of a fair battle and a code of conduct.

"You'll be fine," Taryn told him, just as a BMW X5 drove up and parked in front of the house. The doors opened and an attractive older couple stepped out.

Sam happened to know their ages, but he would guess that anyone else would think they were at least a decade younger than they were. His dad was tall, with dark hair and eyes. Lark was five-eight, with wavy dark blond hair and deep blue eyes. They wore jeans and shirts, like regular people, but Sam knew the disguise was simply to help them blend in. That soon enough they would show their true, weird colors.

But they were also his parents and, despite everything, he couldn't help being pleased to see them. Maybe he was overreacting, he thought. Maybe the visit would be fine. People mellowed as they aged. They could be completely normal.

Lark reached Taryn first and hugged her. "My favorite almost-daughter," she said, and stepped back to study her. "You're so beautiful. I can see you're having regular sex and it's wonderful." She tilted her head. "You're in love."

Taryn laughed. "Yes, I am. You're going to meet him this weekend." She held out her left hand where a large diamond flashed in the light.

"I can't wait to hold him in my arms." Lark stared, then sighed. "Wonderful. Reggie, look. Taryn's engaged."

"Congratulations," Reggie said, hugging her tight. "He's a good man?"

"The best."

Lark smiled. "You know a good sexual relationship is the cornerstone to any marriage. I have some new techniques I want to discuss with you and your young man. It's all about mindfulness and breathing. It makes a man last for hours. Reggie, my love, you'll talk to Taryn's friend about his end of things, so to speak."

"Of course." Reggie dropped a kiss onto the top of his wife's head. "Depending on how shy he is, I'll show him the video of what we've been practicing or just tell him."

Sam hung his head. Yup, these were his parents, and from what he could tell, no one had mellowed.

Kenny slapped him on the back. "This is the best show in town."

"Watch it," Sam warned. "Or I'll ask my dad to give you a private demonstration."

Kenny winced. "Ah, no, thanks."

Lark moved to Jack and hugged him. She studied his face. "Still not giving with your heart?"

Jack shrugged uncomfortably. "It's always good to see you, Lark," he said, and kissed her.

She sighed. "You're emotionally elusive. We have to fix that." She turned to Kenny and smiled. "You know, of all Sam's friends, you were the one I thought would be most interesting in bed."

Reggie rolled his eyes. "You tell him that every time you see him. Give the kid a break."

Kenny grinned. "I like being the favorite."

They embraced and then it was Sam's

turn. He braced himself, knowing the combination of love and space violation would leave him looking for an exit. The worst part was, he never knew which direction the embarrassment was going to come from so it was tough to prepare.

His father shook his hand, hugged him, then turned him over to his mother. Lark studied him for a long time before hugging him so tight his ribs ached.

"I love you so much," she whispered. "I've missed you. You're in my prayers every day."

"I love you, too, Mom."

She stepped back and smiled, then put her hands on his shoulders. "You're in very good shape. I love that I produce beautiful babies. You're still strong and well hydrated. I'm so happy you listened when I tried to teach you about the glory of drinking enough water. It keeps you regular, you know. You're still too young to worry about that, but trust me, in a few years, you're going to care a lot more about your bowels."

"Listen to your mother," Reggie said.

Kenny snickered.

"Come on inside," he said. "You haven't seen Sam's new place."

While Sam appreciated the distraction, he knew that it wouldn't last for long. Nor would it help much. Because his mother never met a boundary she didn't want to cross.

Sure enough, she wandered into the house while the guys brought in their considerable pile of luggage. As Sam, Kenny and Jack carried suitcases to the guest room, Taryn mixed drinks in the kitchen. Sam put down the two bags he'd been holding only to hear the familiar sound of drawers opening and closing. In *his* bedroom.

"Darling, I know a much better brand of condom," his mother called. "And where is that pink vibrator I sent you last Christmas? The one that's shaped to reach a woman's G-spot. I don't see it anywhere."

"Mom, get out of my bedroom."

She appeared in the doorway, her expression one of genuine confusion. "I was just exploring your life, darling. It's how we reacquaint ourselves after being apart for so long."

"Some people just have a conversation," he mumbled.

"I've got the martinis ready," Taryn called from the kitchen.

"Wonderful," Lark said.

They went to the living room. Reggie carried in a tray of drinks while Taryn followed with some appetizers Sam had picked up from Angelo's, the local Italian restaurant.

Taryn pointed to the drinks on the tray. "Straight up with a twist, straight up with olives, straight up with a hint of lavender for the beautiful woman I love so much."

Lark smiled at her.

"Straight up seems to be a theme," Jack whispered, taking one of the drinks.

"As long as it takes the edge off," Sam told him, and grabbed one for himself.

He swallowed half of his in a gulp and glanced at Taryn. She grinned and pointed, as if saying yes, there was a pitcher waiting in the refrigerator. Something he would need to get through the visit.

Once everyone was settled, conversation seemed to flow more smoothly. Lark and Reggie talked about Sam's sisters and how well they were doing. Most of the talk was relatively normal and there was only one mention of his sister Lottie's vagina, which Sam considered a win where his parents were concerned.

"You're on a book tour?" Kenny asked.

Lark nodded. "I never wanted to go on one before. Not when I had to be apart from Reggie for so long." She smiled at her husband. "We try to never be apart for more than twenty-four hours and our goal is to make love at least once every forty-eight hours."

"Mom," Sam said sharply. "TMI."

"You always say that. It's not possible to have too much information. Knowledge is important."

"Not when it's about my parents' sex life."

"You should be happy," Reggie said. "You have the Ridge sports equipment, as my dad used to say to me."

Sam felt the familiar sense of hopelessness that always seemed to swallow him when his parents were around. It wasn't that he didn't love them; it was that he didn't know how to survive them.

Taryn leaned close. "Maybe Kenny or Jack could flash her," she murmured. "That would be a distraction."

"Not a good one."

She patted his hand and took his empty glass. A minute later, she was back and the glass was full.

"You're a good woman," he told her.

Lark leaned against Reggie. "Now that your father is retired, he can travel with me, so we're going on tour together. We're driving and that makes it fun. This country is so beautiful and we've been to the most interesting places. You wouldn't believe all the places we've had sex outdoors."

Reggie chuckled. "We've been caught a few times, but that adds to the fun."

Sam felt the beginning of a headache.

Kenny leaned forward. "Like where?"

Jack laughed. "Any arrests?"

Reggie shook his head. "We had cops tell us to move it indoors once, but then the guy admitted he was pleased to know people of our age still did it. Plus, Lark is a beautiful woman. Anyone would want to see her naked."

Sam glanced toward the door and thought longingly of Mexico.

Conversation continued for another half hour or so. Sam lost track of the number of martinis Taryn poured for him. Finally his friends said they had to leave. Kenny and Jack both said they'd be walking and coming back for their cars in the morning, which meant Taryn had to call Angel for a ride.

"Don't forget, I want to talk to you about that new technique," Lark told her.

"I can't wait," Taryn said.

Lark looked around the room. "Anyone else want in on the discussion?"

Jack and Kenny glanced at each other, as if not sure what to do. Taryn was already following Lark and Reggie. For Sam, it was a no-brainer. He headed for the front door and didn't once look back.

"I LOVE IT," Dellina said, feeling some of her stress fade away. Whatever else was happening, she could count on her sisters to be there for her. It was, she thought, one of the advantages of family. Knowing that she didn't have to deal with any single crisis alone.

Ana Raquel preened as she tore off a small piece of bacon and fed it to Caramel. The tiny dog took it delicately, woofed down the piece, then spun as if to say not only was it delicious, she would very much like some more, please.

Fayrene made a couple more notes, then tasted the last mocktail. "I agree. These drinks are perfect," she told her twin. "With all the different ingredients, the kids can make different flavors and figure out what they like."

"Using different juices is genius," Dellina told Ana Raquel.

"I'm glad you think so. I'm going to use what's left over to flavor the sorbet for the next night so the children can tell their parents how they squeezed juice or used the juicer to extract liquid."

She reached for a hot dog puff and bit off two thirds of it, then handed the rest to Caramel.

"She can eat all this, right?" she asked.

Fayrene patted the Pomeranian. "She seems to like everything in the people food department and her stomach is rock solid." She scooped Caramel up onto her lap where the dog did a graceful roll and settled so her tummy was exposed for rubbing.

"I love the sorbets, I love the mocktails and the appetizers are both kid-friendly and delicious," Dellina said, happy to check so many things off her list.

They'd already gone over the items that would be part of the pasta bar. Dessert was going to be a make-it-yourself sundae. Messy but fun. Heidi had delivered her menu for Sunday; the kids' band and theater troupe was confirmed. She scanned her list for the children's program twice more, then tossed the sheets into the air.

"I am officially ready for at least half this weekend and it's only Tuesday."

"You're more than half-ready," Fayrene told her. "I've seen your other list. You got most of the goodie bag deliveries today. The rest come tomorrow. Which means you're nearly there."

Dellina hoped she was right. "I have dinner tonight at Henri's for the final refinement on the menu and then that's it except for the details."

"A dinner?" Ana Raquel asked. "Not a

tasting."

They were all seated on the floor of her living room with food and drinks spread out on the coffee table. Overnight boxes spilled out of her office into the hallway. Her dining room table was filled with empty goodie bags and her head was swimming with details. It took a second for her sister's question to sink in.

"It was supposed to be a tasting, but then it grew. Sam is coming with me, as are his parents."

"Meeting the parents," Fayrene teased. "You're rushing things."

"It's work and you know it."

"Sam is pretty good-looking," Ana Raquel told her. "I mean, he's no Greg, but still, he is a nice-looking man. You could do worse."

Dellina laughed. "I'm sure he would be desperately flattered by that assessment." She scrambled to her feet. "Thanks for all your help."

Fayrene picked up Caramel, then stood. "She's throwing us out."

"I got that."

Ana Raquel rose and then hugged Dellina. "You'll do great. Call me if you need anything. Otherwise, I'll be up at the hotel at noon on Friday prepping."

Fayrene hugged Dellina, too. "What she

said. You're prepared."

Caramel offered a quick kiss on the nose.

Dellina walked them out, then returned to her office where she studied her master list. It was very possible she was ready. She had her emergency supplies — sunscreen, aloe vera, a jumbo first aid kit, an assortment of phone numbers that included everything from auto repair service to the cell number for a private pilot who lived in town and ran an air service out of the local airport.

Ana Raquel was handling all the food and drinks the hotel wasn't, she'd coordinated with Heidi for the afternoon on the ranch and she and Greg were ready for the wine tasting. Fayrene had the children's schedule memorized, had helped confirm all the vendors and had verified the extra baby-sitters would be in place. The mani-pedis were scheduled, the golf course reserved and —

Someone rang her doorbell. She turned and left her office only to start walking faster when she heard pounding on her front door.

"What?" she demanded as she pulled it open.

Sam stood there. His hair was mussed, his eyes were wide and he seemed to be swaying on his feet.

"They're here," he told her. "They're here and it's worse than I thought."

Dellina got Sam inside. She moved papers around until there was room on the sofa, then pointed to a cushion. He stared at it blankly.

"Are you okay?" she asked.

"Fine. No, I'm not fine. They're here."

"We're talking about your parents, right? Not an alien landing? Because if lizard people are taking over the world, I want to be paid in advance of the party."

His head snapped up and he stared at her. "You think this is funny."

"Sort of." She sat next to him and, without thinking, took his hand in hers. The second they were touching, she was conscious of his maleness so close to her femaleness. Sometimes opposites were a good thing.

"Sam, they're your parents. It's not that big a deal."

"You haven't met them." He shifted on the cushion, then swayed just a little.

She peered more closely. "Are you . . . Are you drunk?"

"Maybe. I don't know how many martinis Taryn poured. Don't worry, I walked."

208

"You left your parents alone at your house?"

"I had to. They were going to have sex. Or a demonstration. Does it matter? Either way they were going to get naked." He shuddered. "Why couldn't I have normal parents? I could accept some level of eccentricity but not this."

She wasn't sure how much of Sam's parents' mythology she believed, but she was sure that it would take a fair bit of stress to get Sam drunk in the middle of a workday.

"They can't be that bad," she began.

"My mother wants me to change condom brands."

Dellina frowned. "How does she know which brand you use?"

"The first thing she does when she arrives at my place is go through everything. My cupboards, my drawers. She asked about a vibrator she sent me. It's pink." He shuddered.

She pressed her lips together to keep from giggling. Partially because it was funny and honestly, in part, out of horror. "Your mother sent you a vibrator?"

"Yes. It's designed to stimulate a woman's G-spot."

"I'm not sure I know what that is."

Sam snatched his hand back and glared at her. "Do *not* under any circumstances say that in front of my mother. Do I make myself clear? If you tell her you don't know where it is, she will have you naked in ten seconds and then show you."

Dellina felt her eyes widen. "She'll . . ."

"Touch it. Yes. Or have you touch it. She'll discuss stimulating it and how it can increase pleasure during orgasm."

While Dellina didn't want Sam's mother anywhere near her girl parts, more pleasure during orgasm didn't sound that bad.

"Do you still have the vibrator?" she asked as casually as she could.

"What? I don't know. Maybe. It's not the point."

"I suppose not," she said wistfully, wondering how gross it would be to do a G-spot internet search. Preferably on sites without pictures because there were just some things she didn't want to see.

"You're not listening," he told her. "These are my *parents.* They're like locusts. They have to be controlled or they'll sweep in and destroy everything."

"Seriously?"

He sucked in a breath. "Fine. They'll destroy my life and leave everything else untouched." He stood and paced the length

210

of her living room, then headed down the hall.

She followed him and they ended up in her office. He walked to the window, then faced her.

"I can't do this," he told her. "I have to leave the country. I'm driving to Mexico. I can't spend a week with them. What was I thinking?"

"You're blowing this out of proportion," she said gently.

"Am I?" His voice was surprisingly shrill. "Let's see about that. We have the dinner at Henri's tonight. If you think they're completely normal, then I'll never complain about them again. If I'm right, I get to stay here while they're in town."

"All I have is that futon in the other room," she said without thinking.

"I don't care if it's the floor." He grabbed her by her upper arms. "They're not human."

She held in a smile. "I'm pretty sure they are. They're just a little strange. All parents are." She was sure if hers were alive she would be complaining about them. For a second she let herself think how nice that would be.

"Oh," she said as an obvious solution occurred to her. "Why don't you put your

211

parents up at the hotel? Is it full? Do you want me to make some calls?"

He dropped his arms to his side. "No hotel," he said flatly. "It's too risky. I like this town and I want to stay here."

"Okay, and that has something to do with your parents how?"

"They don't have boundaries. Not as you know them. They'll walk down the hall to get ice. But they'll be naked. Or they'll have sex in the lobby."

She felt her lips twitch. "Sam, you have to take a step back. Seriously, they can't be that bad."

"You're wrong. They're worse than you think. You'll meet them tonight and then we'll talk."

"I can't wait," she said with a grin.

"You say that now."

CHAPTER TEN

Dellina arrived early to Henri's. She spoke with the catering coordinator, then checked out the private room they would be using. Although it was large for a party of four, she wanted to see how the flow worked. After going through where they would hold the wine tasting, she returned to the private dining room to find that Sam and his parents had arrived.

Dellina stopped in the doorway, studying them before they had a chance to notice her. Sam's dad was tall and rangy. He looked fit and athletic, with an easy smile and a bit of gray at his temples. Lark wore a low-cut dark blue dress the color of her eyes. Her wavy blond hair had been pulled back in two decorative combs. Her makeup was light, her expression pleasant and when she laughed, the happy sound seemed to fill the room.

Sam turned and spotted Dellina.

"You made it," he said. He spoke easily enough but there was a hint of tension in the muscles in his jaw and the tightness by his eyes.

"I was looking at the rest of the venue for Friday night." She walked toward the three of them. "I'm Dellina."

She held out her hand. Reggie introduced himself and his wife, then shook her hand. Lark smiled at her, announced, "You're very pretty, child," then pulled her close for a warm hug that had Dellina suddenly missing her own mother.

Lark released her. "Sam has told us so much about this weekend party. It sounds as if you've been running around, getting everything ready."

Sam's parents looked at her with equally welcoming expressions. She felt herself relax in their presence.

"I'm excited about having it all come together," she said. "We don't usually get weekends this fancy in town."

"We're looking forward to it very much," Lark said as she linked arms with her husband.

A server appeared with glasses of champagne. A second followed with a tray of appetizers.

"Please," Dellina said, motioning to the

drinks and food. "I'm looking for objective opinions. This is our final chance to tweak the menu. I would very much appreciate your honest thoughts on every part of the meal."

They toasted to the weekend and then tasted the appetizers. Dellina was careful to have one of everything and take notes.

"I like the presentation," she said, putting a puff on a plate so it could get cold. One of the challenges of appetizers was that people tended to chat before eating them. Having something that tasted good at room temperature could be difficult.

Reggie looked at her notes. "You're organized."

"I have to be."

"You own your own business?"

She smiled. "Yes. It's just me. Sometimes I think about expanding but then I'd give up control. Plus there are parts of what I do that I really love. I wouldn't want to hand them off to someone else." She paused. "I do think about hiring an office manager, though. I'm not great with balancing my own books."

"I understand that," Reggie told her. "When I retired from basketball, I had to figure out what to do with my life. I had a degree I couldn't use and no experience beyond a great jump shot."

Lark moved close to her husband and leaned against him. "That's not true. You had loads of life skills. You just had to find out the best way to use them."

He nodded. "I went back to college and paid attention in class this time. I got my master's in business. Went to work for a large company and worked my way up."

Dellina smiled at Sam. "So you come by your interest in finance honestly."

"Dad was an influence," he admitted.

Reggie beamed at his son. "Sam's very intelligent. A planner, too. He played football, but was looking to the future. I spent a couple of years being lost after the crowds went away."

"Having Kenny and Jack around helped," Lark added. "They're good friends. They took care of one another. The world of professional sports can be difficult. Not just the physical requirements, but the media attention. Now with so much accessibility through the internet, there's nowhere to hide. But Sam navigated his transition with grace."

She, like Reggie, sounded like an extremely proud parent. Dellina didn't understand what Sam was complaining about. From what she'd seen, his family was lovely.

He caught her gaze and shook his head, as if telling her to wait. It was all going to get worse.

"When did you start writing?" she asked Lark as they moved to the table and took their seats.

The other woman frowned delicately. "About fifteen years ago. I'd always been interested in the link between sexuality and marriage. As the children got older, I started to study the subject more rigorously. I ended up starting a women's support group and we exchanged information. My first book grew from that."

Dellina waited, but Lark only smiled. Just as she'd thought — the outrageousness had been highly exaggerated. She relaxed in her chair and explained about the menu for dinner.

"We'll have tasting portions," she said. "Three different entrees but only a small amount of each. I really do need your honest opinions. We're going to give our guests options on a limited menu."

Lark leaned toward Sam. "Was the party your idea?"

"We thought it was a good way to bring our clients together," he said, his voice a little stiff. "To thank them for all their business."

"It's a good way to bond with the town, too," Lark said. "From what I've seen, Fool's Gold is charming and lovely, but small. You want to stay on everyone's good side. The party allows you to pump money into the local economy, but in a subtle way."

"Thanks," he mumbled, then reached for his wine.

Dellina wanted to grab him by the arm and drag him out of the room for a private conversation. She sensed Sam's tension and was sure his parents felt it, too. And for what? Lark and Reggie were a charming, loving couple. So they touched a lot. Wasn't that a testament to their happy marriage? In an era where so many couples were getting divorced, their love for each other should be celebrated.

She wondered if his failed marriage with Simone had made him so wary of seeing someone else in love. Taryn had mentioned there had been other failed relationships. Had he grown unnecessarily cynical?

The servers brought out the first course. There were three soups and two salads. Dellina studied each offer, then made a few notes.

Lark tasted the first soup. "Delicious," she said. "How long have you and Sam been lovers?"

Dellina swallowed and choked. When she could breathe again, she wiped her eyes, then sipped some water.

"Excuse me?" she asked, her voice a croak.

"You and Sam," Lark said. "You're sexually involved."

Dellina's cheeks burned with heat. "Um, no. We're working together. That's all."

She didn't dare look at Sam. No doubt he was ready to mouth "I told you so" and she didn't want to hear it. Or see it.

Lark shook her head. "Then you were sexually intimate at one time. I can sense the connection between you. What caused the problem? I doubt it was Sam's ability in bed. Although he wouldn't allow me to instruct him, I know he and his father had many conversations on technique. So many men are lost when it comes to pleasing a woman."

Dellina sipped more water and decided she was going to let the others decide the best first course.

Lark looked across the table at her son. "Simone called me the other day. She admitted that while she doesn't regret the marriage ending, she does miss you in bed." Her expression brightened with pride. "She said it was more than the number of orgasms. It was the intensity of her satisfaction that she misses."

Reggie nodded knowingly. "That would be difficult to get over. Self-stimulation only gets you so far. A skilled, caring partner adds that indefinable element."

Dellina wondered if her makeup was enough to hide the intense blush on her cheeks. This wasn't happening. These perfectly nice middle-aged people were *not* discussing sex or orgasms at the dinner table. They couldn't be.

"I talked to her about self-stimulation," Lark said as she pulled one of the tiny salads closer. "You know that squeezing pressure I like so much?"

"Mom," Sam said sharply. "That's enough."

His mother paused. "Well, all right. My point is Simone misses you in bed."

Dellina couldn't remember a more exhausting dinner. It wasn't that anything had happened, but that didn't matter. Now that she'd seen the elder Ridges in action, she didn't know when the next mind-bending statement was going to drop in the middle of the table. The matter-of-fact delivery almost made it worse, because for a second it seemed as if she must have misunderstood.

After the whole Simone debacle, conversation shifted to more conventional topics, but that didn't mean Dellina could relax. Being braced for the next shocker required exactly the same energy as enduring it. By the time dessert was brought out, she felt as if she'd run a marathon — at least emotionally. Not that she'd ever done the other kind, either, but that wasn't the point.

"I'm very interested in the history of the town," Lark said after tasting the chocolate mousse. "The Máa-zib tribe especially."

"I know the basics," Dellina told her. "It's required for all students to learn about how they traveled up from Central America and settled here."

"The matriarchal aspect is intriguing," Sam said. "You'd like that, Mom. Using men for sex, then casting their lovers aside."

Lark shook her head. "I like having your father around. I would never cast him out."

Reggie took her hand. "I appreciate that, my dear, and share the sentiment."

"There's a museum outside of town," Dellina told them. "There was an amazing discovery about three years ago. A lot of gold jewelry and small statues."

"We'll have to go see it," Reggie said.

Lark nodded. "And isn't there supposed to be a statue in town? One by Caterina

Stoicasescu? I feel as if I read that some-where."

Dellina remembered the scandal of the work when it was first unveiled.

"It's on loan," she said. "To a sculpture garden in San Francisco."

Permanent loan, she thought with a grin. If Mayor Marsha had anything to say about it.

"I know her work," Sam said. "She uses metal. What was the one she made for the town?"

Dellina winced. "It was a, um . . ."

"A giant vagina," Lark told him. "I've seen pictures. It was beautiful. Caterina truly understands the importance of sexuality. I'm not saying it defines us, but it's a significant part of our lives. For women, especially. We teach our children to drive, to cook, to balance a checkbook, but we don't teach them about sex."

Dellina glanced at Sam, who was staring at his mother with horror. As if he knew what she was going to say next and could neither stop her nor think of a way to es-cape.

"What they teach in school isn't enough," Reggie said. "Birth control is important but what about the rest of it?"

"The rest?" Dellina asked before she

could stop herself. "You mean —"

"Pleasure." Lark smiled at her husband. "Remember when I taught the girls to masturbate?"

He nodded. "It was a beautiful time."

Sam flinched.

Lark sighed at the memories. "Reggie took Sam away for the weekend. After all, he was a boy and knowing what to do with himself was more easily understood. But the girls didn't have the obvious cue of an erection. I told them about their clitoris and described some basic techniques." Her smile trembled slightly as her eyes filled with tears. "They had the whole weekend to self-explore. I answered their questions." She sighed. "It was a wonderful memory I'll treasure always."

The rest of the meal passed in a blur. Dellina was pretty sure there was coffee and tea and more conversation, but she couldn't get past the rushing in her ears.

After they'd left the restaurant, Lark and Reggie went out to explore the gardens while Sam walked Dellina to her car. As they crossed the parking lot, she turned to him, then came to a stop.

"I was wrong," she said, staring up at him. "So wrong. I'm sorry. I don't know how to say it. Your parents are . . ."

"Indescribable?" he said, his voice only slightly ironic.

"Yes, that and so much more." She shuddered. "Your dad talking about spelling out words, letter by letter, while he . . ." She closed her eyes briefly. "I don't want to picture your parents doing that."

Sam's mouth twitched at the corners. "At least now you know about your G-spot."

Dellina pressed a hand to her cheek. Lark had brought up the subject and she'd made the mistake of expressing interest. Lark had immediately pulled an old receipt from her handbag and had drawn an embarrassingly detailed diagram. She'd then offered to come home with Dellina and show her where it was and suggest various ways to stimulate it.

"Don't take this wrong," she murmured, barely able to look at him. "But I never want your mother in the room when I'm having an orgasm."

"Then we're in agreement on that one."

"I just never thought anyone could be like that," she admitted. "When Taryn and Larissa were talking, I thought they were messing with me. Making her out to be worse than she was. But they weren't."

He drew in a breath. "Welcome to my world."

"No wonder you don't want them at a hotel. They'd probably go from room to room, asking guests if they need help sexually."

"Or worse," he said glumly.

She didn't bother to ask what that was. The limit was her imagination. "She's really sweet. They both are. They love you a lot. They just have an unusual focus."

"Tell me about it. No thirteen-year-old boy should have to eat breakfast while his mother grills him about his wet dreams."

She bit her lower lip. "Did she really teach your sisters to . . ."

"Oh, yeah. Dad took me camping. When I came home both my sisters were locked away experimenting with the wonders of self-stimulation. Then we all talked about it at dinner."

"That's just so wrong," she said, then stopped. "You know, I'm not sure it's wrong. Obviously it goes against traditional social norms, but it's not like she was hurting them. Sex is important and all the articles say that for a woman to have good sex she should understand her body. So on that level she was giving her daughters a great start. It's just . . . strange."

Sam held up both hands. "Hey, I grew up with it. Don't talk to me about what's normal and what isn't. I'm right there with you. Every day of my life I wanted my family to be like everyone else's. A little repression is a good thing."

She glanced at him from under her lashes. "So Simone really misses you, huh?"

"We're not having that conversation."

"Why not? It'll be fun."

"Not for me." He put his arm around her and turned her toward her car. "And as my parents will happily tell you, all pleasure should be mutual."

"Oh, sure. Use their training against me."

She liked the feel of him so close to her. While the conversation at dinner had been uncomfortable, all that talk of orgasms and body parts had reminded her of her night with Sam. And that information about her G-spot had been interesting. Sam probably knew all about it. Not that they had that kind of a relationship, but it was something she should remember for the next time she was with a man.

When they reached her car, she turned to face him.

The sun had already disappeared behind the mountains. The trees were dark silhouettes against the inky sky and Sam's face was in shadow. She wanted to know what he was thinking and wondered if any part of the conversation had been interesting to him. Or if he'd spent the whole time wishing he was somewhere else.

There was no way to find out without asking and they'd agreed they were going to have a "business only" relationship. A smart move, she told herself. Sensible. But wow, she sure wouldn't mind if Sam pulled her in his arms, kissed her senseless, then showed her exactly what could happen when a man knew his way around a G-spot.

As that wasn't going to happen, she needed to get home and finalize the dinner for Friday night.

"What time are you coming over?" she asked as she got her keys out of her bag.

"What are you talking about?"

"You're staying at my place, aren't you? I said I'd meet your parents, and if I agreed with you, you were welcome to sleep on my futon." She smiled. "You know the room, Sam. The one where Fayrene keeps her running list of how to get Ryan to propose."

"Very funny." His gaze sharpened. "You're sure? You don't mind?"

"No. It's fine." She'd had friends stay over before. And while Sam was more interesting, in a hunky male kind of way, she knew it would be dangerous to think of him as any more than a friend.

"Thanks. I appreciate that."

"I can't even imagine," she admitted. "It's not that they'll say something, although that's a problem. It's that you'd have to be terrified of walking in on them doing it in who knows what position."

He sighed. "Thanks for the visual. I'll be there in an hour."

"I'll get out fresh sheets."

"Thanks, Dellina."

"You're welcome." She unlocked her car.

He touched her arm. "Want to talk about ground rules?"

She looked at him and thought that yes, she did. As long as those rules included him having quality time with her G-spot.

What she said instead was, "No, Sam. Ground rules aren't required. If there is one person on the planet I can trust to respect my privacy, it's you."

The flaw in the plan, Sam realized at about two in the morning, wasn't that the futon was uncomfortable. It was, but he'd slept on worse. No, the issue was being in Dellina's house, only a few feet from her bedroom.

He couldn't hear her, but he knew she was

228

there. In her bed.

He wanted to get up and join her. He wanted to kiss her into wakefulness, then touch her everywhere. He wanted them both naked and then he wanted to pleasure her until she was boneless and gasping.

Not an image designed to help him rest easy, he thought as he sat up.

He ignored his erection and walked to the window in the spare room. After parting the curtains, he stared into the night. Not that there was anything to see. They were in a residential area of Fool's Gold. Everyone was asleep. Nothing bad ever happened here.

He opened the window and breathed in the cool air. It felt good on his bare chest, but seemed to tease his groin more than assuage his hunger. Maybe that was simply a function of wanting Dellina. Little could take away that ache except the woman herself.

A voice in his head that was suspiciously close to his mother's whispered that there was another way. But Sam ignored the suggestion. He wasn't a fourteen-year-old anymore. He would deal and eventually his arousal would subside.

To facilitate the process, he left the bedroom, thinking pacing would help. He would walk the length of the living room until he was tired and able to sleep. But on the way, he passed Dellina's office. Her computer sat on her desk. Maybe going online and playing games would help.

He walked into the room and quietly closed the door behind him. He moved to the desk and switched on the light there, then booted up her computer. After sitting down, he shifted a few papers to give him access to her keyboard.

One of the pages fluttered to the ground. He picked it up and recognized the name of one of the vendors. When he saw the amount she'd been billed, he frowned.

As they'd agreed, all billing ran through her. She got an estimate, told him the amount, then placed the order and paid the vendor. He, in turn, paid her. With all they'd been purchasing and the speed with which everything had to be pulled together, he'd given her a retainer so she had the cash to make the purchases.

Per their contract, she billed out her time on an hourly basis. She also added a small percentage to each item purchased. So if the goodie bag contained thousand-dollar watches, she added a 5 percent bump when she billed him. Only the amount on the invoice didn't match what he'd been billed.

Sam turned back to the computer and clicked on the browser button. He went to the Score website where he logged on. Once in the secure section he was able to access his information, including invoicing. Sure enough, there was a discrepancy. Dellina had billed him the amount of the estimate, plus her 5 percent. The problem was the estimate was about three hundred dollars *less* than the actual amount billed. She was absorbing the difference.

He swore under his breath as he looked at the stacks of invoices on her desk and in-boxes in her office. The part of him that guarded his privacy said that he couldn't explore without her permission. The businessman in him said Dellina was getting screwed and that had never been his intention. He didn't work that way. He believed in getting the best deal possible, but not at anyone's expense.

He didn't understand what she'd been thinking. Why wouldn't she bill him the amount she was billed? Was it some twisted sense of pride or a lack of business training? Either way, the problem had to be fixed.

Sam rose and walked toward the box of invoices on the floor. He hesitated for a second, before picking it up and dumping it on a nearby table. Then he started going through the pages one by one.

Dellina tightened her robe around her before leaving the bathroom. She would dress and finish with her hair before making an appearance in the main part of her house.

She knew Sam was up — she could smell coffee. Anticipation fluttered in her stomach. They'd spent the night together. Albeit in different rooms, but still. It was the closest she'd come to any action since their ill-fated night on Valentine's Day.

She'd thought she might toss and turn, but she'd been out the second her head hit the pillow. Now she poured herself a cup of coffee and went looking for the man in question.

She found him stepping out of the bathroom. He hadn't showered yet, or dressed. As an interesting factoid, he wore pajama bottoms but not the top, which meant he was bare chested and his face was stubbly.

It was a potent combination, she thought as she came to a stop and looked at him. Over the next five seconds, her burning goal was to keep her mouth from falling open. If she could do that, then she could probably get through the rest of the day.

His shoulders were broad, as was his chest. He was muscled, but not too much, and perfectly defined. The hair on his chest narrowed at his waist, arrowing toward what she remembered as a very large —

"Good morning," she managed.

"We have to talk."

His tone was determined, almost harsh. She blinked. "Okay. About what?"

"Your invoicing." He pointed to her office.

She led the way, then nearly dropped her mug when she walked inside and saw that her entire office had been attacked by some neat freak. Instead of open boxes overflowing with papers, there were neat stacks of full file folders. What looked like a comprehensive report sat next to her keyboard. Her computer was on and humming happily, but that seemed to be the least of her worries.

"What did you do?" she asked, her voice breathless.

"I apologize." His voice was gruff. "I shouldn't have pried into your personal business. I couldn't sleep and I came in here to play computer games. One of the invoices fell. I picked it up and saw the amount you'd been billed. It was different from what you billed us."

Her head came up as she glared at him. "Wait a minute. We have a contract that allows me to bill you five percent over the cost of goods."

His dark gaze softened. "I know. But you're not. You're sticking to the estimate, even when the actual cost goes up. Dellina, you're losing money on this job and that was never my intention. You're providing an excellent service. You should be paid for that. As for the estimates, that's what they are. An educated guess. You can't bill off an estimate. If there's a difference in price, that's out of my pocket, not yours."

Relief eased her tension. "Oh. Okay. I get what you're saying, but I always feel guilty and maybe a little irresponsible when there's a change in cost. I worry that if the estimate is different from the actual price, clients will get upset. So I don't always pass it on."

"So you're constantly eating a significant percentage of the costs of food and entertainment?"

When he said it like that, it sounded less than intelligent. "Not all the time," she murmured.

"How much of the time?"

She cleared her throat. "You're saying I shouldn't do that."

"Not if you expect your business to succeed." He ran his hand through his mussed hair. "Look, we're both busy right now. My parents are in town, the party's in a couple of days. Let's talk about this after. I want to go over all the billing and make sure you were paid what you were owed."

"I'd like that, too," she told him.

"Good. I'm going to take a shower and get dressed. I'll see you later?"

She nodded but what she was really thinking was that while her shower was small, it was plenty big enough for two. And if it was a tight squeeze . . . all the better.

CHAPTER ELEVEN

"I don't have time," Dellina said as she opened the big box that had just been delivered to her place. It was the last of the items for the goodie bags. She had to say that Sam had good taste. The clients would be thrilled, but jeez, putting them together was going to be a lot of work.

"You have to come," Taryn told her. "We're all having lunch with Lark and you won't want to miss it."

"I don't but look at this."

Her dining table was covered with forty empty large gift bags. Dark blue for the men and a metallic-red for the women. Twelve bright yellow bags lined the kitchen counters.

"I have to fill everything and it's not as easy as it sounds. The children's bags are all different, based on their gender and ages. I have to do the name tags and put in the tissue, then stuff them all. There are also some last-minute phone calls and a meeting with the hotel manager."

Taryn tilted her head. "All I'm hearing is a buzzing sound. You have to eat. Come have lunch with Lark."

Dellina tucked her hands behind her back. "She scares me," she admitted in a low voice.

Taryn grinned. "A believer now, I see."

"Yes. She's very sweet and funny, but the stuff she talks about. It's not right."

"I agree," Taryn said. "Poor guy. I don't know how he survived his family."

Having his ex then write about him in a tell-all disguised as a self-help book hadn't been good, either, she thought.

"Just say yes," Taryn said. "You know you want to be there. I'll help with the bags later."

"Seriously?"

"No, but I can send someone over."

Dellina laughed. "That's more like you." She hesitated. "What time?"

"Twelve-thirty. Margaritaville. When you spend a lot of time with Lark, you need access to tequila."

"I'll be there," Dellina said. "Now leave me to my work."

"Yes, ma'am."

Two hours later Dellina hurried into the

restaurant. She was only a few minutes late, but she didn't like not being on time. The good news was she'd finished all her calls and was nearly ready for the weekend party. With Sam helping her with her billing, she was going to be in good shape financially. Which made this project a win for her. Not that she would celebrate until it was over. She wasn't one to tempt fate.

"May I help you?" the hostess asked.

Before Dellina could ask about her party, there was a burst of female laughter in the back of the restaurant.

"I'm pretty sure I'm with them," she said. "I'll find my way."

Sure enough, her friends lined both sides of a large table. Taryn and Larissa sat on either side of Lark. Felicia, Patience and Isabel had joined them, along with Bailey and Consuelo. The only empty chair was directly across from Lark.

Dellina glanced at Taryn, who smiled innocently while motioning to the seat.

"We saved this for you," Taryn murmured.

"Gee, thanks."

Lark smiled at her. "Dellina. It's so nice to see you again. Reggie and I enjoyed our dinner so much. The food was delightful, as was the company."

"Thanks for your help with everything,"

she said, thinking that when Lark wasn't being outrageous, she was really nice. "Are you ready for your signing tonight?"

"Yes. There will be a question and answer session first. I always adore those. With prepared remarks I never know if I'm engaging the audience. But when they ask me questions, I know they're interested in the conversation. It's much more fun for all of us."

The server appeared with two large pitchers of margaritas. Before Dellina could say anything, the glass in front of her was full. Taryn smiled.

"You weren't thinking of working this afternoon, were you?"

"I don't have a choice." Dellina eyed the massive drink. "I'm going to be very careful."

When everyone had been served, Lark raised her glass. "To new friends and a life well lived."

They touched glasses and drank. Dellina took a sip and felt it slide down all too easily. This could be dangerous, she thought.

Bailey was next to her. The other woman leaned over. "How's the party? I'm hearing it's going to be great."

"Fingers crossed," Dellina told her. "I'm in the panic stage. It all starts tomorrow. I hope I'm ready." She smiled. "How are you doing? Has Mayor Marsha left on her vacation?"

"A couple of days ago. I'm nervous about keeping everything running smoothly, but the whole city government staff is helping out. I just want to get through these couple of weeks without a crisis."

"I hear you."

They touched glasses and sipped again. Dellina felt a little of her tension fade. Maybe one margarita wouldn't be so bad, she thought. It could take the edge off.

The server came and they placed their orders.

Lark smiled at Taryn. "You're doing so well. Happy and in love. It suits you. Any plans to get pregnant soon?"

Dellina had to give Taryn credit — she didn't even blink at the personal question.

"Angel and I are still having that conversation."

"While the need to procreate is biological," Felicia offered, "it's not universal. Generally people who don't want children have found satisfaction with an intense career or are in the arts. Something about creating another way. There are also studies that indicate a traumatic childhood can lessen the desire to have children." She paused and looked at Consuelo. "Did I say too much?"

Consuelo picked up her margarita. "No. You said exactly the right thing. People choose to have a family or not for different reasons."

Felicia, very pregnant herself and drinking herbal tea, looked relieved. "Yes, that's it. Gideon and I knew that we wanted a family. We were blessed with Carter from the start and now we have our daughter on the way."

"Children *are* a blessing," Lark said. "Reggie and I wanted at least two. Of course, having girls meant we had to make a run at a boy. Then we had Sam."

Her smile turned wistful. "He was such a sweet little boy. How he adored his older sisters and he desperately wanted to be playing with them all the time. But he was sick so much." She looked around the table. "Asthma. It was horrible. He would turn blue and we would race him to the hospital. A couple of times we thought we were going to lose him."

Taryn reached for Lark's hand and squeezed it. "You didn't, though."

"I know. He grew big and strong." Lark's mouth straightened. "And then he wanted to play football. I knew sports were in his blood. The whole family was athletic. But I couldn't stand the thought of him risking himself like that. Kicking was a compromise and he turned out to be a star at it."

Chips and salsa were delivered to the table, along with big bowls of guacamole. Taryn visibly flinched. "My downfall on the calorie front," she murmured, pushing the guacamole away. "Some of my skirts are getting tight."

"If you breathe correctly, you can increase your calorie burn during sex," Lark told her, reaching for a chip. "I'll show you later."

"I look forward to it," Taryn said.

Dellina shook her head. The truth was Reggie and Lark were loving parents who had a quirky way of looking at things. They weren't bad, they were just . . . different.

After lunch, Dellina walked out with Patience.

"The T-shirts are in," her friend told her. "I got a text during lunch."

One of the thrills of small-town living, she thought. Her T-shirt order had been delivered to Patience's store because the delivery guy was already going to Brew-haha, anyway, so why not?

She'd ordered shirts for Fayrene and Ryan, along with the babysitting staff. Each of the kids was getting a shirt, too. She also managed to arrange for a tiny shirt for Caramel, which was going to be wildly cute. But still, now she had another pickup.

"I think the box is going to be too big for me to carry," she said. "I'll be by later to pick it up."

Patience touched her arm. "No way. I'm delivering it to you as soon as I get back to the store. Are you kidding? You have to be running in circles. The whole big party starts tomorrow night."

"Thank you," Dellina said. "I owe you, big-time."

"Are you ready?"

"Nearly. I hope. I'm going to be stuffing goodie bags into the night. I've triple-checked everything, I have my lists."

"You'll do great," her friend told her. "I love what you did last year with Charlie's wedding. That was perfect." Patience grinned. "Any hints as to what Taryn is planning?"

"She hasn't said a word to me. Maybe they're going to elope."

"No way." Patience laughed. "Taryn needs to wear a designer gown by some French person we've never heard of. She can't do that if she elopes. She'll probably talk to you soon."

"After Sunday," Dellina said. "I couldn't handle it before then."

"I want details."

"I'm sure we all will."

Patience walked with her along the street. "So how's it working with the handsome football players? Sparkage?"

Despite the stress and her exhaustion, Dellina laughed. "Sparkage? Who says that? I'm only working with Sam, and while he's a great guy, we have a professional relationship."

Patience's eyes brightened with amusement. "This would be the same Sam you slept with on Valentine's Day night?"

"Yeah, that one."

Patience raised her eyebrows. "I'm not buying the business-only thing, just so you know."

Because she and Patience had known each other all their lives, there weren't many secrets.

"We might have kissed, but it didn't mean anything." Dellina paused, then grinned. "Beyond the sparkage."

"I knew it. I really love being right. How's Fayrene doing? Is she still on that campaign to get Ryan to propose?"

"Yes, and it's ridiculous. Ryan worships

her. She needs to tell him she's changed her mind."

"I know, but sometimes it's hard to say that kind of thing." Patience shook her head. "Everyone else can see how he feels, but I keep thinking her insistence that the proposal comes from him isn't about convention so much as fear."

"What do you mean?"

"Maybe she's scared he's changed his mind. That he doesn't *want* to marry her anymore. We all create elaborate stories when the truth is too painful."

They stopped in front of Brew-haha. "This is me," Patience said, giving her a quick hug. "Come on inside. We'll load up the T-shirts and I'll give you a ride home."

"Thanks," Dellina said as she followed her inside the store.

But her mind wasn't on the party anymore, or even her sister. She kept thinking about what Patience had said about people making up stories when the truth was too painful to admit.

Did she have a story? She was so clear on not wanting to get married because she'd already raised her family. That was true — she wasn't just saying it. Because if she was, then there was a greater truth. A more painful one. Like maybe she had already lost so

245

much, she was terrified of losing again, and that was why she didn't want to risk her heart.

"Most yardage passing," Jack said, tossing the football to Kenny.

"Regular season or play-off game?" Kenny asked. He caught the ball and then tossed it across the table.

"Regular season," Sam said as the ball spiraled toward him.

They were in the conference room with a football. When Taryn found out, she was going to hit the roof. Sam wondered why they took such delight in messing with her. She always got them back somehow and yet they couldn't seem to help themselves. A couple of months ago, a wayward pass had shattered the built-in television. Taryn had replaced the regular milk by the coffee machine with soy milk for over a week. While any one of them could have gone to the store and bought a quart of regular milk, they hadn't. Instead they'd swallowed the soy and promised to never toss the football indoors again.

"Against the 49ers," Kenny said. "October 2011. It was raining. We won that game."

"Because I kicked a field goal with five seconds on the clock," Sam reminded them.

"Three points, gentlemen. The difference between being a god and getting your ass handed to you."

Their receptionist stuck her head in the room. "Kenny, there's a young lady here to see you."

Sam looked at Jack, who was already hooting and whistling.

"A young lady," he said. "I hope she's over eighteen."

Sam chuckled. "Look at you, Kenny. Having them meet you at the office. Afraid to show them where you live?"

Kenny walked toward the door. "Sam, I was going to let you stay at my place while your folks are in town, but you can forget that."

Sam nearly said that he was staying with Dellina, but kept his mouth shut. No one needed that information. His partners would make too big a deal of it.

They went with Kenny down the hallway to the foyer. At the entrance, the three of them stopped and stared at the two girls waiting there. Because they were girls. Maybe seven or eight years old. One was thin, with bright red hair and green eyes. She was with a blonde girl who wore glasses.

The redhead smiled shyly at Kenny.

"Chloe?" he said, walking toward her.

"What are you doing here?"

"Allison and I need your help," she said. "Allison is making her mom a jewelry box for her birthday. It's her summer project for the FWM. Her dad was supposed to help her finish it, but he had to go out of town on business. Her mom's birthday is Saturday. All it needs is painting and then varnish. Can you help us with that?"

She stared at Kenny as she spoke, her eyes wide, her expression hopeful. Jack chuckled.

"Someone's got a crush," he whispered. "That's so cute."

Which was code for later Jack would torment Kenny about the kid.

Kenny, all six feet four inches and well over two hundred pounds of him, shifted uneasily from foot to foot. "Ah, maybe one of your mom's friends could do it. I'm not good at art projects."

"It's not an art project," Allison said quickly. "The box is made. We just have to paint it. We have money for the paint and varnish. We'd ask Chloe's mom, but she's working. You know Chloe doesn't have a dad, right?"

Sam winced. "She hits below the belt. He's a goner."

"Totally destroyed by two little girls," Jack said admiringly. "You have to respect their tactics. Simple but effective."

"They'll be ruling the world in less than a decade."

Kenny looked over his shoulder. "Could either of you two —"

Jack and Sam were already backing away.

"Sorry, bro," Sam said. "I have my folks to deal with."

"I'm busy," Jack told him.

They rounded the corner, then turned and headed to the conference room.

"It's nearly lunchtime," Jack said. "Want to go to Jo's Bar?"

Sam shook his head. "I'm not sure where my mom is. Let's order in."

"Good idea."

By nine-thirty that night, all the kids' bags were stuffed and standing neatly in boxes that lined the wall of Dellina's living room. The T-shirts — a bright yellow that would be easy to spot if anyone wandered off — were rolled and wrapped in ribbon and resting on the very top of the bags. Big name tags hung from the handles. She'd spoken to Fayrene and confirmed the pickup time for the morning. She had rented a delivery van to get everything up to the hotel.

Now, as she worked on the gift bags for the adults, she went item by item, confirming that she wasn't missing anything. With the women's bags, she was going to nestle the Tiffany's box on top. The pretty blue would be an eye-catcher. Dellina had to admit she'd been hoping the store would throw in a buy-ten-get-one-free bonus, but no such luck. There were three extra pairs of the watches, but she suspected Sam had ordered them specifically for him and his partners.

She had just placed the heavy packages at the bottom of the guys' bags when she heard her front door open. She glanced into the living room and saw Sam walking toward her. He looked pale and shaken.

"The book signing?" she asked.

He pulled out a chair and sank into it. "Oh, yeah."

"There wasn't a, um, demonstration, was there?"

"No." A heavy sigh accompanied the word. "She kept her clothes on and my dad stayed in the audience." He raised his head. "At first it was fine. She talked about marriage and staying connected, both emotionally and sexually. Then she took questions. A woman who had read her previous work asked about a sexual technique and for the next fifteen minutes my mom explained the importance of clitoral stimulation."

Dellina sank into a chair on the opposite side of the table. She couldn't decide if she was happy or sad that she'd missed the event.

"Did that clear the room?" she asked.

"No chance. The women were all nodding and poking their husbands in the arm, as if wanting to make sure they got the importance of the message."

"Well, sure," she murmured.

Sam stared at her. "Are you trying to help?"

"Not really."

He grinned. "Fine. I'll carry my pain on my own."

"How can you build character otherwise?" She stood. "Can you talk while I work, because I still have to finish these bags, then go over the schedule one more time."

"Sure. Let me help." He rose and moved next to her. "Tell me what goes where."

She pointed to the list on the wall. "In that order, please. I've played around with how to fit everything into the bags without them getting crushed. Then we put them in the large boxes for delivery in the morning."

Which all sounded so professional when what she was really thinking was how well Sam had known his way around her clitoris

251

that lone night they'd been together. And that while the lessons his mother taught could be embarrassing, they had a purpose. Education was important. Like her learning about her G-spot and how she still wanted to know where it was, exactly, and what it felt like when it was happy.

But those fantasies were for another time, she told herself firmly. Right now she had gift bags to prep and a thousand details to get to before she could sleep.

Dellina drifted in that blissful not-quite-awake semi-sleep. She'd been up until after midnight, but it had been worth it. When she'd finally gone to bed, it had been with the knowledge that she was as ready as she could be. There was no need to panic. She was prepared for whatever the day might offer.

She opened her eyes and sighed. She'd slept really well. Given the short night, she'd expected to be more tired. But she was energized. As if she'd gotten her full eight hours instead of a mere —

She turned to her clock and screamed. Eight-thirty? Eight-*thirty*? No! She'd set her alarm, hadn't she? She was going to get up at six and be ready. Fayrene was bringing the van at nine. They had to be at the hotel by ten. She'd paid extra to have access to the meeting rooms this morning. There was still so much to do.

She jumped out of bed and collected her clothes, then dashed down the hall. She threw herself into the bathroom, slammed the door shut and turned on the water.

In record time she'd brushed her teeth, washed her face and leaped into the shower. She didn't have time to wash her hair, so she pinned it on top of her head. Wash, rinse and she was out. Naked and dripping, she reached for her towel just as the bathroom door pushed open.

Dellina remembered instantly that she hadn't locked the door. She'd been too much in a hurry, plus she hadn't been thinking that she had a temporary room-mate. And while him seeing her dripping and naked was embarrassing, it wasn't the end of the world. He'd seen her without her clothes before.

She closed her hand around her towel, all the while expecting him to apologize and then back out of the room. Only he didn't. He stared at her with a combination of desire and need that made her legs shaky.

He swore softly, reached for her, swore again, then took a step back.

"The door wasn't locked," he said, his

voice gritty and thick.

There wasn't any time, she thought. This was insane. They'd already agreed on ground rules. There were a thousand reasons to say, "Hey, no problem," and then cover herself. To pretend this had never happened. It was the smart thing to do. It was sensible. It was impossible.

"Sam," she breathed.

His jaw tightened. For one agonizing second he didn't move. Then he ripped open his shirt and dropped it to the floor even as he surged toward her. His arms came around her as she clung to him. Then his mouth was on hers and nothing else mattered.

CHAPTER TWELVE

He claimed her with a kiss that shook her to her toes. Lips pressed. Breath mingled. Dellina parted instantly and he pushed his tongue inside her mouth. She stroked hers against his, wanting the friction and teasing arousal. But it was difficult to concentrate on his kisses when his hands roamed over her bare, wet body.

He explored her back, then her rear before cupping her curves and squeezing. She arched against him and felt that he was already hard. Very hard. His hands moved around to her front, then up to her breasts. His long, skilled fingers found her already tight nipples and brushed against the very tips.

Wanting burned so hot, she melted. Between her legs she ached as her body swelled in anticipation. She fumbled with his belt and got it open, then undid his jeans and pushed them down.

He pulled back enough to shove off the rest of his clothes. He was already barefoot. He kicked everything out of the way, then dropped to his knees and eased her thighs apart. She barely had time to grab the sink for support before he was holding her open with his fingers and licking the very heart of her.

It was too much, she thought, gasping for air as his tongue moved back and forth against her clitoris. Too good, too soon, too early. But she didn't want him to stop. Not when he did those little circles, pausing only to suck deeply.

He moved his hands to her hips and shifted her slightly, then raised her left foot so it rested on the tub. She was exposed and waited to feel embarrassed. But before she could summon the emotion, he pushed two fingers deep inside of her and curled them upward. She felt delicious pressure, then an odd rubbing.

It was as if he was caressing her clit from the back. But more than that. Deeper. She pushed down to increase the pressure. She gasped as those fingers rubbed and stroked and his tongue circled. The sensations blended until she was at their mercy, unable to do anything but breathe and feel and then surrender to the inevitable climax that gripped her so tightly she had no choice but to scream her release.

"Oh, Sam!" she gasped as she started to come. "Please!"

He touched her from the inside and the outside, drawing every last quiver until she was spent.

"Condoms."

The word came out in a near-guttural moan. She opened her eyes and watched him stand. He was hard and shaking and staring at her with an intensity that nearly made her swoon.

The meaning of what he wanted sank in. She turned and pulled open the medicine chest, then handed him an unopened box.

The paper lid went flying. He pulled one out, had it on and her turned back to him in less than three seconds. A heartbeat after that, she was on the counter, her legs spread and he pushed inside of her.

His sharp exhalation told her how close he'd been to the edge and the knowledge made her shiver. She wrapped her legs around his hips and pulled him in closer.

He filled her deeply, making her arch against him. More, she thought hazily. If he did this for a little bit longer, she would come again. If he just —

His hands returned to her breasts. Her

257

nipples were still tight, but so sensitive from her recent climax. When he began to massage them, she nearly told him it was too much. Only then he was rubbing and touching her nipples all the while pressing his fingers in just below them. And he found a spot that connected directly to her very core.

Her eyes flew open and she found him watching her.

"What are you doing to me?" she asked.

He smiled as he pushed in again. At the same time he squeezed and pushed or twisted and —

Who cares, she thought as she lost herself in a second climax. She pulled him in as deeply as she could. Her body convulsed around his. He pumped harder and faster until he, too, came and then they were holding each other and trying to catch their breath.

"Your mother is amazing," Dellina said when she could speak again.

Sam looked at her and started to laugh.

"We are so late," Dellina said as she picked up clothes off the towel rack and ran into the hallway. "Late, late, late."

Sam knew she was right, but he couldn't begin to care. Damn, talk about a great way to start the day.

He pulled on his briefs, then his jeans and followed her down the hall. His reward was the sight of her slipping on her bra, then adjusting her breasts. She shimmied into jeans, pulled on a blouse and wrapped it around her. She turned and saw him.

"Stop it! You have that smile."

He leaned against the wall. "What smile?"

"The one that says you just got laid. Do you want everyone to know? What time is it? Oh, my God. It's nine. Fayrene will be here any second. Get your shirt on."

She was frazzled, he thought with satisfaction. *Rattled* and *scattered* and all those other words that describe a woman after she'd had her world rocked. Yeah, that was good and he was the man who'd made it happen.

From outside came the sound of a vehicle pulling into the driveway.

Dellina shrieked and ran into her bedroom. She came back in flats and was pulling pins out of her hair. "Get dressed," she told him as she raced past. "Fayrene can't suspect. Do I look guilty? I feel like I look guilty."

"You look beautiful."

She paused and smiled at him, then shook her head. "Don't talk nice to me. We have to be completely normal."

"I am nice when I'm normal."

"You know what I mean."

She walked to the door and smoothed her hair. "Okay. This is fine. I'm ready." She reached for the handle.

"Dellina?"

She turned to him and raised her eyebrows. "Yes?"

"In case you were wondering, that was your G-spot."

Kipling lived a half-life of near-consciousness. Even when he was out, he was aware of the pain, but when the drugs were working, he didn't care. It hummed in the background but didn't touch him. But when the drugs faded, then there was the agony of a thousand shattered bones. Shards and swelling and lacerations. The carefully stitched seams from his surgeries.

He'd been moved. He knew that. And he could breathe on his own. The nurses were less quiet, less worried, in this new room. They still monitored him too closely and talked about fluids in and out in such a way that he knew he must be on a catheter. That particular hell was one he didn't want to think about.

"Kip?"

The soft voice was familiar. Perhaps the

only one in the world he had always loved. He forced his eyes open. The room swam at first, then settled and he saw Shelby standing by his bed.

He saw her eyes first. Big and blue. Like his own. They had that in common, along with their dark blond hair. Both inherited from their mutual father. They had different mothers, though. That showed in the rest of their features. Shelby was small boned and delicate. Like a fairy princess come to life. Only no fairy princess should have a fist-size bruise on her face.

"I'm going to kill him," he said, or at least he tried. His mouth was dry and speaking was harder than he'd thought it would be.

"Kip." His baby half sister leaned close and kissed his cheek. "Oh, Kip, I've been so worried. They said you nearly died."

She took his uninjured hand in hers and squeezed. "I came as soon as I heard."

"I wish you hadn't."

She'd flown halfway around the world and for what? To watch him lie in a hospital bed? He'd been injured before — they both knew the drill. Although what he would never admit was that he hadn't been hurt this bad before. He wouldn't acknowledge the chill of fear that whispered this time was different. This time meant he would never compete again, never ski professionally. This time, maybe he wouldn't walk.

The doctors hadn't said anything and he didn't ask, but he wasn't a fool. And the possibility of how bad it could be terrified him.

Shelby touched his face. "You look terrible."

"Always with the compliments." He freed his hand and pushed the button to raise the bed, then studied her. "Dammit, Shelby, what are you doing back home?"

"You know why I'm there."

He did. Shelby's mother had cancer. She'd been in remission for a while, but it was back. Staying with her mom meant staying with her dad. And when Nigel Gilmore drank, he was a mean sonofabitch.

"She only has a few more weeks," Shelby told him. "I can stand it." She pressed the back of her hand against her cheek. "Normally I stay out of his way, but she'd had a bad night and he caught me sleeping."

Kipling closed his eyes against the image of his father hitting Shelby while she slept. He swore. Normally he would fly to Colorado and go see his father himself. Those ugly visits usually kept Shelby safe for at least a couple of months. But he wasn't going anywhere for a very long time.

She took his hand again. "I'm okay. I'll be fine. The second she's gone, I'll leave. You know that, right? I'd never stay there if it wasn't for her."

He nodded because he believed her. Fortunately Nigel had never hit his second wife. Kipling didn't have a clue as to why she was immune, but what the hell.

She bent down and kissed his cheek. "I love you, Kip."

"I love you, too."

She was his family, his heart. She was the best of him — of all of them.

She settled back in the chair and pulled an issue of *People* magazine out of her bag. "So, you ready to get caught up on the latest gossip? I hear Katy Perry has a new boyfriend. You always had a thing for her."

"It was the blue hair," he said, closing his eyes. "How could anyone resist that?"

Dellina arrived at the hotel behind the big van. Her heart was pounding and she was pretty sure she was shaking all over. The thing was, her reaction had nothing to do with the upcoming weekend and everything to do with her close encounter with Sam.

Talk about amazing. The things he did to her body. She wanted to believe it was all about technique, but she had a feeling there was more to it than that. Obviously they had chemistry. Their first time together had been spectacular, too. But this time had been different. There'd been a little extra oomph — probably because she now knew him and liked him. Connection made a difference.

"Connection isn't a relationship," she told herself as she parked. "And I can't deal with this now."

There would be plenty of time for introspection after the weekend party. For now, she had to get her act together and take care of business.

"If only clichés paid in cash," she murmured as she grabbed her bag and headed for the van.

An hour later, the goodie bags were unpacked and she'd gone over the list of rooms with the front desk manager. She settled herself in a quiet corner of the shaded porch and called all her vendors to get last-minute confirmation.

"You know this is the third time you've called me," Angel said when he picked up the phone. "I'm ready. You're kind of a nightmare to work with."

She grinned. "You're lying. I've met your fiancée so I happen to know you like it when a woman takes charge."

264

Angel chuckled. "Don't tell anyone. Yes, the obstacle course is ready. I'll have plenty of water on hand for hydration. There's a first aid kit, everyone who works here knows CPR and the weather is good. Now can we be done?"

"We can. Thank you."

She called Ana Raquel next.

"The wine is delivered, the food all came in this morning and looks great. Greg and I are prepping, we have our schedule and I'm thinking I might make a banana layer cake because I'm in the mood. How are you?"

Dellina smiled as she curled up in the chair. "You are one of my two favorite sisters. Have I said that recently?"

"No, but it's always on your mind. I can tell. Sis, you gotta relax. We're all ready. It's going to be a great weekend."

"Planning makes that happen."

They chatted about a few more details, then hung up. Dellina moved on to the next call.

Close to noon, she and a bellman delivered the goodie bags to the guests' room. There was a schedule of events, but she wanted to hand those out personally during check-in. She adjusted temperatures, checked linens and made sure each minibar was stocked. By two she'd taken her suitcase to her own room and changed into a pretty summer dress and slightly nicer flats. She was going to be on her feet until around midnight. She had to be sensible.

As she touched up her makeup, she found herself remembering being in a different bathroom that morning. With Sam. Her body shuddered slightly as she flashed back to how he'd touched her and how she'd reacted to that touch. She wanted a repeat performance. Or fifty. She was still smiling as she made her way downstairs.

On the main level, she confirmed that no guests had checked in yet. She made sure she had the welcome packets set up at the small desk the hotel had provided.

"You look official."

She saw Jack and Kenny approaching. At the sight of the two handsome football players, she felt her stomach drop a little. Not in reaction to them, but if they were here, then so was Sam.

"I don't have a name tag," she told him. "It's not official without a name tag."

Kenny shook his head. "We forgot that. Talk about stupid."

"You know, sometimes we're just a bunch of football jocks."

Taryn hurried over to them. "Did I miss it? Where's Sam? Is he late? I swear, if he's late to this party, I'm going to beat him with a stick."

"I'm here."

Sam appeared next to Kenny.

The second Dellina saw him, she suddenly forgot how to breathe. Had he always been so good-looking? How did the other women in the room keep from ripping off their clothes and begging him to take them — which was what she desperately wanted. Which, of course, she couldn't. Nor, it seemed, could she look at him. Because when he smiled at her, she ducked her head and prayed she wouldn't blush.

At first she didn't understand what was wrong, but then she got it. She was shy. Apparently hot, fast, mind-clearing sex left her elated and a little unsure. What was he thinking? Did anyone know? She didn't want that. She was on the job and her professional reputation was important to her. Sleeping with clients was not going to be good for business.

"We appreciate all you've done," Taryn said, drawing Dellina back to the moment. "Me, especially. Because I refused to have anything to do with planning the party, and if you hadn't stepped in, it would have been a disaster."

Kenny glared at her. "Are you saying the

three of us couldn't have pulled it off?"

"Yes."

He shrugged. "You're right."

Jack handed Dellina a blue bag. A familiar blue bag because she'd just handled twenty exactly like it.

"Thank you," Taryn said. "From all of us."

The guys nodded. She thought maybe Sam's gaze was a little more intense than the others, but she couldn't be sure.

She took the bag and looked inside. The blue Tiffany's box was bigger than the ones she'd seen. So she wasn't getting the same diamond stud earrings.

She untied the white ribbon, then lifted the cover of the box. Inside was a beautiful bangle. A center row of diamonds with a twisted rope of gold on either side. The piece was gorgeous, but not so huge that she couldn't wear it every day.

"It's beautiful," she murmured. "Thank you."

"Sam said you weren't the diamond stud earring type," Taryn said, helping her with the bracelet. "That this was something you could wear every day. Seriously, you've done a great job with the party. Thank you for everything."

"You're welcome."

Dellina looked at the bangle on her wrist

and knew she'd never owned anything so nice before.

Taryn hugged her. Kenny and Jack did the same. Sam touched her last, briefly pulling her close, then releasing her.

"All right, I have to go unpack," Taryn said.

"How many suitcases?" Jack asked. "Three?"

Taryn sniffed. "Just one. It's only two nights."

"You're lying," Kenny said conversationally. "You can't go anywhere with just one suitcase."

"Yes, I can. Angel is letting me use part of his." With that, she turned and walked away.

Kenny and Jack followed, leaving Sam next to her.

"You okay?" he asked when they were relatively alone.

She made herself look into his dark eyes. "Yes. You?"

One corner of his mouth turned up. "Never better." His mouth straightened. "About this morning," he began. "It was unexpected."

"I know."

"And great."

Now she smiled. "Better than great. But private."

His expression relaxed. "Exactly."

"Because it isn't anyone else's business and we have to work together this weekend." Not to mention the fact that she had no idea if it had been a one-time thing or if they were going to see each other again.

"Hello, my love."

Dellina saw Lark and Reggie approaching. "Parental alert behind you."

"I knew my luck was too good to last," Sam muttered before turning. "Mom. Dad. You made it."

"Of course we made it," Lark said as she pulled him close. "I'm very excited to meet your clients. Plus we get to spend more time with you."

She stepped toward Dellina as Reggie hugged his son. But before Lark drew Dellina into what she knew would be an enthusiastic embrace, Lark hesitated. Her blue eyes widened and she smiled broadly.

"Reggie, look," Lark said, her voice carrying through the foyer of the hotel. "Sam and Dellina had sex today. And from the glow on her face and the way she's carrying herself, the orgasms were especially delicious."

Dellina carefully pulled up the side zipper of the black taffeta dress she wore. It was by a designer whose name she couldn't pronounce. One of Taryn's castoffs from their clothing exchange a couple of months before and the only one Dellina had thought could be let out enough to actually fit her.

The bodice had lots of shirring and was fitted to the waist. The skirt flared out to just above the knee. A designer friend had worked her magic, inserting matching panels into the side seams, giving Dellina the extra few inches she'd needed. The V in front was low enough to be evening appropriate but not so low as to show anything. Tonight wasn't about her. Despite being invited to the party, she was staff, not a guest. Staff who had slept with the boss.

Dellina pressed her hands to her cheeks. She'd redone her makeup, hoping to cover what seemed to be a permanent blush. While not everyone had heard what Lark had proclaimed, Taryn, Jack and Kenny had, along with the front desk clerks, a couple from Omaha and a few others she didn't know. At least none of the Score guests had arrived yet.

Still, she was humiliated. Not because of what she'd done, but because it made her seem unprofessional. She was good at her job and she didn't want people thinking less of her.

Someone knocked on her door. She opened it and found Taryn in the hallway.

"How are you holding up?" her friend asked as she walked in.

"I've had better moments," Dellina admitted. "And I'm sorry about . . ."

Taryn waited, her blue-violet gaze more amused than judgmental. "Yes? I don't think you're sorry for sleeping with Sam. You liked it the last time."

"Well, it's more about work than anything else."

Taryn shook her head. "It's not you, it's Lark. We all get that. I'm not going to say anything and the guys aren't going to say anything. No clients heard. I figured you were upset and I came to say don't be."

Dellina wished letting go was that easy. "I'm worried about tonight."

"Try to let it go. I had a little talk with Lark and Reggie and they promise to be on their best behavior."

"Is that enough?"

"They can be controlled for short periods of time. It's fine." Taryn headed for the door, then turned back. "About Sam," she began. "Like I said before. Don't break his heart."

"I won't." An easy promise. Sam wasn't interested in her that way.

Taryn smiled and then left.

Dellina finished getting ready. She put on simple gold hoops, then slid on the beautiful bangle she'd been given earlier. She took her tote and her ever-present lists, then headed out.

When she got to the dining room, Sam was already there. He wore a dark suit and white shirt, both of which looked really good on him. He'd obviously showered and shaved, and when she looked at him she felt a distinct quiver deep in her chest.

Attraction, she told herself. Nothing more. And if it was something else, then it was Taryn's silly comments about not breaking his heart. As if she could.

"I've already checked the place settings and talked to the head server for the dinner," he said.

"That would be my job."

"I know, but I wanted to talk to you." He moved close and lightly touched her cheek. "Are you okay?"

"Of course. Busy, but otherwise, just peachy."

His mouth twisted. "My mother is a problem."

"She's always interesting, I'll give you that."

"I'm sorry about what she said. We both

273

wanted to keep that private. Taryn and the guys won't say anything and none of our guests heard. I talked to her and she's promised to be on her best behavior for tonight."

"Taryn talked to her, too."

"She mentioned that." He paused. "You know it's not personal. She blurts things out without considering the consequences."

Dellina nodded. "She can't help herself. It would be better if she weren't so intuitive."

"I agree."

He looked worried, which was sweet. And he'd come down early to talk to her. The concern was nice. She smiled. "I'll be okay. It's just one of those wacky things. I don't regret this morning."

Heat flared in his eyes. "Me, either. You were spectacular."

"I can live with that description."

CHAPTER THIRTEEN

Fayrene pulled on the hem of her T-shirt and told herself she was dressed appropriately and that she wasn't the least bit bitter that while she was with twelve children, her sister got to preside over an elegant dinner. That was for later. For now, she had a crisis.

Ryan had gotten stuck at work. He had texted to let her know he would be a few minutes late. She'd reminded him to stop by her apartment and pick up Caramel. She'd left the dog home alone for a few hours, but now that everything had been delivered to the hotel, she planned to have the little Pomeranian spend the weekend with her. Because right now Fayrene could use a friendly face.

Twelve children of varying ages all stared at her. They didn't know one another and they didn't know her. The extra babysitters, the ones who did this sort of thing on a regular basis, were checking on dinner, which meant Fayrene was alone in a room that was way too quiet.

"I want my mom," a little girl of maybe seven or eight said. "Why does she and my dad get to go to a nice dinner while I have to stay here? It's not fair."

"This is stupid," one of the boys said. "We're supposed to be having fun and we're not."

Fayrene swallowed against rising panic. She'd taken the job with the kids for a number of reasons. For one, she wanted to help her sister. For another, the reference and experience would be good for business. But more important, she'd hoped that hanging out with a bunch of kids would allow her and Ryan to talk about what it would be like when they had their own children. Which would lead to a conversation about getting married. Which would mean he would finally propose.

But none of that was going to happen if she had a mutiny on the very first night. Dellina would not be happy if the kids broke ranks and sought out their parents.

Fayrene looked around the large room they were using for their first event. There were balloons and a working jukebox and tables with ingredients. But no activity and no conversation. She didn't know what to

276

do or how to make it better, but she'd best come up with something fast.

Ana Raquel strolled in. Fayrene rushed to her.

"Help. They're not having fun. Do something."

Her twin raised her eyebrows. "I'm a chef, not an entertainer."

"Give them food, then. That will distract them."

"We're supposed to have the mixology class in a few minutes, and make appetizers. Greg is bringing the rest of the ingredients before he heads off for the wine tasting. We can't start until he brings the rest of the food."

"We have to do something."

"You know this is your gig, right? There's technically no 'we.' "

Fayrene was about to beg when Ryan walked in. He held Caramel in his arms. When she spotted Fayrene, she wiggled to get free and rushed over to greet her.

Fayrene picked up the happy dog and held her close. Protection at last. Ryan gave her a brief hug and kissed her cheek.

"It's quiet in here," he said. "Too quiet."

"I know. I thought they'd be more interactive. We have to do something." She'd figured they would supervise, not be in charge of helping them get along. Weren't kids supposed to be friendly and outgoing? She remembered having tons of friends when she'd been young, and talking to virtually anyone who would listen.

Ryan picked up a pen and wrote his name on a tag, then put it on his shirt. "No worries. Watch the master at work."

He took Caramel from her and carried the dog over to the milling children.

"Who here likes dogs?" he asked.

A few hands went up.

"Who's afraid of dogs?"

Fayrene saw one of the littler girls stare at the ground, but no one said anything.

"Can you tell me what kind of dog this one is?" Ryan asked.

There were blank stares.

"A Pomeranian. Her name is Caramel. She's got a lot of fur, but underneath, she's tiny."

"She has really little feet," a young girl said. "But she's pretty."

"She is. She's also friendly and loves people." He winked at a blonde girl in sandals. "She likes to lick toes."

The girl giggled.

"I'm going to put her down and let her get to know all of you. While we're doing that, let's get on our name tags. We don't have much time before the activities start."

"What activities?" one of the older boys asked. "Because it's not fun yet."

Ryan patted him on the shoulder. "Patience, my man. You know what a cocktail is?"

The kid grinned. "We get to have them?"

"Almost. We're making mocktails — cocktails without the alcohol. And appetizers. Oh, and there's going to be a band later."

"A live band?" one of the girls asked.

"Yup." He put down Caramel and pointed to the table. "Let's figure out who we are and then we'll get going on the fun."

Fayrene breathed in deeply, then exhaled with relief. This was going to be okay. Ryan was here and, as far as she was concerned, he was her hero. She would reward him later, but for now, she had a dog-wary little girl to help out.

She crossed to the petite brunette and smiled at her. "What's your name?"

"Sally."

Fayrene sat on the floor in front of the girl. "Do you have dogs at home, Sally?"

"No. My dad's allergic. I've never been around dogs before." Sally watched Caramel move around the room. "Does she bite?"

"Not at all. Why don't you have a seat and I'll introduce you. It's easier to make friends after you've had an introduction."

Sally's hair was in a thick braid down her back. Her eyes were big and solemn. She hesitated, then dropped to the floor. Fayrene called Caramel over.

The little dog came running and jumped gracefully over Fayrene's crossed legs, then sat facing Sally. She was panting a little, which made her look as if she was grinning.

"The best thing to do with a dog you don't know is ask the owner if it's friendly. If the owner says it is and you can pet it, you want to introduce yourself first." She petted Caramel. "Now close your hand into a fist and let her sniff you. That's dog for saying hi."

Sally bit her lower lip, then slowly extended her small fist to the dog. Caramel leaned in and sniffed delicately before giving her a quick lick.

Sally jumped, then looked at Fayrene. "Does that mean she likes me?"

"It does. You want to pet her?"

Sally nodded. She inched closer and reached out to touch Caramel's back.

"She's soft!"

"I know. And feel how much fur there is. She's really small underneath."

Sally continued to pet her. Caramel jumped over Fayrene's legs again and moved next to the girl. She flopped onto her back, exposing her tummy. Fayrene showed her how to rub her chest and her stomach. Caramel sighed in contentment.

Sally laughed. "Dogs are funny," she said. "But I like this one."

Fayrene silently thanked her temporary pet and mentally promised bacon every morning for a week. One kid won over, eleven to go, she thought. But with a little more optimism than she'd had before.

Dellina was up before six on Saturday morning. The previous evening had gone perfectly. The wine tasting had been a hit and the dinner had gone over well. There had been good food, lots of conversation and most of their guests had gone up to their rooms feeling a little tipsy. She hoped that meant they'd slept well.

Dellina was downstairs by six-thirty, going over preparations. Today was the big busy day. After a morning stretch and yoga class, there was a buffet breakfast on the terrace. Then the vans arrived. The adults would head off to CDS for their obstacle course while the kids went bike riding. At eleven everyone reunited before they all headed to town for lunch and some in-town time during the Summer Festival. At three-thirty the vans brought them back to the hotel.

At four, the kids spent time with Max and his therapy dogs. Angel and the Acorns were going to be there to introduce the new puppies. There would be a demonstration of what therapy dogs could do. For the adults, it was the trickiest part of the weekend — Lark's lecture. Then there was a big barbecue with the children joining their parents. Dellina's hope was that, by nine, everyone would be exhausted and make an early evening of it.

She had already confirmed with Josh, Angel and the van company. Although she was itching to make a few phone calls, she resisted. She had to trust the people she'd hired.

At seven, a yawning Fayrene joined her. She wore shorts and a T-shirt and had Caramel with her.

"I'm exhausted," her sister said as she sat in the chair opposite, Caramel on her lap. "Twelve children is too many. But it went well."

"Everyone had a good time?"

"Uh-huh. This little girl and Ryan were hits. I was more a background person." She yawned again. "I need coffee and to rally myself for bike riding." She rose. "We're all set, by the way. We have sunscreen and water. Josh is providing the bikes and the helmets. I double-checked that everyone knows how to ride a bike. There's going to be a short talk on the Tour de France with pictures for the kids to look at."

"Sounds great. You doing okay?"

Fayrene nodded. "Just exhausted. I appreciate the business but I'm longing for a simple receptionist temp job. Right now sitting down and answering phones for eight hours sounds like a vacation." She waved and walked toward the coffee cart in the lobby.

Dellina spoke with the catering manager and confirmed the buffet was on track, then went to get herself some coffee. Halfway across the lobby, she saw Lark was already at the cart, waiting for her latte.

Dellina paused, not sure if she should approach or retreat. She hadn't spoken directly to the other woman since the previous afternoon when Lark had announced that Dellina and Sam had recently had sex. Apparently Taryn's talking-to had worked because Lark had been charming through dinner, but had steered clear of any questionable topics. Now she collected her latte, turned and saw Dellina. She waved her over.

"Everything is going so well," Sam's mother said. "Reggie and I enjoyed our-

283

selves so much last night. We just love Kenny, Jack and Taryn. Spending time with them is delightful. I only wish Larissa had been here."

"She's in Los Angeles visiting her family," Dellina said, then placed her order with the teen manning the cart. "Apparently her sister just found out she's pregnant."

Lark lowered her voice. "I'm so sorry about yesterday," she said quietly. "I wasn't thinking. I was just so happy to know that you and Sam had been together. He's been avoiding relationships for a while now and I worry about him."

Dellina was torn between the obvious concern of a loving mother and clarifying that she and Sam weren't in a relationship. Not that saying that made things any better. Fortunately Lark didn't need a whole lot of participation to have a conversation.

"I do have to admit, he has had a rough time with women," she continued. "His first serious girlfriend turned into a stalker. When he tried to break things off, she slashed his car tires."

"You're kidding," Dellina said. "Was she arrested?"

"She was and that seemed to snap her out of it. She pleaded guilty and agreed to move across the country. Then there was Simone.

That ended with the book."

"A nightmare," Dellina said, collecting her latte. She and Lark walked toward the outside terrace.

"He was determined to learn from his mistakes, so he kept his next relationship quiet. Too quiet, because she slept with both Kenny and Jack, then asked Sam if he wanted to be in a foursome." Lark's mouth drew into a straight line. "I'm as open as the next person when it comes to sex, but I do believe in fidelity to one's partner. Besides, Sam is hardly the kind of man to enjoy that sort of thing."

Dellina did her best not to choke on her coffee. A foursome? Maybe it made her boring, but she wasn't interested in that, either.

"He's a cautious man," Lark said. "Rightfully so, I suppose. I just keep hoping he finds the right woman. A partner." She looked meaningfully at Dellina.

"I hope he finds that, as well," she murmured, and took another sip so she didn't have to talk. "If you'll excuse me, I need to check on the buffet."

"Of course."

She walked toward the restaurant. As she'd already spoken with the catering manager, she didn't actually have an appointment, but that didn't matter. Getting away from Lark seemed judicious. She appreciated the apology and Lark's concern about her son was admirable, but talk of partners wasn't anything she wanted.

She and Sam weren't even dating. Not really. She liked him — a lot. He was a great guy. Handsome and caring and surprisingly funny. He was competitive without being a jerk about it. And the things he could do in five minutes of hot, hungry sex stole her breath. She desperately wanted to see what he had to offer with a whole hour at his disposal. Because while their February encounter had been great, she hadn't known him. And knowing Sam made being with him intimately all the better.

Maybe after the weekend, she thought wistfully. She would like that a lot. But as to the rest of it . . .

At the end of the hallway, she saw Ryan and Fayrene. He had his arm around her and whispered something that made her laugh. For all her sister's craziness about the proposal, she was obviously wildly in love with Ryan. Ana Raquel had also found happiness. Being a part of something, being connected and in love, appealed. Sort of. Only she wasn't sure she really wanted that. Not that she was looking forward to spending her life alone.

"A problem for another time," she told herself as she glanced at her watch. She had a yoga class to get started.

By seven-thirty, the stretching-yoga class was going strong. Dellina walked back into the hotel and nearly bumped into Bailey.

"I was looking for you," the other woman said. "Your phone is turned off."

"Oh, no!" Dellina pulled it out of her pocket and saw the mute button was on. "I did that last night at the dinner," she said. "I forgot."

She checked her messages and saw that Bailey had been her only call. "Thanks so much for telling me. Is that why you drove up here?"

Bailey smiled. "Sort of. I also wanted to know if you needed help with anything. Chloe spent the night with her friend Allison and they're spending the day together. Later they'll be here for the therapy dog demonstration." Bailey shrugged. "I have nothing planned for today. Seriously, if you need anything, just ask."

Dellina appreciated the offer. She also had a feeling that her friend was feeling at loose ends without her daughter around. Since the death of Bailey's husband and Chloe's father, the two had only had each other. At least until the town had figured out what had happened and had reached out to them.

"We're taking our guests into town this afternoon," she said. "Want to offer a walking tour of downtown Fool's Gold?"

"Sure. With my job as Mayor Marsha's assistant, I've been studying local history. I know more facts than anyone could ever want to know. Plus, the festival is going to be fun."

Dellina suggested a time and place for them to meet.

A woman in yoga pants and a fitted tank top hurried up to them. Dellina recognized her as one of the wives. She grabbed Dellina's hand and pulled her toward the terrace.

"You have to come see this," she said. "Hurry!"

Bailey walked with them.

"What on earth," Dellina began, then stopped talking when she caught sight of what was happening on the large lawn just off the hotel.

About twenty guys were playing football. They were fit, handsome guys in shorts and T-shirts on a bright, sunny morning with a view of the valley behind them. Jack was quarterback on one team. He took the snap, then stepped back and threw the ball.

Dellina had never been to a professional football game before. She'd attended a college game once, but football wasn't her thing. She didn't understand the game and didn't get the point. But when she saw Jack throw, she understood the power and grace inherent in every professional athlete.

One of the clients' husbands caught the ball and ran toward the makeshift goal. Based on the cheering, Dellina would guess he'd scored. Male laughter filled the stillness of the morning.

Light glinted off muscles. Powerful legs bunched and released as the men moved.

"All they need is a sound track," Bailey murmured as she stood next to Dellina. "Oh, look. Sam's the quarterback for the other team."

Dellina saw she was right. That when they lined up, Sam took the center position and caught the ball when it was snapped.

It turned out that while he might have been a star kicker, he had a hell of an arm, too. He dodged a tackle and threw the ball nearly the length of the lawn. Kenny flew past the other men and caught it. He was moving toward the goal line before he even touched the ground.

"Oh, my," Bailey whispered. "That was impressive."

"Tell me about it," Dellina said, her gaze locking on Sam as he gave Kenny a high five.

This had been his world, she thought. On a grander scale, but the basics were here. Athletic prowess, winning and being part of a team. She noticed the other women lining up to watch the show and wondered how many of the wives were thinking their husbands looked pretty good out there.

Despite being on different sides, Sam, Kenny and Jack huddled together for a moment before stepping back into the game. When Sam used the hem of his T-shirt to wipe his face, she saw a flash of bare belly and the muscled contours below. Somewhere behind her, a woman sighed.

"If I weren't married, I'd want me some of that," she said.

Dellina agreed. And lucky for her, she wasn't married.

Sam had discovered shortly after moving to town that Fool's Gold was a place that loved its festivals. He and the guys had been bombarded with prepared meals during the Great Casserole Cook-Off and he'd taken his older sister to the Tulip Festival. She'd been impressed by the acres of flowers that stretched for what seemed like miles.

The Summer Festival seemed to be part arts and crafts, part music celebration with lots of food and plenty of tourists. Sam walked with several clients as they explored the various booths. His group didn't have any kids with them but he knew some of the others did. Dellina had arranged for Fayrene and the babysitters to be on hand if any extra care was needed.

Fayrene had brought the Pomeranian she was taking care of with her and, from what he could tell, the little pooch was a hit. One of the wives had stopped him in the hotel that morning to say that her daughter had had a wonderful time the night before and couldn't stop talking about the darling little dog who had been so warm and friendly with them all. Apparently Caramel was an equal opportunity cuddler. Something Sam could have respected when he was younger, but not so much now. He preferred to keep his personal life simple and that meant one woman at a time.

Not that he'd been involved in a while or was now, he thought as he stepped aside for a couple of teenage boys on skateboards. They barely made it to the corner when a deputy stepped in to put a stop to their fun.

He liked Dellina a lot. She was great. Funny and sexy and someone he could count on. But he knew what would happen if things got serious — it would all go to hell. He'd reconciled with the truth a long time ago — he had the worst luck when it came to women. Always had, always would. As much as he wanted that to change, it hadn't.

Which left him wondering about his future. He wanted a traditional family. A wife and a few kids. How was he supposed to make that happen when his personal life went from one disaster to another?

Up ahead the door to The Christmas Attic opened and a woman stepped out with large shopping bags in each hand. She had two kids trailing behind, although the little boy seemed more interested in the festival than keeping up with his mother.

"Stay with me," the woman called as she started for the corner.

Sam figured her car was in the lot there and, once she put her bags away, she would be fine. It was the getting there that was going to be difficult.

Her son, a boy of maybe four or five, spotted the ice cream vendor and grinned. He moved toward the curb instead of following his mother. The woman turned and looked for him, then frantically called out a name.

"I'll be right back," Sam said as he jogged

toward the boy and scooped him up. As he did so, he waved at the woman. "I've got him."

He maintained eye contact as he approached so she wouldn't think he was trying to kidnap the boy, then put him down as soon as they were close.

"Let me help you with your bags," he said. "Then you can keep hold of what's really important."

She gave him a grateful smile. "I should have made two trips," she admitted. "It's just the Christmas store is having a sale and there's a nativity set I've wanted forever. Noelle called to tell me she was holding it for me." She picked up her son and took her daughter's hand. "Thank you for helping."

"No problem." He took her bags and they walked to her small SUV. He put the bags in the back. "Enjoy your weekend."

She smiled at him and he returned to his guests. One of the wives linked her arm with him.

"This is why I like your company so much," she said. "You all have heart."

"It's a small town," Sam said, not sure what to do with the compliment, but liking it all the same. "Helping out is part of the culture."

"It's so nice to see," she told him. "Living here must be very special."

Sam nodded. The woman released his arm and returned to her husband's side. Sam continued to walk with them, but his thoughts were elsewhere.

When the guys had first visited Fool's Gold, they'd all been impressed by the location. Although Taryn loved everything about Los Angeles, the guys were ready for a change and Fool's Gold had offered that. But once they'd bought the new building, Sam had wrestled with second thoughts. Did he really want to live in a place where everyone would know his business? He'd grown up with that and didn't feel the need to recreate it as an adult.

Because of that, he'd held back a little. Jack and Kenny had made friends everywhere, but Sam had kept to himself. He'd resisted requests to speak to local business organizations and hadn't done any community service work. He saw now that he was never going to feel as if he really belonged if he didn't simply take the plunge. It was like what had happened with Dellina. He'd been so busy thinking the worst, he'd missed out on someone great. She'd not only saved the client party, she'd turned out to be someone he could trust. And in his world, that was to be treasured.

Sam walked out of the elevator and saw Kenny and Jack handing Taryn money. Judging from the wad of cash she held, he would guess three or four hundred dollars each. They were making a bet — something he usually participated in. Only not this time. Because he knew what they were betting on. Maybe not the exact verbiage, but he could guess the subject matter.

"What?" he asked as he approached.

His friends turned to him. Kenny and Jack both looked guilty while Taryn appeared smug.

"Showing a video versus just talking," Taryn told him. "I'm convinced she's not going to do anything to embarrass you. Jack says there's going to be sex on a video while Kenny's going for an over the clothes demonstration."

Kenny held up both hands. "I've been to her talks before. We all know what happens."

"You in?" Jack asked.

Sam tried to ignore the steady thumping of a headache coming on and shook his head. "There's no win for me. Taryn, I appreciate your support, but we both know that we're talking about my mother. There's no way she's not going to do something."

"You want to bet on the video versus talking?" she asked.

"No. I want her to be normal."

"We don't have a pool for that."

"I wonder why," Sam muttered as he walked toward the room at the end of the hall. He planned to sit up front, but on the side. That way he could rush the stage if necessary. He wasn't sure what he would do when he got there, but when it came to Lark, being ready for action seemed more important than having a plan.

CHAPTER FOURTEEN

"It's safe to relax," Dellina said as much to herself as to Sam. They were off the terrace at the rear of the hotel after a long, successful day of entertaining clients.

Behind them, large grills were heating as the hotel chefs prepared for the evening's barbecue. To the north was a big fire pit that would be lit closer to sunset. The tables were set, the music already playing, and in a few minutes their guests would arrive. The weekend event had passed the halfway mark. Dellina hoped to have an easy time of it from now until tomorrow afternoon when she was going to collapse and sleep for at least twelve hours.

"From everything I've heard, people had a great time in town," she told him. "The kids loved their bike ride with Josh and the therapy dog event was a hit."

He looked at her. "What you really mean is my mother didn't take off her clothes or have sex on the stage during her lecture."

"It had been a concern," Dellina admitted. She'd stayed in the back of the room while Lark had taken the stage. She wasn't sure if she was there so she could run if necessary or to show other people the way out if they felt the need to bolt.

"She was okay," Sam admitted. "For her, the lecture was tame."

"And informative," Dellina added.

Lark had spoken about the importance of sexual happiness in a marriage. When she'd hit a button on the computer next to her and lit up the screen, Dellina had been prepared for anything from porn to detailed, anatomically correct photographs. Instead Lark had shown tasteful drawings of both male and female anatomy, then had discussed pressure points and breathing exercises.

"She only said clitoris three times." Sam sounded relieved. "So we got through it."

"Or at least the part we were both worried about." She glanced at her watch. "Okay — I've checked on the food. The bar is ready. There's a mocktail station for the kids, if they want to re-create their favorite drinks from last night. We can —"

She stared as the first couple in their group stepped out onto the lawn. She knew them by sight and name, had spoken with them. They were in their forties and had left their college-age kids at home.

While the couple had been friendly with each other, Dellina couldn't remember them holding hands. As she watched, the wife glanced up at her husband and laughed. He stopped, faced her, then cupped her face with his free hand and kissed her. Using tongue.

"What?" Sam said, spinning toward the hotel. "Are my parents naked?"

"I have no idea, but if they are, they're not out here."

He looked around, then back at her. "What are you staring at?"

"Bill and Marie."

Sam glanced at them and shrugged. "They're here."

"They're kissing!"

"I don't get the big deal."

Dellina started to smile. "Oh, I think you will in a little bit. This is going to be one interesting and mellow barbecue."

"I have no idea what you're talking about."

Another couple joined Bill and Marie. They spoke to each other, as they had all weekend. But there was a notable difference.

Dellina put her hand on Sam's arm and

turned him toward the couples. "Look at them. What do you see?"

"I don't know. People I know."

"People you know who just had mind-blowing sex. I'm going to guess that more than a few of your guests used your mother's techniques and enjoyed them."

"Holy crap," Sam muttered. "You think so?" He groaned before she could answer. "You're right. Look at them. What have we done?"

She stepped in front of him. "We've helped happy couples reconnect in an intimate way. This is a good thing. I know your mother can be intrusive and that she doesn't respect boundaries, but that doesn't mean her information isn't valid. Don't you think this is going to make your clients feel even better about working with your company?"

"I don't want them talking about sex or doing things my mother taught them in front of me."

She laughed. "Yeah, that would be uncomfortable for all of us. But I say just go with it."

He sighed. "Why couldn't I have been born into a normal family?"

"Then you wouldn't be who you are."

"I guess." He shook his head. "Okay, time

for a barbecue."

"I'm on it."

She started to walk away. Sam grabbed her hand and held her in place. She turned toward him.

"Yes?"

"Want me to show you those pressure points later?"

Dellina thought about how he'd made her feel the day before and that was without trying too hard. If he really put some effort into it, who knew what would happen?

In less than a second, her skin burned and she felt swelling in all the girl places.

"Is it possible to die from too good an orgasm?" she asked.

He grinned. "No."

"Then, sure. Let's have a lab experiment with the pressure points. You know my room number."

"I do."

For Dellina, the evening couldn't pass quickly enough. The barbecue seemed to take forever. She'd never known people to eat so slowly. Part of it was how the other couples were so attentive to each other. She saw more than one pair feeding each other.

But as soon as the kids started to get sleepy, parents hurried away. She stayed until the last of their guests had headed upstairs, then checked with the staff to make sure everything was ready for the morning brunch.

Once her work was complete, she was free to leave. There was only one problem — she hadn't seen Sam in over an hour. Had he forgotten their plans for the evening? Had he just been kidding?

This was what was difficult about sleeping with someone she wasn't dating. There was no good way to ask. If she and Sam were actually together, then they would have a pattern. Or at least regular conversation. Although in truth, Sam had been with her for much of the weekend. And he'd been living with her for the past few days.

"I'm tired," she told herself as she made her way to the elevators. "I'll figure it out after all this is done."

She would give him fifteen minutes after she was in her room, then she was going to take a shower and crawl into bed. While not as exciting as a couple of hours in his arms, being rested had its benefits.

She stepped out onto the floor and headed for her room. After using her card key, she let herself inside.

Her room was of the standard variety. A bed, a couple of chairs and a bathroom beyond. She had a view of the mountains, not that she'd had the chance to look at it. It wasn't as if she'd had time to relax over the past couple of days. Still, she knew what to expect and what she found this evening was different.

The first thing she noticed was how a few of the lights were on, but not the bright ones. The covers had been pulled back on the bed and there was a standing ice bucket by the nightstand, along with a bottle of champagne.

She turned to her left and saw Sam sitting in one of the chairs. He was in shadow, but she could see enough of him to know he was wearing jeans . . . and nothing else.

Funny how the sight of a bare-chested, handsome man could get her tummy to dancing, she thought as she put her purse on the table by the door and stepped out of her flats.

"Did I give you a key to my room?" she asked.

He stood. "No."

"I didn't think so. Should I ask how you got in?"

"If you really want to know."

He crossed to her. His expression was unreadable. Intense, she thought. Hungry. Unable to help herself, she put her palms flat on his chest and felt warm skin and hard muscle. He was *sculpted* and *beautiful* in the most masculine definition of the words.

She was tired and stressed from the weekend, ready for it all to be over. What she needed was sleep. What she wanted was him.

She slid her hands down his rock-hard belly to the waistband of his jeans. She unfastened the button, then lowered the zipper. His erection made the latter difficult, but she persevered. She tucked her thumbs inside the waistband, by his sides, and then pushed the denim down. As she moved she caught the top of the briefs and dragged them along.

When she reached about midthigh, he took over and shoved his clothes to the floor, then stepped out of them.

He was completely naked and she was, except for her shoes, fully dressed. There was something kind of cool about that, she thought. Exciting. Heat seemed to bubble up inside of her, making her skin extrasensitive. Just looking at him made her want to touch. Touching made her think about them being together, and that was more than enough to make her breasts ache and her center swell.

He was aroused. His erection jutted toward her. She wanted him inside of her, but she wanted other things, too.

She stepped to his side and put her palm on his belly. Her pinkie and ring finger were nestled in the hair at his groin. She moved behind him. She rested her free hand on the small of his back before slowly — oh, so slowly — lowering it over his butt.

The curve was muscled and hard, like most of the rest of him. It was also warm, and touching him like this was arousing. She'd seen him play football the previous day. Sam really was a gifted athlete.

She continued to move that hand around his side, while keeping the other still on his stomach. She eased closer, so that her belly pressed against his ass while her lips nibbled along his right shoulder blade. Her left hand kept moving down his hip, then across to the top of his thigh.

She felt his stomach muscles contract. At the same moment she reached for his penis, she slipped her left hand between his legs and cupped his testicles.

His breath caught. She moved the hand holding his balls, shifting to get into position.

"I think I'm supposed to do something like this," she murmured into his back, searching for the pressure points Lark had described. At the same time, she closed her fingers around his arousal and began to stroke him.

"If I find them and push on them," she continued, "you'll get unbearably close, but won't go over the edge. What did she call it? Orgasm without release?"

Using her middle finger the way Lark had explained, she gently applied pressure just under the apex of his scrotum. She found the other positions for her fingers. As she continued to move her right hand up and down, she increased the pressure with her left until Sam's breath increased and his body began to shake. She could feel him getting closer and closer, but if Lark was right, there was no way he was going to have an orgasm. The other woman had claimed a man could go like this for hours.

"Dellina," he began.

"Shh. Let me enjoy this for a few more minutes."

"What if my mother's wrong?"

She considered the question, then pressed her mouth to his spine. "I suppose I'll have to let you make me come a couple of times while we wait for you to recover. I'm not sure I see a bad in that."

She decided to test the theory and moved her hand faster and faster. She felt him get even bigger, and if his rapid breathing was anything to go by, he was incredibly close. But no matter how she caressed him and how his breath caught and he trembled, he didn't climax.

She slowed her hand. Lark had been very clear to stop that stimulation before releasing the pressure points, or there was going to be a mess everywhere. After giving him a second to catch his breath, she drew away both hands.

She was about to say how fun that was, but before she could speak Sam was spinning her to face him. In less than a nanosecond, her shirt was off, her bra was flying, his hands were on her breasts and he was kissing her with more passion than she'd ever felt before in her life. His lips claimed, his tongue demanded and as she wrapped her arms around him, she thought maybe this standing thing was highly overrated.

She hung on, loving the feel of him so close. He teased her breasts, concentrating on her hard, tight nipples. He touched and stroked until she was writhing. Her jeans were heavy and very much in the way. She wanted them both naked, preferably with him inside of her.

"Sam," she breathed against his mouth.

He drew back just enough to bend over and pick her up in his arms. She shrieked and hung on as he carried her to the bed. He set her down on her back. After unzipping her jeans, he took them and her panties off.

Better, she thought, liking that he was still incredibly hard. All that for her.

He had already poured a couple of glasses of champagne. Now he took a drink from one but didn't swallow. He got on the bed, slipped between her legs and gave her an openmouthed kiss right on her clitoris. He was hot, the champagne was cold and fizzy and she couldn't help gasping. Or possibly shrieking.

The sensations were incredible. Especially when he moved his tongue through the champagne. Hot and cold mingled, as did the bubbles dancing across her most sensitive spot. He swallowed and sat up enough to reach for the glass again.

This time she was prepared, or so she'd thought. Because she wasn't the only one who had been paying attention during the lecture. As Sam gave her another openmouthed kiss, he pressed his knuckle right at the base of her clit. He moved it up and down in tiny increments. She braced herself because Lark had warned them that when the man found the right —

"Oh, please!" she gasped, not caring that

she was begging.

He'd found it. The nerve, the connection, the whatever it was that made her hypersensitive to everything he was doing. If his tongue on her was usually a nine, this was a two hundred. She could feel the individual champagne bubbles, and when he moved his tongue, she went from aroused to on the verge of climaxing in a single exhale.

Only she didn't. She was there — right there. So close she could see it. Feel it. Beg for it. But there was no over the top.

He swallowed the champagne and continued to stroke her with his tongue. She gasped, she writhed, she pumped her hips. So. Damn. Close. Right on the edge.

With every stroke, she knew she was finally going to fall. She'd never felt anything so arousing. But she couldn't get to the other side.

He shifted and pushed two fingers inside of her.

"Sam, I don't think I can handle that," she gasped.

"If you don't like it, I'll stop," he promised.

She nodded and sucked in a breath.

She was so in tune with all he was doing. Every nerve ending was electrified. She felt the delicious pressure of his fingers sliding through her swollen body. Deeper and deeper before he slowly — oh, so slowly — curved up his fingers to that magical G-spot. At the same time, he pushed in with his knuckle and sucked her clit into his mouth.

She gasped as pleasure poured through her. The fingers inside of her stroked and circled. His tongue danced against her center. She got closer and closer, so near that she started to shake. Her leg muscles trembled, her hands shook.

"Please," she begged, tossing her head back and forth. "Please."

The knuckle released and the intensity faded a tiny bit. He withdrew his fingers and at the same time raised his head. Her arousal rate dropped enough that she could breathe but the deep, aching need to climax didn't fade.

"Is that what I did to you?" she asked.

He shifted onto his knees and reached for a condom. "Pretty much."

"I'm sorry."

His mouth curved into a slow, sexy grin. "Don't be."

"But I left you hanging."

"I knew we'd get there eventually."

He slid on a condom.

"Top or bottom?" he asked.

An interesting question.

She put her hand on his wrist and guided his hand between her thighs. He began to rub her. She spread her legs more and let herself sink into the sensation of him rhythmically circling her swollen center.

"If I'm on top, can you do that pressure point thing again?" she asked. "Help me hold back until you're ready."

Something bright flashed in his eyes. "I can do that."

"Then top."

"You're my kind of girl."

She wasn't really, she thought as she watched him lie down. She enjoyed sex, but she wasn't usually so . . . comfortable. Maybe it was exhaustion, or the pressure points. Either way, she didn't care. She felt sexy and alive. Her body hummed. She had never in her life guided a man's hand to her body the way she just had with Sam, yet it had felt completely right.

She sat up, then moved over him. As she shifted, her breasts hung down and she thought it would be nice to have him touch her there. She paused to put his hands on her breasts. He immediately began to massage them. When he gently squeezed her nipples, her breath caught.

"Like that," she whispered. "Only more."

He did as she asked. Arousal poured

311

through her. She wasn't sure it was possible for her to be more swollen, more ready. She straddled him, then slowly sank onto his erection and closed her eyes.

He filled her completely. She braced her hands on either side of his shoulders and prepared to start moving.

"Wait," he told her.

She opened her eyes and found him watching her.

"Sit up. Shift your weight back so you're straight, not leaning forward. But go slow because I'll go in really deep."

She did as he suggested and felt him fill her even more.

"Spread your thighs while pulling in with your stomach," he told her.

She was unprepared for the results. The tip of his erection settled firmly on her nerve-filled G-spot. Her whole body convulsed with pleasure.

He smiled again. "That's it." He reached for her and used his thumb and forefinger to start massaging her clitoris while using a knuckle from his other hand to find the pressure point.

He moved hard and fast against her swollen spot of pleasure. She urged him on, wanting more, straining to have the friction on the inside match that on the outside.

More and more, she thought hazily. Faster and faster.

Her breasts got uncomfortable, but not from how close she was. Instead she realized it was from bouncing up and down. Somewhere in all of this, she'd started riding Sam. Up and down and up and down.

She supposed she should be embarrassed by her wild behavior. But that was for later. Instead she cupped her breasts in her hands and held them, all the while going up and down faster and faster.

With every drop, the head of his penis pushed against her from the inside and drove her closer and closer. But the pressure just below her clit meant she wasn't coming. The truth was oddly freeing, she thought.

Sam swore.

The sound shocked her into her opening her eyes. He was staring at her. His expression was one of intense concentration — a man on the edge.

"I don't want to come," he gasped. "Watching you. But I can't —"

Several things happened at once. She realized that he'd been enjoying the show of her riding him. She was momentarily embarrassed. But then he relaxed his finger, releasing the pressure point. So all she was left with was sensation and she came with a scream that echoed through the room.

She came over and over, unable to stop. Riding him up and down. She put her hand over his, to keep him rubbing her as she climaxed for what felt like a lifetime. At some point she was pretty sure he got his, but she was so lost, she wasn't sure.

She'd never felt anything like this. As her release slowed, she found it hard to breathe — maybe because somewhere along the way, she'd started crying.

Dellina wanted to die. It wasn't enough she'd put on a show. Now she was shaking — and not in a good way — and sobbing. With her luck, she would pee the bed or something next.

But instead of running, Sam pulled her close and held her. He stroked her back and hip and murmured softly. There weren't words, just sounds. Eventually she calmed enough to catch her breath.

"I'm sorry," she whispered.

"It's okay." He drew her onto her back and settled between her thighs. "It's okay."

"It's not. I've never freaked out like that." She touched his lower lip with her thumb. "Thank you for not running. I wouldn't have blamed you."

"I wouldn't do that."

Something hard probed between her legs. Before she could figure out what was happening, he was in her again. Hard and filling her.

"Sam?"

"Relax."

She was going to ask what he was doing. No, not what. That was clear. But why? Hadn't he already . . .

But then she realized she was ready for this. Wanted this. She wrapped her legs around his hips and sank into the feelings of him filling her. After last time she would have thought she had nothing left. Instead she came within seconds and he quickly followed, shuddering as he finished.

She opened her eyes. "I don't understand."

"Mom left out that part of the pressure point lecture. It's the orgasm of your life with the added benefit of making you want to do it again." One corner of his mouth turned up. "I thought calmer might be better for you."

"Oh. So you've done this before. The pressure thing."

She wasn't sure why that news disappointed her so much. It wasn't as if she and Sam were virgins or something.

"I've experimented with it," he told her.

"But not like this. Never to climax. As for the aftereffects, I'd only heard about them. I never experienced them myself." He bent down and whispered in her ear. "We definitely have to try that one again."

She felt herself blushing. "I don't think so."

"Why not? Didn't you enjoy it?"

"I rode you like an I don't know what. I screamed. I cried. My enjoying it isn't the point."

He frowned. "I think it is. Besides, you were hot. Seriously hot. If I'm ever alone on an island with no female companionship, you're going to be my only fantasy."

An unexpected and very strange compliment. But one she liked.

Sam stretched out next to her. She rested her head on his shoulder. He drew her hand to his groin.

"Nothing's going to happen," he told her. "But it's nice to have you touch me."

"I like it, too."

They stayed like that a long time. They talked about the day and the success the weekend had been so far. Dellina was able to keep up with the conversation, even as she flashed back to their passionate encounter. As she thought about how Sam had made her feel, she remembered Felicia talking sometime the previous year. The other woman had explained the biology of sexual bonding. That after intercourse, a woman generally felt closer to the man, while he felt a sense of conquest.

If a woman bonded during regular sex, what would happen to her after an experience like she'd just had? Sam had an amazing hold on her body. How difficult was it going to be to keep him from also possessing her heart? Something she happened to know he didn't actually want.

Fayrene sat in the passenger seat of the van, Caramel on her lap. The little Pomeranian was exhausted from her time at Castle Ranch. She'd played with the children, discovered goats and had enjoyed the cheese sampling. Fayrene was also tired, but the feeling didn't come with any sense of accomplishment. Yes, she'd gotten through the two and a half days. But they'd been a lot more work than she'd anticipated.

Ryan was in the back with the boys. He'd been so great with all the kids. He was patient, funny and knew how to defuse nearly any situation, even if that meant calling over Caramel to offer a well-timed doggy kiss.

The van pulled up in front of the hotel

and the kids spilled out. Their parents were waiting for them. Fayrene watched all the greetings. The kids seemed happy, the adults were relaxed. Obviously the weekend had been a huge success for Score.

Fayrene gathered a nearly limp Caramel in her arms and stepped out of the van. Ryan was saying goodbye to the kids and shaking hands with the parents. A few of the children called out to Fayrene, but most were already heading to the hotel to collect their belongings before leaving.

From a business perspective, Fayrene knew she'd done fine. Everyone had been entertained and kept safe. She'd managed her babysitting team well. But she hadn't been all that comfortable with the kids themselves. Ryan was much more relaxed around them than she had been. She'd wanted this to be a bonding experience for the two of them. She'd wanted him to see that she was going to be a great mother and that he should marry her right away. And none of that had happened.

He walked up to her and touched her chin, then kissed her mouth.

"What's wrong?" he asked.

"Nothing. Handling twelve kids is harder than I thought."

"Why wouldn't it be? There's too many of

them." He grinned, then put his arm around her. "We'll practice with Caramel for now, then later, after we're married, we'll take our own on one at a time."

She sniffed. "You still want to marry me?"

He stepped in front of her and put both hands on her shoulders. "I love you, Fayrene. I have from the first moment I saw you." He smiled. "You were running around like a crazy person, yelling that the babies were coming."

"Not my finest hour."

"It worked for me." The smile faded. "I love you," he repeated. "For now and for always. When you're ready, I'm going to propose and we'll get married. That hasn't changed."

I'm ready now. Only she didn't say the words. Somehow she couldn't speak at all — not with the lump in her throat.

He put his arm around her again and led her toward the hotel. "Maybe Mayor Marsha won't come back from her trip and we can keep her dog forever."

Fayrene kissed Caramel's head. "I'd like that. To be honest, I don't remember her ever having a dog, so I'm not sure where this sweet little girl came from."

Caramel yawned and settled more comfortably in Fayrene's arms, then closed her eyes. Fayrene told herself to accept the blessings she already had. A career she loved with a business that was growing. A great guy who only wanted to make her happy. Family, a town that took care of her. She had everything. All that was missing was a ring on her finger. And the truth of that situation was, she only had herself to blame.

CHAPTER FIFTEEN

Sam followed Jack into Taryn's suite. Kenny was already there, opening a bottle of champagne. Taryn had kicked off her heels and was barefoot. She tucked her feet under her and accepted the first glass of champagne. Kenny handed them out to everyone else, then raised his in a toast.

"To a hell of a weekend," he said. "Dellina pulled it off."

"She sure did." Jack winked at Sam. "To Dellina."

Sam had no problem toasting the woman who had made the Score client weekend such a success. Thankfully he would have felt exactly the same this time yesterday, so there was no reason to worry that his pride in her achievement was in any way influenced by what they'd done together the previous night.

Taryn sipped. "Does anyone else think it's strange we didn't invite Dellina here to be celebrated in person?"

"I asked," Kenny told her. "She's debriefing the hotel staff, then will be going through all the guest rooms personally to make sure no one left anything behind. She'll get the bell staff to load her car. After that, she said she plans to go home and sleep for three days. She told me she's open to being celebrated on Wednesday."

Sam listened attentively and did his best not to look guilty. Dellina had been working hard on the weekend and would have started the event already tired. But last night hadn't helped her get any rest. They'd stayed awake until nearly two simply talking and touching. As if what they'd been through had required continued connection.

This morning he'd sensed her every time she was near him. Not in a possessive way — more because they'd shared something so unique, they could never be completely separate again.

Insanity, he told himself. And he had his mother to blame. Although her pressure points sure took things to the next sexual level. It was balance, he told himself. There was always the bad to counteract the good.

Everyone settled onto the sofa and chairs in Taryn's suite. Conversation flowed.

Taryn glanced at him. "By the way, Sam,

you're giving a lecture on finances to the local business community."

He was grateful he wasn't swallowing. "What?"

"You helped Dellina. She mentioned it to a couple of her friends and they approached me. I said you'd love it."

Jack toasted him. "Way to give back."

Sam ignored that. His instinct was to say no. Or, hell, no. But then he remembered how he wanted to connect more with the community. He wasn't like Jack or Kenny, but he understood finances.

"Sure," he said. "I'll do it."

Kenny raised his eyebrows. "That's a surprise."

"I can't help being brilliant, bro."

Everyone laughed. He took another drink. The champagne was good, but the company better. They didn't have as many times like this anymore, Sam thought. The four of them together. He wasn't sure why. Was it because Taryn had Angel? Was she the one who pulled them all together? Which meant if either of his friends ever fell for someone, they'd drift even further apart.

He glanced at Kenny. The other man had a thousand reasons to never trust his heart. Or maybe just one. The biggest one possible. Losing a woman was one thing, but to

lose a child. And the way it had happened . . . Sam shook his head. His friend
was one strong guy. He'd kept going and
managed to fool nearly everyone into thinking he was fine.

Jack, on the other hand, never let anyone
get close. There was always a wall around
his heart. Sam knew why and respected his
friend's reasons. Some things were never
going to be okay. Some burdens were too
big to survive. Jack did the best he could
and faked the rest of it.

Sam's gaze shifted to his only female
partner. A few months ago he would have
been comfortable explaining why she was
alone. Only she'd found the right guy and
he'd never seen her happier. Watching Taryn
in love made him long for what he'd always
wanted. A wife. Family. A traditional life-
style in a place he liked surrounded by good
people.

Fool's Gold offered that. He wasn't fitting
in as quickly as Jack and Kenny, but he was
okay with that. He was more reserved with
his feelings. He knew he was welcome here.
But that was only a piece of what he wanted.
There was also the matter of the wife and
kids. Of trusting a woman enough to give
her his heart.

For a second he thought of Dellina. From

what he could tell, she was exactly who she seemed. Warm, loving, honest. She didn't play games and she wasn't out to win. She'd given up her own dreams to take care of her sisters. He liked her. A lot. She was smart and funny and when they were in bed . . .

He took a sip of champagne to hide his satisfied smile.

But there was more to love than sex. There was trust and he didn't think he had it in him. Not yet. Not after what had happened. How was he supposed to believe that she wouldn't turn into God knew who in a few weeks or years. He would never have guessed Simone would write a tell-all. Or that his demure, soft-spoken girlfriend would sleep with each of his best friends. Or that the girl he'd fallen for in college would stalk him, slash his tires and end up moving across the country to avoid him. With his luck with women, his next one true love was going to be a hermaphrodite.

Better to be alone and be safe, he told himself. As he always had tried to do. But for once, the price of that safety seemed high. Maybe too high. Which left him with a difficult dilemma.

Dellina hesitated before walking into Jo's Bar. She loved meeting her friends for lunch, and having the Score party behind her meant she had a lot to celebrate. What made her stop for a second before pulling open the door was her concern that everyone would take one look at her and know something had happened. Something amazing and wonderful and . . .

Even as she tried to get annoyed, she couldn't help smiling. Aftershocks from her time with Sam continued to ripple through her. Just when she thought she had recovered from their incredible lovemaking, she got a little ping from somewhere deep in her belly. That sensation made her remember and remembering made her want to do it again.

She had loved being with him, she thought. Well, loved what they did together. She didn't love the man. She was susceptible, not foolish. She wasn't looking for love and Sam thought all relationships ended in disaster. What she meant was —

"Hey," Larissa said, coming up behind her. "I heard you were a wild success. I'm sorry I missed the party."

Dellina opened the door and stepped inside. "Me, too. I could have put you to work."

Larissa laughed. "You say that like I should be scared, but I spent the weekend with my mother and sisters. Trust me, you have nothing on them. My mother's campaign to get me married and pregnant continues."

As always, Larissa was casually dressed in an oversize T-shirt and yoga pants. Her long blond hair had been pulled back into a ponytail and she had on athletic shoes. She was tall and lithe and moved with the grace of a natural athlete. As a kid, Dellina had preferred books to sports. As an adult, that hadn't changed.

"Do you get along with your family?" she asked as they walked to the large table in the middle where Patience and Isabel already waited.

"I do," Larissa told her. "Mostly. It's not so horrible. It's just I'm the oldest and my two younger sisters are already married."

Dellina realized she was kind of in the same position. While Fayrene wasn't married, she was settled with Ryan.

"They both already have kids," Larissa continued. "The pressure is on for me to settle down and produce grandchildren. I finally had to threaten to never speak to my mom again to get her to stop."

"Intense," Dellina murmured, thinking she wouldn't mind a little pressure from her mother. Or complaints or any kind of conversation at all. Because that would mean they weren't gone. Not that she would say that to her friend.

"You did so well," Isabel said as they approached. "Congratulations. Everyone has been raving about the party. It was fun and went smoothly. Brace yourself — you're going to get a lot of business out of this."

"That would be nice," Dellina said. "I like to stay busy."

She pulled out a chair. Larissa sat next to her.

"The people seemed really nice," Patience told her. "They came into my store and tipped really well. I appreciate that."

Dellina grinned. "I'll pass on your approval."

Noelle hurried in and joined them. She hugged Dellina. "You kicked butt! Yay you. I can't tell you how much your people bought at the store. It was a very happy Saturday for me."

Before Dellina could respond, the door opened again. Taryn and Lark walked in together. Dellina felt herself starting to blush. Oh, no. Not Lark. She would take one look at Dellina and know instantly what had happened. Dellina looked for an exit, but before she could find one, the other two women had joined them.

Taryn hugged her. "My new favorite person ever. You were fabulous. Everyone had a great time. The weekend was perfect. You're a goddess."

"I wish," Dellina murmured. "But I did enjoy the corporate aspect of it."

Taryn settled next to her. "You should look for more accounts like that. What about CDS? They have those corporate weekends but it's really just about the obstacle courses."

"She's right," Patience added. "Justice has to work with the companies all the time, telling them what's in town and where to stay. He really doesn't like it." She leaned forward. "You should get together with him and talk about coordinating a package or something. Where he can just give them your name and you can pull meetings together."

"I'd like that," Dellina admitted. Plus, if Sam was able to show her what she was doing wrong with her bookkeeping, she might be more financially successful. And wouldn't that be nice?

She smiled at Lark, thinking a distraction would keep the other woman from reading her aura or whatever it was she did. "You were brilliant. Everyone loved your lecture."

"That's true." Taryn grinned. "I'm sure

there was a lot of sex happening in the hotel that night."

"I hope so." Lark reached for her water. "It's so nice when a couple who's been together for a long time finds a new level of sexual energy and compatibility."

"Where do you go next?" Larissa asked her.

"New Orleans. Reggie and I will drive there. We'll have a week on our own, then have a small seminar. Only five couples who want to experience the ultimate pleasure."

Dellina felt her eyes widen. She glanced at Isabel, who looked about as startled as she felt.

Patience's mouth formed a perfect O. "So you show them what they should be doing?" she asked, her voice sounding slightly incredulous.

"Yes. We start with some basic techniques, then quickly go through to the more advanced positions, breathing and pressure points. Each couple will have an opportunity to make love in front of us so we can offer suggestions."

Even Taryn looked startled at that one. "I don't think I would be up for the pressure."

"There's no pressure," Lark told her. "We're there to be supportive. Sometimes one of the partners can have a little trouble getting aroused. We have ways of dealing with that."

Larissa leaned toward Dellina. "I can't decide if I want to ask what they are or stick my fingers in my ears and hum."

"I know. It's really scary."

Jo walked over and discussed the specials, then handed out menus. Other people arrived to have lunch. A few of the women had small children with them.

During the lunch hour, there was a play area set up in one of the corners. Mothers with toddlers could lunch and watch their kids at the same time. Lark looked over at two little girls sharing a miniature stove.

"I remember when my girls were that small," she said wistfully. "We were all so happy. I breast-fed them until they were ready to move on to a glass. Both my girls waited until they were nearly four, but Sam wanted a sippy cup by the time he was eighteen months. He was always independent." She smiled at the memory. "I encouraged my children to be naked as much as possible, to be comfortable with their bodies, but Sam wouldn't have it. He insisted on getting dressed every day. Such a little man."

Dellina had a feeling that next up would be Lark reminiscing about the time she walked in on Sam in the shower or something. Honestly, the woman had no boundaries. Sam's personal life and preferences should be respected, not the subject of casual conversation.

"Did any of you know Mayor Marsha has a dog?" she asked, in a not very subtle attempt to change the subject.

Jo returned with their drinks in time to hear the question. "No, she doesn't."

"I agree," Isabel said. "I've never known her to have a pet."

"Well, she left an adorable Pomeranian with Fayrene while she's in New Zealand."

Taryn's knowing gaze settled on her face. Dellina figured Taryn had guessed what she was trying to do.

"You think she has a secret pet?" Taryn asked.

"I don't know. Caramel is very sweet and highly socialized. She was a big hit this weekend. The kids loved her."

"She was lovely," Lark said. "And the right size for travel. Maybe I should talk to Reggie about getting a little dog. He or she could go with us on our trips."

"I'm working with an organization that might have to do a chiweenie rescue," Larissa said. "They're small."

"Chihuahua and dachshund?" Lark asked.

"An interesting blend."

"They're cute," Larissa told her. "There's a woman being investigated. We think it was a regular breeder situation that got out of hand. That can happen."

Taryn sighed. "Yes, Larissa is very good at finding causes. Remember when you hand-fed imprinted swan babies?"

"Cygnets," Larissa corrected. She nodded. "Their mother had been killed and a family took them in. But then the cygnets imprinted on humans and there were five of them, so I took in a couple."

Taryn leaned toward Dellina. "What she means is she volunteered and Jack ended up with baby swans in his living room."

"Cygnets."

"Whatever."

Dellina nodded, not that interested in Larissa's need to rescue the world. Of more importance to her was the fact that they weren't talking about Sam anymore. More specifically, that Lark wasn't blabbing about her son to anyone who would listen.

They got through lunch without any more oversharing. Dellina told herself to be grateful and simply move on with her life. Only she couldn't stop thinking about all Lark had said about Sam. Not just during this

333

meal, but every other time they'd spoken. She wasn't angry, exactly. More frustrated. As they all walked out of the restaurant, she pulled Lark aside.

"What is it?" the other woman asked.

Dellina tried to tell herself it wasn't her business. That she shouldn't get involved. Only she couldn't seem to help herself.

"I'm sorry. I know this is just my opinion, but you can't keep doing that," she said quickly. "Talking about personal things. It's fine when it's your business. You have every right to share as much as you want. But not when it comes to Sam. Maybe the girls, too, but certainly him."

Lark frowned. "I don't understand."

"You say things that make him crazy. Like talking about when he stopped breast-feeding and that he wouldn't run around the house naked."

"But he was a charming child."

"I believe that, Lark. I know you love your son, but talking about him that way is intrusive and disrespectful. He wouldn't want you to do it. I can't figure out if you simply don't understand that or if you don't care about his wishes."

She paused to wonder how deeply she'd stepped in it. "I get that you're a warm, loving family. I wish my mom was alive to drive me crazy. You obviously care about your kids a lot. But Sam is different from you. He needs his boundaries to be respected."

Lark's blue eyes filled with tears. "I've upset you, Dellina. I'm so sorry."

"This isn't about me. It's about Sam. Why can't you see that?"

Lark sniffed. "Look at you, standing up for him." She hugged Dellina. "I'm so glad he has you on his side."

Dellina hugged her back, even as she wanted to shake her. "Lark," she began.

The other woman shook her head. "Not another word," she said. "I understand everything."

But Dellina knew there was no way that was true.

Kipling kept his breathing even. He knew the argument for painkillers. That being in pain stressed the body and impeded healing. It made sense medically, but the information wasn't the issue. Instead he had to deal with what was happening in his gut. The knotted anger and helplessness that had nothing to do with broken bones and damaged organs.

Shelby had left for home. Her mother had taken another turn for the worse and Shelby wanted to be with her. Kipling had told her to go — he knew she would, anyway. But leaving meant putting herself in danger. She would walk into the house of a monster and there was no way he could protect her.

In a twisted way, not taking his pain medication made him feel as if he was in control. Something his coaches would tell him was bullshit. But right now, it was all he had.

He shifted slightly on the hospital bed, then hissed out a breath when the fire ripped through his body. Moving was never a good idea. Not at this stage. Not until he'd healed a little more. Which meant Shelby was totally on her own.

Before he could rail at the unfairness of the situation, his hospital door opened and an old lady stepped in. She was of average height, with white hair and blue eyes. She wore a jacket over dark pants and pearls around her neck. Pearls? In a hospital in New Zealand?

"Hello, Mr. Gilmore," the woman said. "I'm Marsha Tilson."

"I don't give a shit who you are, lady. I'm not in the mood to give autographs, so get out of my room."

Instead of leaving, or even seeming upset, the old woman pulled the visitor's chair closer and sat down.

"How are you feeling?"

He raised his good arm and motioned to the pulleys and casts, the drip lines and the beeping monitor. "How do you think?"

Her expression turned knowing. "You're not taking your pain medication. I understand why. I hope you understand your logic is flawed."

She was American. Probably mid-sixties. With her lack of accent, he would put her from the West Coast, maybe. Or Nevada or Colorado. The one thing he was sure of was that he'd never seen her before.

"Get out," he said, turning away from her. "Just get the hell out of my room."

"I will. I promise. But first I need five minutes of your time."

He sighed. What the hell. It wasn't as if he had anything else going on today. He closed his eyes and hoped he could fall asleep while she talked.

"I'm the mayor of Fool's Gold. That's a town in the foothills of the Sierra Nevada. Our town is in California, not too far from Sacramento. We're at twenty-five hundred feet, so we get all four seasons, but none of them are especially brutal. There's good skiing up the mountain. Not that you'll be doing that for a while."

He turned back to face her and opened

337

his eyes. "I really appreciate your support."

She lightly touched the fingers sticking out of his cast. "I'm sorry, Mr. Gilmore, but we both know the truth. You'll never ski professionally again. While that's very sad, you did win two gold medals at the Olympics a few months ago, and over the years have won nearly every major event in your sport. So if you had to go out, better to do so on top."

"Thanks for the tip," he said. "I feel much better now."

"You don't, but you will." She drew in a breath. "I'd like to offer you a job. Not now, of course. You have some healing to do. But later. We're going to be starting a search and rescue group in Fool's Gold. I'd like you to run it. You'll be outdoors much of the time, yet connected to a community. The best of both worlds, so to speak."

He pushed the button to raise his bed and ignored the white-hot pain that shot through him when he moved.

"Get out," he told her. "I don't know you and I sure as hell don't want to talk to you about a job."

"Mr. Gilmore," she began, then paused. "Kipling. Our town is a unique place. Friendly, warm and we take care of our own. We always have. Maybe it's our history, maybe it's just dumb luck. Regardless of the reason, you would be safe there. More important, Shelby would be safe there."

Kipling stared at her. "What do you know about my sister?" he asked, his voice a growl.

"I know that she loves her mother and that she's having to deal with a father who enjoys hitting helpless women. I know you're not scared for her. Because being scared doesn't come close to describing what you're feeling. You are terrified, and while you're in this hospital you can't help her. I, however, can."

Kipling closed his eyes. What was happening? Was it real? Could he trust this old broad and how did she know about the situation with Shelby?

"I know a couple of people," Marsha Tilson continued. "Gentlemen who have served our country with honor and distinction. I have already spoken with them and they are willing to take care of Shelby's problem."

He stared at her. "How?"

"Shelby's mother doesn't have much time. My friends will explain to your father that he needs to make his wife's last weeks pleasant. They will make sure that Shelby is safe, and when her mother finally passes, they will assist with the details of the estate. Then they will bring her to Fool's Gold, where she'll be given a safe place to stay while she decides what to do with the rest of her life."

"And my father?"

The old lady gave him a spooky smile. "We won't break the law, Mr. Gilmore. But it's possible your father will get a taste of his own medicine."

"You keep Shelby safe and I'll follow you to hell, Ms. Tilson."

"Mayor Marsha, please. That's what everyone calls me." She rose and lightly touched his hand. "You don't have to be alone in this, Kipling. Nor do you have to go all the way to hell. Just come to Fool's Gold when you're able. We'll be waiting for you."

She pulled a business card out of her pocket and handed it to him. "My cell number is on the back. You can reach me anytime. Let me know when you've moved back to the States for your physical therapy and I'll come visit. We'll talk about the search and rescue team you'll want to put together."

He glanced from the business card back to her. "Is this for real? You'll take care of my sister?"

"I will. You have my word. I've already called my friends and they're on their way to see her right now. Once they arrive, your sister will never be alone with your father again, Kipling."

She reached for the button on his morphine drip. "May I?" she asked.

He nodded.

She pressed the button. Seconds later the drug entered his system and the pain began to ease.

"Be well, Kipling," she said. "When you're ready, come to Fool's Gold. I think you're going to like it there."

He nodded and she left. A few minutes later, one of the nurses came in.

"I saw you had a visitor," she said with a grin. "Was that your granny? Oooh, what a handsome man she was with. A few years younger, judging by appearances. She's, what, sixty? And he didn't look a day over fifty. You have to respect that. He reminded me of that actor fellow. Now what was his name?"

The nurse kept up her cheerful chatter, but Kipling wasn't listening. Instead he turned the business card over and over in his hand and hoped Mayor Marsha Tilson of Fool's Gold had been telling the truth. That Shelby was safe and that his old man would get what was coming to him.

■ ■ ■ ■

Sam carried two suitcases to the car. While he was happy to get his house back to himself, he always felt a little sad when his parents left. Yes, they drove him crazy — but they were still family.

His mother was waiting for him when he returned to the house. She took both his hands in hers and smiled up at him.

"You've grown into quite the man," she began.

He held in a groan. There was no telling where this was going. "It was great to see you, Mom. You and Dad. The lecture went well. I was proud of you."

She studied him. "Were you? I sometimes wonder. I know . . ." She drew in a breath. "I don't mean to embarrass you," she told him.

He drew back his hands. "I know that."

"Which is not the same as saying I don't."

"No." He shifted uncomfortably. "Mom, you and Dad are great, but I don't get how you can just talk about what you do and be the way you are in public."

"I can see that. You'd never have sex on-stage."

"I wouldn't even think about sex while

onstage."

"You're missing out," she began, then shook her head. "No, you're not, are you?"

"Not as far as I can tell." He searched for something supportive to say. "I know you help people with what you do. They're grateful. And you do have a lot of information. I want to hear about your work, but I don't want you going through my closet or telling me about how you and Dad did it last night."

She nodded. "Last night was actually very traditional," she began. "With your father on top and —"

"Mom!"

"I'm sorry." She led him over to the sofa and urged him to sit, then she did the same and angled toward him. "Sam, I remember your first asthma attack. It was the most terrifying thing I'd ever seen and I have to say it was still the worst experience of my life. Watching you unable to breathe, seeing you turn blue. I would have given my life for you."

"I know."

"I love you."

"I love you, too. You and Dad."

"We know. It's just you were so sick for so long. And then when you started to outgrow your symptoms you wanted to test yourself.

343

I was frightened."

He wasn't sure what this had to do with her sexual oversharing but he was willing to go with it.

"I worried. We both worried and yet we had to let you be. But in my heart, you were always that little boy, gasping for breath."

"Mom," he started, but she held up her hand.

"I don't try to embarrass you on purpose," she continued. "I'm open and excited to share every part of my life with the people I love. I want to know everything about you."

Which would be the problem, he thought. "I'm not comfortable with that," he told her.

"I know. I think I've always known, but as your mother, I thought I had special privileges."

"You do."

"Not in that way. I can demand your attention and tell you what to do, but in truth, you're a grown man and I need to respect that. Your boundaries aren't my boundaries, but they are still important. I'll do better in the future. Change is never easy and old habits are very seductive. But I will do my best to remember that you don't need me commenting on every aspect of your sex life, or even going through your closets. I want

344

things to be different between us."

He sighed, then pulled her close and hugged her. "Not too different," he told her. "If you weren't asking about my scrotum, you just wouldn't be my mom."

She laughed and hung on tight. "I'll still ask. Just not so much and maybe not in a crowd." She drew back. "You're a very good man."

"Thank you." He stared into her eyes. "Dellina?"

"I have no idea what you're talking about."

But her gaze was shifting as she spoke and he could feel her starting to squirm. His mother was so honest, she had a horrible time lying, or even withholding the truth.

"You talked to someone and she's the only one I can think who would take you on."

"Fine. Dellina mentioned that I was driving you away. That I needed to respect you and pay more attention to your needs." She waved a hand. "Some version of that. Don't be mad at her. She's got your back."

"I know."

Not many people were willing to say something like that — especially to Lark. But Dellina had. His friends hadn't ever taken on Lark, mostly because they enjoyed the show. But Dellina had been worried about him. He liked that. He felt an odd

345

tension inside his chest. Affection, he told himself. Gratitude. Nothing more.

CHAPTER SIXTEEN

"I have a plan," Fayrene said.

Dellina dropped small faux makeup kits into bright pink goodie bags. She had a party for twelve nine-year-olds later in the week and wanted to get ahead of schedule by filling the bags now.

"I don't want to hear it," she told her sister.

"This time it's different."

"It's not. You have some crazy idea to get Ryan to see that marriage is the only possible road to total happiness. Which very well may be true, but all these plans are nothing more than you being scared to tell him the truth."

Fayrene put one hand on her hip. The other held a very relaxed Caramel, who snuggled against her. "You're not very supportive."

"I love you and I want you to be happy. I also know that in the end it all comes down to trusting the man you love. Just tell him you want to get married now. He adores you. Every day he doesn't propose is proof of how much he cares. He's doing what you asked. You're making a big mistake trying to trick him into betraying his resolve."

Fayrene's eyes unexpectedly filled with tears. "I want him to propose."

"He did. You asked him to wait. He's not going to change his mind. Just admit what's in your heart."

Fayrene shook her head and flounced out.

Dellina waited until the front door slammed to continue filling goodie bags. But as she started to work again, she felt an uncomfortable sense of déjà vu. Her weekend with Sam had been extraordinary. Being with him was fun and comfortable and exciting. Defining their relationship was impossible, yet she found herself wanting to do just that. Could she do it? Admit what was in her heart? Maybe the more pressing question was what, exactly, she thought her feelings might be.

Sam continued to study the invoices in front of him. He'd asked Dellina for paperwork from all the suppliers, including the gifts purchased. He compared that to what she'd billed and found that was where the problem occurred. Despite their conversation on the topic, she was reluctant to bill more than what she'd estimated, even when the estimate was significantly less than the final cost. The times he'd changed his mind, switching items, she billed the correct amount, but when the item didn't change but the final price was more, she absorbed the difference.

"No way to make a living," he murmured as he went on to the spreadsheet he'd started to track the changes.

He wondered how many times she's gone through this before. She handled a lot of weddings and parties. From what she'd hinted at, she was struggling financially. He could see why. The difference in what she charged her customers and what she was paying vendors ate into her profits. He would guess there had been several jobs where she'd lost money, despite the hours she put into the project.

He pulled out her contract and read it through again. There was a section that detailed how estimates and actual prices were handled. The words clearly explained that the client would pay the actual price. The problem was Dellina herself.

He glanced at the clock and saw he only had a few minutes until she was due to arrive. After printing out the spreadsheet, he carried all the paperwork over to his small conference table, then started toward the hall to greet her in the foyer. She walked in before he had a chance to head out.

"Hey," she said, smiling when she saw him. "I've had an extra cup of coffee so I'm ready to talk numbers."

She wore a green dress that made her eyes seem more hazel than brown. Her hair was curled, her expression relaxed and friendly. She was pretty, but not classically beautiful. Average height. To the untrained eye, she wouldn't stand out in a crowd.

But he knew better. He knew that she loved her sisters fiercely, even when they frustrated her. That she was honest and concerned, without being a sucker, and that she was willing to stand up for what she believed.

"Sam? You okay?"

He crossed to her and took her in his arms. "You stood up to my mother," he said as he kissed her.

She stiffened and drew back. "I, ah, have no idea what you're talking about."

He cupped her face in his hands. "My mother apologized for getting into my business and going through my things. There's only one way that would ever happen." He smiled at her. "Okay, two, but as far as I know, hell didn't freeze over. So someone talked to her and I'm betting it was you."

"You're not mad?"

"That you looked out for me? No. I'm not."

"Okay, then it was me."

He chuckled, then kissed her. The second his mouth touched hers, he wanted to do more, but they were in his office in the middle of a workday.

He led her to the conference table and they sat down. He pulled the papers toward them.

"We talked about this before. You need to bill the cost of an item rather than the estimate. You have a clause to cover it in your contracts. Your clients know about it — you have a place for them to initial, saying they've read it."

"I know," she said with a sigh. "It's just I start to feel bad when everything is going over the estimate. Sometimes it's because of changes, but sometimes it's not."

He showed her the spreadsheet. "Here's the total on the estimates for our weekend. Here's the hours you billed."

She pointed to that last number. "Then why don't I have that in my checking account?"

"Because here's what you actually paid for the items. By only billing Score the estimated amount rather than the actual invoice, you lost forty percent of your billable hours. Multiply that by every job you take and you're not working for minimum wage."

Dellina pulled the spreadsheet closer. "This makes it really clear. I can't keep losing money this way. Why couldn't I figure this out on my own?"

"You're a one-person business. You don't have time to be a financial genius."

She glanced at him, her mouth curving up at the corners. "Like you?"

"Exactly."

She gathered the papers and stood up. "I'm going to rebill you."

"Good. And in the future?"

"I'll bill the actual amount, not the estimate. I'll feel guilty, but I'll do it."

"That's my girl." He rose.

She put the papers into her tote, then kissed him. "Thanks, Sam. This has been really helpful. You're good at this and you explain things clearly. Thank you."

"You're welcome." Wanting stirred. Not just for sex, but for her. "Can I see you tonight?"

The smile returned. This time it was filled

with promise. "I'd like that a lot."

At about three, Jack strolled into Sam's office. He sat in one of the chairs across from the desk and leaned back. He tossed a football into the air, then caught it.

"Good party," Jack said.

"That's the feedback we're getting."

"We should do it every year. Invite different clients, but keep the events the same."

Sam glared at him. "No. That's not happening. Do you know what that weekend cost? And the work involved. We're not doing it again. Ever."

One eyebrow rose. "Don't get your panties in a bunch."

"It's easy for you to say that. You didn't do anything but show up." Sam paused for breath, then studied his friend. "And you're kidding."

"Pretty much, but you put on a good show."

Sam relaxed in his chair. "Okay, then. Glad to be the entertainment."

Jack tossed the football again. When he caught it, he put it on the desk. "Dellina's nice."

An odd observation. "Okay. Sure. Why does that matter?"

"You're seeing her." Jack held up a hand.

"Don't deny it. If I can figure it out, it's obvious to everyone."

Sam did his best to avoid shifting in his seat. "We're hanging out," he said, not willing to admit much more.

It wasn't that he wanted to keep things a secret from his friends. It was more that if he defined it, named it, then he would have to acknowledge that he liked her. And once he went down that road, it was only a matter of time until the next disaster.

"Not every woman is your ex," his friend reminded him.

"She doesn't have to be. When I get involved, it ends badly. Every single time."

"So you're due for some good luck." Jack's mouth twisted. "Face it, Sam, you want to get married and have a family. You're a traditional guy. You're going to have to be willing to trust at some point."

"No, I'm not."

"Then you'll never end up where you want to be."

Sam understood his friend was trying to help and a case could be made that Jack was onto something. In theory Sam could adopt a couple of kids on his own and truly avoid the whole man-woman thing. Only he didn't want to. He wanted a partner, someone he could count on and be there for. He wanted to introduce the love of his life as the woman he'd married. Hell, he was open to a minivan.

"It's not going to happen," he said grimly. "If I get involved with Dellina, everything will change."

"You're already involved. You can pretend you're not, but we can all see it. You know her. You like her. What's the worst that could happen?"

Sam raised his eyebrows.

Jack sighed. "Yeah, don't answer that."

"You're an odd one to be giving advice," Sam pointed out. "It's not like you're swimming in commitment."

Jack leaned back in the chair. "We're all so screwed up. How did that happen?"

"Dumb luck?"

Jack smiled briefly. "Taryn figured it out. She found Angel. He's a good guy."

"Any regrets?" Sam asked. Because years ago, Taryn and Jack had gotten married. The circumstances hadn't been ideal. She'd gotten pregnant and he'd insisted they fly to Las Vegas to make it all legal.

"About Taryn?" Jack asked. "No. I still have her around. We were never in love." He hesitated for a second. "I wonder if I'm capable of loving anyone. Romantically, I mean. I never have. I don't need to get married. I have Larissa."

Sam raised his eyebrows. "Really?"

Jack rolled his eyes. "Not that way, asshole. I mean Larissa takes care of me. She makes my life run smoothly. Anytime something messy and emotional comes up, I pass it on to her."

Which all sounded great, but there was a flaw. "You do realize that one day she's going to want more. What happens when she gets married and has a family of her own?"

Jack's features tightened for a second, then he relaxed. "She'll still work for me."

"I don't know. I think she's the type who will want to stay home and look after the kids."

"Well, hell." Jack tensed. "No way. I'll give her a raise. I'll pay her so much, she won't ever want to quit."

"That's one way to handle it," Sam said, thinking the truth between Jack and Larissa was a whole lot more complicated. Not that either of them would admit it.

"When the time is right, you'll figure it out," Sam told him.

"Is that what you say to yourself?"

Sam shrugged. What was there to figure out? He knew exactly what had gone wrong in every one of his relationships. The same could be said for Jack and Kenny. Although

Kenny's circumstances were unique. And painful.

Jack stood and grabbed the football. "I don't want you dying old and alone," he said.

"Because young and alone is better?" Sam asked.

"You know what I mean."

Sam grinned. "I'm better with money than you. When you lose it all, I'll let you live above my garage. Then neither of us will be alone. How's that?"

"I'd rather have a woman, if it's all the same to you."

"And if that doesn't happen?" Sam asked.

"Then sure, I'll move into the apartment above the garage. You going to get me one of those lifts to carry me up to the second floor?"

"Sure. With the biggest motor they make."

"Because it's all about speed." Jack crossed to the door. "Think about Dellina. She seems like one of the good guys."

Sam didn't respond and, when his friend had left, he leaned back in his chair.

Jack was right — somehow he'd gotten involved with Dellina. One second they were working together, and the next, it was a whole lot more. But to risk anything else seemed impossible.

He understood that to get what he claimed he wanted he was going to have to take a leap of faith. To gamble on believing in someone. Otherwise, he was destined to always want and never have.

Sam hadn't known what to expect for his first Finance for a Small Business lecture. In truth, he couldn't figure out why he'd gotten roped into the series in the first place. Sure he'd helped Dellina, but that was different. He'd been able to figure out what was wrong immediately, but that was because they were working together. It wasn't as if he had insight into every business in town. But he'd given his word, so he showed up on time, his presentation ready to go.

There were already several people waiting in the meeting room at city hall. He recognized Patience, the owner of Brew-haha, along with several other small-business owners. Three women, obviously related and one from each generation, sat near the front. Dellina had an appointment, but she'd promised to stop by before he was done with his talk.

Sam walked to the front of the room and clipped on the microphone. He looked out at the people watching him and felt unexpected nerves. He was used to speaking before large groups. He did it all the time. But those talks were about sports or having a winning attitude. He wasn't used to lecturing on finance.

"Success in business can be measured in many ways," he began. "Market share, customer loyalty, brand recognition. But at the end of the day, if you can't pay your bills, none of that matters. I'm sure you're all familiar with the failure rate of small businesses. After five years more than fifty percent of them have closed. So what makes the difference between the ones that succeed and the ones that don't make it? How can you use what you already know to your advantage? How do you make sure you're in that successful fifty percent?"

"You're going to answer all those questions, aren't you?" an older woman asked. "Because just asking them isn't helpful."

Sam glanced at her and recognized her as one of the old ladies who showed up regularly to watch the morning basketball games he played in. Eddie or Gladys, he thought, not able to tell them apart.

"I'll do my best," he told her. "One of the most important aspects of a small business is managing cash flow. You have to pay for inventory before your customers can buy it.

359

You can do your best to get terms that minimize payments you have to make, but you're going to have to pay for what you have in your store, which means you need to get your customers to pay you as quickly as possible."

He clicked on the screen and pushed a button on his laptop. The first slide came up. Sam explained about inventory control and billing, in general terms. Dellina had told him to use her mishaps as an example. He had re-created invoices from fictitious companies, plugging in the numbers, but keeping her information private, and went over the difference between an estimate and what was actually billed. He'd worried about boring his audience, but they all scribbled frantically as he talked. When he was done, nearly every hand shot up as the participants began to ask questions.

When he'd finally answered them all, his audience began to get up and leave. He saw both Taryn and Dellina sitting in the back and started toward them. Patience stopped him in the aisle.

"You're going to keep doing these, aren't you?" she asked. "It's so helpful. I took night classes at the community college, but your information is more practical."

"Sure," he told her. "If there's interest."

"There is," she said. "Nearly all the businesses in town are small. We survive on tourist dollars for the most part. It's important we're doing everything to maximize those dollars." She smiled. "Thanks for making it all so clear."

She stepped away and the older lady — Gladys or Eddie — took her place. "You did good," she told him. "You're more than a pretty face and a great butt."

Sam stared at her, not sure how to respond to that.

"I enjoy those basketball games of yours. Eddie likes Kenny because he's bigger, but you have style when you play. You remind me of a gentleman friend of mine." She sighed. "He was handsome. Successful in business, like you. He showed up in Fool's Gold maybe ten years ago and cut a swath through the single ladies of a certain age. I heard some of them allowed him to buy into their businesses." She shook her head. "Not me. What's mine is mine. No man's going to take it away from me. But he sure knew what he was doing between the sheets."

Sam looked around frantically for an exit. This was worse than dealing with his mother. At least he could tell her to stop. Politeness dictated that he not interrupt a woman old enough to be his grandmother.

Taryn and Dellina strolled up.

"Are you torturing Sam?" Taryn asked.

Gladys grinned. "Maybe. But I think he's man enough to handle it."

Sam wanted to say he wasn't. Not at all. But before he could figure out how to make that confession, Dellina was guiding Gladys away.

Taryn watched her expert maneuvering and smiled. "You found a good one with her, Samuel. Dellina takes care of you."

"You know it's not like that," he said.

"You're involved." She watched Dellina chat with Gladys before the old lady left. "At some point you're going to have to get over yourself."

"Now you sound like Jack."

"He can be insightful on occasion." She looked around at the emptying room. "Nice job. You impressed our business neighbors. They're going to love us even more."

"I'm happy to share what I know."

She linked arms with him. "I appreciate the distraction. Angel's gone for a couple of days and it's boring without him."

"Where did he go?"

"He didn't say. Mayor Marsha had a special project for him. Ford went along, too. He didn't share details. I doubt it's dangerous, but it's possibly not legal." She sighed. "He's just so sexy."

"Yeah, and could we not talk about that?"

Taryn laughed. "I'd accuse you of being jealous, but you have your own thing these days." Her humor faded. She faced him. "Seriously, Sam, I had my reservations, knowing what you'd been through, but Dellina's a sweet girl. Smart, funny, pretty. I know what you've been through. I know you don't trust easily, but at some point you need to take a risk. I don't want you old and alone."

Two conversations about the same material in two days? What were the odds? Of course he knew his friends cared about him.

"Jack's going to live over my garage if that happens. We'll be bachelors together."

Her violet-blue gaze never left his. "That's not enough. I know what you want. You're not going to be happy until you have a family and all the trappings that go with it. That will require you to believe in someone."

He understood the words, but didn't like being pushed. Sure, on the surface, all was well with Dellina. But what about the long-term? How could he know she wasn't like all the others?

Dellina got Gladys out of the room, then

returned to Sam's side. Taryn waved and left.

"You did great," Dellina told Sam. "Everyone was really impressed."

"I was happy to help."

He stared at her, as if seeing her for the first time. She had the feeling he was looking for something, but she didn't know what.

"You make numbers look sexy."

He grinned. "Thanks. Then my work here is complete. Do you have time for lunch?"

"Sure."

He took her hand in his and they walked out onto the sidewalk.

"Margaritaville?" he asked. "We could split nachos. You could get a salad and pretend it has no calories."

Because she did that sometimes, she thought, nodding in agreement. "Sounds perfect."

"Good."

They headed toward the restaurant. Sam said something about the lecture. Nothing that required a response. Which was a good thing. Because out of the blue, with no warning at all, she knew.

Maybe she'd known for a while. Maybe she'd been hiding the truth from herself because, well, she wasn't sure why. Or maybe she'd just figured it out this second.

She loved him. She loved his honor and sense of duty. She loved how he made her feel, how he protected those he cared about, and that even though stepping up in front of the town was his personal idea of hell, he would do it because the business lectures would help people. She loved that he was quiet and sexy and that he called when he said he was going to call. She loved how she felt when she was around him.

She loved Sam.

How totally ridiculous. She'd fallen for the one guy she knew who absolutely, positively, never, ever wanted to get involved in a serious relationship. Talk about stinky luck.

CHAPTER SEVENTEEN

Fayrene glanced anxiously at the clock. Her guests were due to arrive at six. She'd just put in the bubbly feta and sweet pepper dip that she was going to serve as her appetizer, but they needed to be served immediately. Which meant if Montana and Simon Bradley were late, she was in trouble.

Exhaustion swept through her. She wasn't sure how much longer she could do this. Convincing Ryan to propose had proved to be a lot more complicated than she'd realized. But she wasn't going to give up. Tonight's dinner guests were blissfully happy. Montana was also weeks away from giving birth. Fayrene hoped talk of babies and being in love would get the message across.

The back door opened and Ryan and Caramel came in.

"The barbecue is ready," he said as he walked to the refrigerator and pulled out the tray of marinated chicken pieces. Fayrene had gotten the recipe from Ana Raquel's *A Fool's Gold Cookbook.* The salad was ready, along with dessert. Ryan would grill corn with the chicken.

"They should be here any second," she told him. She scooped Caramel into her arms and cuddled the little dog. Caramel settled in close and gave her a reassuring puppy kiss on the nose.

"How do you know Montana?" he asked, pulling a beer out of refrigerator and opening it.

"I've worked with her and the therapy dogs. Max, her boss, sometimes gets in several puppies at once and socializing them takes a lot of work." She leaned against the counter. "I'll admit, it's one of my favorite temp jobs. I get to spend the day playing with puppies and taking them into town so they get used to different situations."

"Like when we took one to the high school football game last year?" he asked.

"Exactly." She petted Caramel. "I'm going to miss you, baby girl."

"Me, too," Ryan admitted, scratching the dog's chest. "She's been great. We should talk about getting a dog. After we're married."

Fayrene held her breath. Was it now? Was

he going to ask her now?

The doorbell rang.

"I'll get it," Ryan said.

Fayrene sighed. She told herself that at least the arrival of their guests for dinner meant the appetizer wouldn't be ruined, but it was cold comfort.

She walked into the living room and greeted Montana and Simon. The other woman was huge and moved awkwardly. Fayrene's back gave a twinge in sympathy.

"How are you?" Fayrene asked. "Feeling okay? Should you be out?"

Montana, a pretty blonde with brown eyes, laughed. "Out is so much better than home. It distracts me. Plus Simon is less likely to hover so much in person."

Dr. Simon Bradley shrugged. "I worry about you. Live with it."

As he spoke, his gaze lingered on her, as if there was no one else he would rather see. Simon was an interesting guy. A gifted surgeon who specialized in helping burned children achieve normal again. He knew what they suffered. One side of his face was so handsome as to seem unreal, while the other side was a twisted wreck of savage burns.

He'd come to Fool's Gold temporarily, but had fallen in love with both Montana and the town and had decided to stay. Fayrene remembered the triplets' wedding, with Montana and her two sisters marrying the men of their dreams. Fayrene was hoping a little of that marriage magic would wear off on Ryan.

"Why don't we go outside," Fayrene said. "The evening is so lovely."

The heat of summer had started to fade and nights had grown cool. But in this hour, the temperature was perfect.

She and Ryan got their guests seated. Montana insisted on holding Caramel, who immediately flopped onto her back for a tummy rub and a snooze. While Ryan offered drinks, Fayrene pulled out her dip and slid the accompanying pita crisps onto a serving plate. She joined her guests outdoors.

Ryan handed Simon a beer, Fayrene a glass of wine and Montana a glass of lemonade. He took a beer for himself and settled next to Fayrene.

"This is so nice," Montana said with a smile. "Quiet. I adore my daughter, but once she learned to talk, she never stopped."

Simon's smile was full of pride. "She's a smart girl."

"Which means she takes after you."

"You're smart."

"Uh-huh. I think we all know who has the brains in the family. That's fine. I'll take being the heart."

"You have mine," Simon told her.

Fayrene felt the need to look away. Being around Simon and Montana was like watching something so intimate as to be private. Their love was a tangible presence in the room.

Montana nuzzled Caramel. "And then there's this little girl. What a sweetie."

"I've enjoyed looking after her."

Montana stroked the dog's cheek. "I'll bet you have. When do you return her?"

"When Mayor Marsha is back."

Montana looked at her. "She's back already. I've seen her around town."

"I didn't know that." Fayrene frowned. "I'll give her a call in the morning." Not that she wanted to give up the sweet girl, but still. Caramel wasn't her dog. How strange that the mayor hadn't been in touch with her when she arrived home.

"We could get a puppy," Montana told her husband.

Simon shook his head. "We're going to have a new baby. We already have Skye and our other pets. Isn't that enough?"

"I guess. But puppies are fun."

"There are other ways to have fun."

Simon's voice wasn't all that suggestive, but Fayrene had a feeling he wasn't talking about playing board games. She glanced at Ryan to see if he was picking on the passion and caring radiating from this couple. She smiled, thinking this had been a very good idea. When dinner was over and their company left, she was going to guide the conversation back to —

"Oh, no!"

Montana spoke loudly, then groaned. She started to stand up. At the same moment a huge gush of fluid soaked through her chair and dripped to the ground.

Simon was on his feet in an instant. He took Caramel from Montana and passed her to Fayrene, then looked at Ryan. "We'll need to borrow a couple of towels, please. Montana, look at me. How long have you been having contractions?"

His wife shrugged. "A few hours. They were pretty minor so I thought we'd have time. They just got stronger."

"Then we're going to the hospital."

Ryan returned with an armful of towels. Simon wrapped one around Montana's middle, then guided her back into the kitchen and toward the front door.

"I'm so sorry about the mess," Montana called over her shoulder. "And for missing dinner. I'm sure it would have been delicious."

Then they were gone.

Fayrene stared at the mucky puddle. Whatever it was, it wasn't water, she thought and turned away.

"I'll get the hose," Ryan said.

She nodded and carried Caramel inside. Once she put down the little dog, she walked over to the sofa and sat down. So much for a romantic evening, she thought glumly. At this rate, she was never going to get her proposal.

Sam watched Dellina pull up the zipper on her skirt. She tucked in her blouse, then reached for a brush.

"I'm so late," she told him. "And it's all your fault."

They'd spent the night together and when her alarm had gone off that morning, he'd silenced it before pulling her into his arms. Now they were both running behind, although his morning was a lot less pressing than hers. He didn't have clients to attend to.

"Want me to apologize?" he asked, tucking his hands behind his head and watching her pull her hair back into a ponytail. She put on earrings, then disappeared into her closet to dig for shoes.

"No." She reappeared with navy pumps in her hands and a smile on her lips. "I had a good time."

"Me, too."

He always did. She was easy to be with. His recent conversations with Jack and Taryn had made him wonder if he was making a mistake. If he should break things off with Dellina before they got too serious. He'd come over the previous evening to discuss that with her. But somehow going out to dinner and then staying with her had made more sense.

They enjoyed each other's company. They had fun together. Nothing about that was bad. He knew how to keep his feelings at a distance. As for Dellina, she knew his past and understood the rules. She wouldn't push him. He believed that. So why not enjoy what they had.

"I have to go," she said as she hurried to the bed. She kissed his mouth, then straightened. "I'm so late."

"I'll call you later," he told her.

"I'll answer."

With that, she was gone.

He got up and took a shower, then dressed. He would head to his place to shave before going into the office. He walked toward the back of the house. Before he left, he wanted to make sure the back door was locked. He'd just stepped into the kitchen when the front door opened and someone yelled.

"It's me. Are you here?"

Fayrene, he thought, recognizing the voice.

"Dellina's already gone," he said as he secured the lock, then moved toward the living room. "She had an early appointment."

Fayrene stood by the front door, her little dog in her arms. She looked tired.

"Is something wrong?" he asked before he could stop himself.

"Yes. No." She dropped onto the sofa. "The usual. Ryan and I had another couple over for dinner last night. I thought it would help him see we need to get married. But things didn't go as I planned. Her water broke and, let me tell you, that's a lot grosser than I ever thought."

Sam glanced at the door and thought about bolting. This wasn't his area of expertise. Yet even as he inched toward freedom, he realized that he knew exactly what she was doing wrong. His mother would be so proud.

He took a seat across from Fayrene.

"This has to stop," he told her. "Put on

your big-girl panties and tell Ryan what you want."

She rolled her eyes. "I can't."

"You won't. There's a difference. If you're not prepared to ask for what you want from a man who loves you very much, then you're not ready for marriage. It's a full-time commitment. It requires everything you have, and being honest about how you feel is the cornerstone to success. If you can't be honest about this, what else won't you be able to talk about?"

Fayrene's eyes filled with tears. "That's really harsh."

"It's really the truth. Ryan is doing what you asked. He didn't want to wait, but he is. That is a good quality in a man. Now you're playing some twisted game, trying to get him to violate his own code of ethics. Because you believe if he really loved you, he could read your mind. Well, he can't. No one can. If you don't get smart pretty soon, you're going to lose the man you want to marry."

Fayrene's mouth dropped open.

Sam waited a second. When she didn't say anything, he rose. "Good luck," he told her, then walked out of the house.

Shelby Gilmore stared at the two men in

front of her.

"I don't understand," she admitted.

It was hard to talk. Her jaw was swollen. Not broken, she thought. At least she hoped it wasn't. She was less sure about her ribs.

Pain dodged her every step. She was exhausted from not sleeping. She couldn't. Not only might her mother need her, but it wasn't safe. Her father loved to sneak up on her when she was most vulnerable and do his worst.

"Who are you?" she asked.

"Friends," the younger of the two men said.

They were both big enough to be frightening. One — she thought his name was Ford — had an easy smile, but she could see the darkness in his eyes. The other man, a few years older, terrified her. He had a scar across his neck — as if someone had tried to slit his throat. Who would have been that stupid?

"A friend of ours knows your brother," Ford told her. "We're here to take care of you."

Shelby told herself not to bother believing. Because nothing good was ever going to happen again. She was trapped with a monster because her mother was dying of cancer. Her mother wouldn't leave and

Shelby couldn't leave her alone. Only a few more weeks, she told herself. But her escape would come at the loss of one of only two people she loved in the world.

"Kipling sent you?" she asked.

The two men exchanged a glance.

"Sure," the older one said. "Here's what's going to happen. Your dad thinks he's smarter than everyone else, but he's not. We've collected evidence on his criminal activities. It's enough to keep him locked up for a long, long time. The police are arresting him right now."

Her father in jail? Was it possible? She didn't have a whole lot of information on what he did to fill his day, but she knew it involved people who lived outside the law.

"We'll take you to the police station later," Ford added. "Not to confront him, but so you can know he's behind bars. The district attorney will want to talk to you and the police will need to search the house later to gather evidence."

Shelby struggled to take in all the information. Her father arrested? Jailed? Was it really possible he wasn't coming back for a long time?

She only needed a few weeks. Her mother wouldn't last much longer. Then she would walk away and never come back. After that, she didn't care what happened to the man.

The older man, the one with the scar, sat next to her on the sofa. His gray eyes were surprisingly kind.

"A nurse will be here shortly. She's going to help with your mom." He pulled a business card out of his shirt pocket. "This is the name of a therapist we want you to see."

"About my mom dying?" she asked.

"That and everything else you've been through."

He reached toward her. Shelby had to consciously keep from flinching as he lightly touched her jaw.

"You have that looked at?" he asked.

"I'm fine."

"We're going to let a doctor decide. We'll go as soon as the hospice nurse arrives."

"How did my brother do all this?" she asked, fighting tears, knowing she just might not be in this alone anymore. "He's still in the hospital in New Zealand."

"Let's just say he has a friend who is taking care of things for him," the man told her.

Someone knocked on the front door. Ford went off to answer it. Shelby looked into the gray eyes of her rescuer.

"Who are you?"

"You can call me Angel."

Despite the pain in her jaw, she managed a smile. "Seriously?"

He made an X on his chest. "It's the name I was born with."

She knew she should say something funny. Something that lightened the mood or showed that she was tough. Only she couldn't think.

Ford returned with a petite brunette in bright pink scrubs.

"Hi," the woman said with an easy and compassionate smile. "I'm Nancy. I'll be taking care of your mom."

Shelby started to speak, only the words got stuck and then she was crying. Angel drew her into his arms.

She usually hated when men touched her. If they were close, she couldn't see where the hit was coming from. But somehow Angel was different. Maybe it was because he had so much power he didn't need to hurt those less strong than himself. Maybe it was exhaustion. Whatever the reason, she relaxed into his embrace and gave in to the tears that had been waiting for so long. She surrendered to the possibility that maybe, just maybe, she was going to get out of this alive.

Fayrene and Caramel walked through city

hall. She'd called ahead to confirm that Mayor Marsha was indeed back from her vacation and in her office. Which begged the question of why the other woman hadn't come to pick up her dog.

"Don't take it personally," Fayrene told the Pomeranian. "You're totally adorable. I don't want you to go back. But she is your owner."

Caramel gave her a doggy smile that both assured and comforted. As if she were confident that every outcome would be to her advantage.

Fayrene led them into the foyer of the mayor's office. Bailey sat behind her desk.

"You're right on time," she said. "Go on in."

Fayrene frowned. "On time? I didn't have an appointment."

"I know, but Mayor Marsha said you'd be in this morning."

Okay, that was weird, Fayrene thought as she walked through the open double doors.

Mayor Marsha stood when they entered and smiled. "Fayrene. Thank you for stopping by. I trust you didn't have any trouble with Caramel."

"No. She was wonderful. Ryan and I adore her."

Fayrene waited for the little dog to dash

forward to greet her owner, the way she did whenever Fayrene returned from an errand. She would bark and spin and dance on her hind legs. But instead she stayed calmly at Fayrene's side. Her tail wagged, as if she were interested in Mayor Marsha, but there was no real excitement.

The mayor motioned to a sofa and chairs in the corner. "Shall we?" she asked.

Fayrene followed her over and settled on the sofa. Caramel sat on her lap, as she often did, again showing little or no interest in Mayor Marsha.

"Um, how was New Zealand?" she asked, feeling awkward.

"As beautiful as everyone says. I had a lovely time, but I'm very ready to be back home." The older woman smiled. "I hear you've had some excitement in your life."

"Me? Not really."

"Didn't Montana's water break while she and Simon were visiting? That can't have been comfortable."

"It was strange," Fayrene admitted. "Have you seen their new baby?"

"I have. I was at the hospital the very night Henry was born. Such a handsome boy."

"But that was a few days ago," Fayrene said before she could stop herself.

"Yes, I've been home about a week now."

Fayrene instinctively drew Caramel close. "You left your dog with me all that time?"

The mayor's expression softened. "Oh, child, I thought you knew what was happening. Caramel isn't mine. I took care of her for a few weeks while I figured out where she belonged. She's in her forever home now. With you and Ryan."

Fayrene opened her mouth, then closed it. "You're giving her to me?"

"I think of it more as Caramel making her choice. Unless you want me to take her back. I can find her another home."

"No!" Fayrene closed her arms around the little dog. "No, she doesn't need to go anywhere else. I'm happy to take her." More than happy. Relieved not to have to give up her little girl. "But why didn't you say that before?"

Mayor Marsha smiled. "Because you would have told me all the reasons you couldn't have a dog. And in your head, they would have made sense. I've known you all your life, child. You and your sisters faced terrible tragedy at a young age. You got through it and now you're thriving. But you've always been a little stubborn. You see things a certain way and nothing else will do. A trait that is both admirable and sad. By ignoring the possibilities in favor of what you've already decided, you can miss out on some of life's greatest pleasures."

Like Ryan, Fayrene thought, her mind barely able to keep up with what the mayor had told her. She needed him to propose a certain way because that was what she saw in her head. Nothing else would do.

"I . . . Thank you," she said as she stood. She tucked Caramel under her arm. "Yes, of course we want her. And you're right. About all of it."

She turned and hurried out of the office.

By the time she got to the sidewalk, she was shaking. A thousand thoughts crashed in on her. She saw clearly how much she'd risked with her rigid rules and expectations. Sam had been right. Dellina had been right. Everyone had been right and she'd been too stubborn to listen.

Once outside, she put down Caramel. The little dog seemed to understand her urgency and hurried along beside her. Ryan would be at work, Fayrene thought as she went up to Fifth Street, then turned. She could only hope he was in the offices and not out at the manufacturing facility.

She practically ran through town. As she waited at a light, she picked up Caramel. The little dog was panting from running to keep up. Still holding her new pet, she hurried across the street.

When she reached Hendrix Construction, she paused long enough to catch her breath, then went inside. The receptionist wasn't at the front desk, so Fayrene went through the swinging half door and back toward Ryan's office.

He was there! She paused in the doorway, studying him, taking in the familiar, handsome lines of his face. He hadn't seen her yet — he had his back to the door. As he talked about tolerances and adjustments, he picked up a photo of the two of them and lightly ran his thumb alongside her face.

"Sure, Joe," he said. "Get the information and give me a call back. I'll be here all day."

He hung up, then saw her. He smiled and rose. "This is a nice surprise, Fayrene. What are you —" The smile faded as he moved toward her. "Honey, what's wrong? Are you okay?"

She flung herself at him. Caramel was between them, but the little dog simply relaxed into the double embrace and gave them both kisses.

Ryan hung on as if he would never let go. Fayrene breathed in the scent of him and knew she'd been a fool for too long.

"I'm sorry," she said, drawing back enough to see his face. "I'm stubborn, and when I get an idea in my head I won't let it go. Sometimes that's a good thing, but sometimes it's a pain in the butt. Like with my plan. When I said I wanted my business to grow before we got married, I meant it. But now I don't want to wait. I love you, Ryan. I want to get married now. Only I didn't know how to say that and I really wanted you to be the one to propose. Now I'm not even sure why. I guess I was telling myself that if you really loved me, you could read my mind. But that's ridiculous."

She paused to draw in a breath. "Oh, and Mayor Marsha said Caramel is our dog and I'd really like to keep her."

Ryan studied her. "Wow. Okay. That's a lot to take in." He took the dog from her and set Caramel on a padded chair, then pulled Fayrene into his arms.

"I love you. I want to be with you. I hope you know that."

She nodded and sniffed. No way she was going to cry and ruin this. "I know."

"But I can't read your mind."

"I know that, too."

"Is this why you invited Montana and her husband over?"

"Yes. And Pia and Raoul. And why I thought the Score weekend would be so good. I was trying to show you how great it would be to be married."

"I already know it's great. Because I get to be with you every day." He cupped her face in his hands and gently kissed her. "Fayrene, you're my world. I want to be with you always."

He released her and walked around to his desk. He pulled open the bottom drawer and reached behind the hanging files. Then he pulled out a box from Jenel's Gems.

"I bought this the day you told me you loved me," he said. "I was going to wait for however long you wanted, but I also wanted to make sure I was ready when I finally got to do this."

He stepped in front of her, then dropped to one knee. "Fayrene Hopkins, will you marry me?"

She nodded. Her throat was tight and the tears were just so close. "Yes," she managed. "I love you."

He rose and kissed her. "I love you, too."

He opened the box. She stared at the most beautiful round solitaire she'd ever seen. The ring was perfect. Simple and elegant. He slid it on her finger and kissed her again.

After a couple of minutes, he drew back and picked up Caramel.

"I'm thinking flower girl," he said. "Can't

you see her in a little dress with lots of bows?"

"I love it," Fayrene said. "And you."

"I love you, too." He glanced at the dog. "Ready to make us your family?"

Caramel yipped once, then gave them both kisses. Ryan chuckled.

"I have to make a call," he said. "Then let's get out of here."

"Where are we going?"

"Anywhere we can be alone. I just have to phone Joe and tell him I won't be available for the rest of the day." Ryan chuckled. "And maybe not tomorrow, either."

CHAPTER EIGHTEEN

"Can I help you?" Sam asked as he glanced up and saw a little girl standing in the doorway to his office. She was thin, with bright red hair and pretty green eyes. He would guess she was seven or eight. He remembered he'd seen her before. About painting a box, maybe.

"Chloe?" he asked.

She nodded. "I'm looking for Kenny."

"Okay. I can take you to him." Poor Kenny, dealing with a very young crush.

"Thank you," Chloe said politely. "My mom is Bailey Voss. She works for Mayor Marsha." Chloe sounded proud of that fact. "I'm in the Future Warriors of the Máa-zib. Angel and Taryn are our grove leaders. Kenny helped me with knots and my friend's jewelry box."

"I remember," Sam said as he led her down the hall. "His office is this way."

Sam ushered Chloe inside. "You have a visitor."

Kenny looked up from his computer. His brows drew together. "What's up?"

Chloe smiled. "Hi, Kenny."

Kenny looked both pleased and terrified. "Uh, hi, Chloe. What's up?"

Sam was about to leave when Chloe spoke.

"We're having a barbecue this weekend and I want you to come."

Simple words. A common and uncomplicated invitation. Only it wouldn't be that for Kenny, he thought. Not unless he and Bailey were friends and she had a clear understanding of how things were. Sam hesitated, not wanting to intrude, but needing to know if he had to protect his friend.

"Do I know your mom?" Sam asked.

Kenny answered. "She works for Mayor Marsha. Red hair, green eyes. Tall. Pretty."

"You know her," Chloe said confidently. "And if you don't, you can meet her at the barbecue. We're going to have lots of people over. It'll be really fun. Mom makes great cakes. Everybody likes cake."

"What about your dad?" Sam asked, wanting to help his friend. But as the words came out, he remembered what Allison had said the last time she'd been at Score.

Chloe's happy expression faded. "He was

a soldier. He died last year."

"I'm sorry," Sam said automatically, thinking while that was tragic, Kenny's problem was more immediate.

"Thank you." Chloe looked at Kenny. "Can you make it?"

Kenny was a big guy. Well over six feet with plenty of muscle. He could run like the wind and had magic hands that could catch anything thrown at him. But right now he looked incapable of moving. He was trapped by a seven-year-old girl who had no idea what she was asking.

"Kenny's not going to be in town this weekend," Sam told her.

"Oh. That's too bad."

"Yeah, it is." Sam motioned for her to follow him. "We need to let him get back to work."

Chloe sighed. "Maybe another time."

Kenny's mouth formed a straight line. "It was nice to see you," he told Chloe, rather than respond to the invitation.

Sam saw the girl out, then returned to his friend's office.

"I'm sorry, man," he said. "I didn't know why she was here. She was here before and I figured it was a town thing."

"Yeah. That makes sense." Kenny shifted in his seat. "No problem."

Sam hesitated, wanting to say more. But what? Kenny had his demons. All Sam could do was offer cover when possible.

He returned to his office, still not sure why Chloe kept coming by. Was she looking for a substitute dad? If so, Kenny was the wrong guy. He might look like a good candidate on the surface, but it didn't go further than that. The last thing he needed in his life was a woman with a kid that wasn't his. That would be beyond cruel.

Dellina vowed she would not freak out. She'd done more with less, she reminded herself. The fact that she couldn't remember when didn't matter.

"Over there," she called out to the catering staff she'd hired to help with the event. "Stack the plates at the end of the buffet."

She turned and eyed the flowers on display. They were beautiful and fresh. Most important, they were practically fragrance free. Few things could destroy the desire to party faster than the overwhelming scent of too many fragrant flowers.

The party was being held in the Condor Valley Winery. The main floor was perfect for entertaining. The rustic decor added charm, while the open area allowed for plenty of mingling. She'd set up the buffet

391

along the wall opposite the tasting bar.

Pulling together Fayrene and Ryan's engagement party with less than forty-eight hours' notice had been a challenge but the outcome was worth it. Word had gone out to all their friends. Dellina had arranged for the catering and serving staff. Ana Raquel and her husband took care of the food and the drinks were easy. Tonight the choices would be coffee, tea, soft drinks and Condor Valley wines.

Ana Raquel came out with a large tray in her hands. It was covered with rows of tiny sandwiches. Dellina helped her place it on one of the buffet tables.

"The puffs are ready to go in the oven," her sister said. "We're also doing mini quesadillas. Dessert is more complicated. I wanted to do a wedding cake, but there wasn't time, so I called the bakery and they had several undecorated sheet cakes. They're going to do two layers with a chocolate buttercream filling for each level. We should get about four layers in total." She shrugged. "It'll kind of look like a wedding cake. Square rather than round, which is okay. They'll cover it with vanilla frosting, then drizzle chocolate ganache over it. Not exactly elegant, but it will work."

Dellina hugged her sister. "Thank you,"

she said earnestly. "I couldn't have pulled this together without you."

Ana Raquel grinned. "I know. I'm amazing." She laughed. "Greg's done most of the work. He's brilliant in the kitchen." She hugged Dellina back. "I love you, sis, but I gotta go."

She waved and raced back to help with the final preparations.

Dellina made one more round to check on everything, then ducked into a nearby office to change. Normally she wasn't concerned about what she was wearing. Her job was to disappear into the background. But this party was different.

She pulled off her jeans and T-shirt, then slipped into the simple navy sheath she'd brought. She exchanged flats for strappy sandals and put on gold hoop earrings. There was a mirror on the wall and she used that to touch up her makeup. She carried her overflowing tote to her car and locked it inside, then went back into the winery. A quick check of her watch told her that guests would start arriving any second.

She'd barely registered that fact when Fayrene and Ryan walked in. Her sister rushed over to her and showed off her beautiful engagement ring.

"It's perfect," Dellina told her.

"I know. I'm so happy. Isn't Ryan wonderful?"

"He is."

Ryan joined them and kissed Dellina's cheek. "Thanks for all this," he said. "I can't believe you got an engagement party together so quickly."

"It's what I do. I'm glad the engagement is official."

"Me, too," Fayrene said, her expression impish. "It took me long enough to come to my senses and realize I had to ask for what I wanted."

Ryan took her hand in his and kissed her knuckles. "We're together now, my sweet. That's what matters."

Dellina smiled, happy for both of them. She glanced past them and saw several guests arriving.

"Go mingle," she said, shooing the young couple toward the front doors of the winery. "Accept congratulations and drink champagne. I have a designated driver for you, so not to worry."

Fayrene hugged her sister again. "Thank you," she whispered. "For everything. I love you."

"I love you, too."

Dellina watched them go. Although she still had a million things to do, she gave herself a second to revel in her sisters' happiness. They were both settled. Happy, successful and in love. When her parents had died, Dellina had been overwhelmed by the sudden responsibility of two younger siblings. They'd all gotten through it together. They'd stayed close and connected. She had a feeling her parents would be proud of all three of them.

She turned toward the kitchen, prepared to tell Ana Raquel that the guests had started arriving, but her sister and Greg were already walking toward the buffet with large serving dishes. Dellina sighed. She loved it when a plan came together. When she had to —

The back of her neck prickled. She glanced over her shoulder and saw Sam had arrived. In the few seconds before he saw her, she took in the sight of him. Her stomach did a little shimmy, her girl parts quivered in anticipation and her heart . . . Well, her heart was overflowing with love. Maybe falling for him was a mistake. Maybe she would regret it later. But right now loving Sam was the best part of her world.

Sam hadn't been to the Condor Valley Winery before. He liked the use of wood and high ceilings in the tasting room and looked forward to trying the wine.

He still had trouble believing that only a couple of days ago Fayrene had been waffling about telling Ryan her true feelings, and now they were engaged and there was a party to celebrate the happy couple. Things moved fast in this town. Obviously Fayrene had come clean about wanting to move up the wedding. Sam wasn't surprised Ryan had been enthused about getting engaged. He obviously loved Fayrene. But pulling a party together this fast?

That was Dellina's doing, he thought as he searched for her in a crowd. She knew how to make the magic happen.

He spotted her talking to Josh Golden and his wife. Charity? Sam wasn't sure. He knew she was the city planner and that they had a couple of kids.

He let his gaze linger on Dellina. She was smiling as she talked. Moving her hands. She always listened intently, as if whoever was speaking was the most interesting person in the world. She had a way with people. And a way with him.

He liked her. He liked being around her. Taryn and Jack hadn't been subtle in their advice. It was just a matter of time until Kenny took him on. It wasn't that he didn't want a happy ending with a beautiful, funny, sexy, caring woman like Dellina. It was that he didn't think it was possible. Their relationship was going to end badly. The trick was putting off that end as long as possible.

He walked over to the wine bar, then moved to the edge of the room to watch what was going on. As he studied the growing crowd, he realized he knew most of them by name. Pia and Raoul. He'd met Heidi at the ranch a few weeks before. Heidi of the goats. The guy with her was her husband and his name was Rafe.

"Are you being antisocial?" Taryn asked as she walked over to him.

"Observing. There's a difference."

"Maybe on the inside, but on the outside, they look the same." She linked arms with him and drew him toward the center of the room. "Angel is back so my world is restored," she told him. "You see before you a happy woman."

"I'm glad."

"He won't say what he was doing, which is a little annoying."

"I'm sure you have ways of making him talk."

"I do, as a matter of fact." She smiled.

Mayor Marsha walked up to them. "How are you two?"

"Great," Taryn said with a sigh. "Did you

have something to do with Angel and Ford disappearing?"

Sam expected the older woman to be confused by the question. Instead she nodded.

"Yes, they were helping me. A young woman was in trouble and they went to make sure she was safe."

Taryn's eyes widened. "Seriously?"

"Of course. Her name is Shelby and she was trapped at home with an abusive father. He's been arrested and charged with multiple crimes. Shelby will be receiving some counseling to deal with the trauma of all she's been through. Even worse, her mother is dying of cancer."

"How do you know her?" Sam asked.

"I don't. I know her brother. I suspect they'll both be moving to town in the next few months." She turned her attention to him. "I heard your business finance talk went over very well. Thank you so much for doing that. The business community needs strong leadership. I'm hoping you can fill that role."

"I, ah . . ." Sam cleared his throat. The mayor continued to stare at him until he found himself saying, "Yes. Of course. Happy to."

"Good."

Taryn squeezed his arm. "So, how was your trip to New Zealand? Meet any handsome men?"

"At my age?" Mayor Marsha smiled. "Don't be silly. Now if you'll excuse me, I want to congratulate the happy couple."

She walked away.

Taryn watched her go. "I think she has supernatural powers."

"Not possible."

"You're about to be a leader in the business community, Sam. You're more than capable, but you do your best to never get involved. So why did you say yes?"

He shrugged, not sure of the answer.

"See," Taryn told him. "She used mind control."

He got Taryn a glass of wine, then spoke to more people he now somehow knew. All the while, he watched Dellina manage the party. She smiled at him, but before he could join her, she was pulled into the kitchen. There was plenty of time, he reminded himself. He would find her by the end of the evening. Find her and take her home. He smiled. It was going to be a very good night.

"There you are."

Dellina turned and saw Sam approaching.

399

Her heart rate immediately increased and she felt herself smiling.

"I could say the same thing," she told him. "You've been quite the social butterfly this evening."

He grinned. "Hardly."

"Every time I spotted you, you were chitchatting with someone else. Careful, Sam. People will think you're a native."

"I'm getting there." He put his arm around her waist and drew her close. "I've missed you."

Words to make her already in-love self sigh. "I know. This party has taken every second."

"But you pulled it together in forty-eight hours. Impressive."

His dark gaze was possessive, his hand firm on her back. He drew her into a corner and she didn't resist. Not when she was pretty sure of the outcome.

Sure enough, as soon as they were in a relatively private space, he wrapped his arms around her and kissed her deeply. She relaxed into his embrace and let her body melt against his.

She let herself get lost in the feel of his tongue against hers before reluctantly drawing back.

"I know," he said before she could speak.

"You're still on duty."

"Until the party is over."

He kissed her lightly. "I'll wait. Want to go back to my place?"

She put her hands on his chest. "Really?"

"Why are you surprised?"

"I've never been to your place."

"You have."

She shook her head. "Nope. I've never seen where you live." Something she was sure was deliberate. Or had been at first.

"Then it's past time."

Dellina found herself oddly nervous as Sam pulled into his driveway. He'd followed her to her place first. She'd dropped off her car and grabbed a few things so she could stay the night, then had gotten into his car. Now as he parked in front of the ranch-style home, she felt fluttering in her stomach and it had little to do with how good-looking he was.

It was close to nine and the sun had set over an hour ago. Lights spilled from most of the houses around them. The sound from TVs and kids playing could be heard. An ordinary neighborhood in an ordinary town, she thought, although she wasn't totally convinced by her words.

She got out before Sam could open the

door, but let him carry her small bag. He led the way up to the front door and opened it, then flipped on lights.

The house might have been built in the sixties, but it had been extensively remodeled. The whole middle section had been opened up. There was a kitchen to the far left and a huge great room large enough to support two sofas and nearly half a dozen chairs. Big windows would let in light during the day.

Sam flipped on a few lamps. She saw a fireplace with an old-fashioned brick hearth. The mid-century touch suited the room.

"Nice," she said as she glanced around..

"Want to see the rest of the place?"

"Sure."

They went into the eat-in kitchen. It was open, with plenty of counter space and lots of cupboards. There were plenty of gadgets, including a complex-looking espresso machine and massive stove with a built-in grill.

Beyond that was a formal dining room. There were two spare bedrooms with an adjoining bath at one end of the house. The master was probably at the other.

The colors were all muted guy-tones. Beige, sage, taupe. She assumed he'd employed a professional decorator. Minimal artwork covered the walls. It was mostly abstracts or landscapes. Chosen more for the decorative value than because he liked it, she would guess.

"Where are you?" she asked when they returned to the great room.

He raised his eyebrows. "Should I state the obvious and point out I'm right here?"

She smiled. "I meant, where are you in this house? It's great and beautifully decorated. But it's not you. The muted colors are very neutral. That's you on the surface, but underneath, you have a lot of passion. Where are the bold touches? The whimsy only you would see." She put her hands on her hips. "Wait a minute. You're some famous football guy."

He winced. "Famous football guy? Is that how you think of me?"

She laughed. "You know what I mean. You have to have stuff. Where is it?"

He didn't answer right away. She wondered if he was going to try to deflect her. And if he did, should she let him? But then he took her hand in his and led her toward the other end of the house.

He dropped her bag outside a partially closed door, then motioned for her to lead the way. She pushed the door open as she entered and found herself in what she would guess was the heart of the house.

The room was huge. Probably the result of two bedrooms being combined. There were bookshelves all along one wall. But instead of books, the shelves were crowded with awards. Statues and plaques, glass swirls and silver bowls. There were dozens of them. Maybe hundreds.

Black leather chairs — big and comfortable looking — faced a huge flat-screen TV mounted on the wall. The wall opposite the bookcases had been painted a dark crimson. Framed L.A. Stallions posters showed Sam, Jack and Kenny in action. Below was a built-in cabinet that went the length of the wall. Complicated-looking equipment gleamed. Remote controls sat in a basket. There was a refrigerator, a small microwave and wine cellar.

All the comforts of home, she thought, knowing this was where Sam allowed himself to relax.

She studied the posters of him, passing over the ones of his friends. There were three — two of him kicking and one of him right after the kick had scored. When his teammates had carried him on their shoulders.

"Which game?" she asked.

"Super Bowl."

Right. Because Sam had kicked a field

goal in the final seconds — winning the game for his team. A fact she had known but never really internalized.

"That must have been something."

"We'd worked hard to get to that game. Everyone played well. I was fortunate to be able to add the final points."

Which all sounded like an ESPN sound bite.

"It must have been a lot of pressure. Don't a couple of billion people watch the game every year?"

He shrugged. "Sure."

She walked to him and grabbed him by his shirtfront. "Sam, come on. That was a huge moment. You won the Super Bowl. You didn't throw to someone, or catch a ball someone else had thrown. You did it yourself. You and the goal and the ball. You did it."

His mouth twitched at the corners. "There's no *I* in *team.*"

"How many clichés do you have?"

"How much time you got?"

She dropped her hands to her sides. "Just tell me it was cool."

"It was." His mouth curved again and this time he smiled. "It was better than cool. It was like swallowing lightning."

"Best night of your life?"

Some of his humor faded. "So far. I was hoping it would be overshadowed by having a kid, but until then, yes."

"Don't you get a ring?"

"We do. Want to see it?"

She nodded.

He walked over to the bookcase. As he approached it, she saw a center display. A ring sat in the middle of an acrylic or glass case. A huge ring with the L.A. Stallions logo and plenty of diamonds. Bold letters announced World Champions.

He opened a drawer underneath and pushed several buttons on a pad. There was a faint click as something unlocked, then he pulled out the ring and handed it to her.

She took it and studied the design. "I've never seen you wear it."

"Look at it. This isn't the kind of ring you wear every day."

"I suppose it would get in the way."

The ring was heavy and attention-grabbing. She slid it on her middle finger. It was impossibly huge.

"Still," she said, handing it back to him. "Very cool. What a moment. You'll always have that, no matter what. You have to be proud of that."

He put the ring away. "I am proud. But what feels like the bigger feat is having a life

406

after football. Not all the guys figure that out."

She moved toward him. He opened his arms and drew her close. "You're the kind of person who will always be successful," she told him. "You would insist on it."

"You're giving me too much credit."

She stared into his dark eyes and let her emotions flood her. Love, she thought. So much love. "Not possible," she whispered, right before he kissed her.

His mouth settled on hers. Familiar wanting grew. She wanted to be with him tonight, she thought. For all the other nights to come. She wanted it all. But what about Sam? Could she convince him they were worth taking a chance on?

Questions for another time, she told herself, surrendering to the passion. She would come up with a plan. She would be brave, because they were worth it. But later. Tonight there was only the man and how they made each other feel.

Sam knew right away something was up. While he and Larissa got along, she didn't generally hang out in his office. Plus, there was something worried in her eyes and she couldn't stop smoothing her long ponytail.

"Just say it," he told her, knowing if she

expected his help with one of her weird-ass rescues, he was going to send her to Jack. No way he was getting involved with some three-legged tiger or Thanksgiving turkey breakout. Larissa was great and he liked her a lot. Her massages kept him functional. But when it came to seeing the world as one giant need, she was the queen and he wanted no part of that kingdom.

"You're not going to like it."

"Then let me help. No, you can't put an ant farm in my living room, or a pig in my garden or whatever it is you want to do."

That earned him a smile. "You're so mean," she told him.

"Not mean. Firm. Unlike Jack, who lets you walk all over him."

"No. That's not fair. Jack supports my causes."

Because Jack liked Larissa. And because he had a guilt complex, Sam thought. He was forever trying to make up for something that wasn't his fault. With Larissa as his front, he could convince the world he was giving back. The problem was he never felt it himself, so the guilt didn't go away.

Sam frowned. He was way too insightful this morning. It wasn't like him.

Sam returned his attention to the woman fidgeting in front of him. "I have a phone call in ten minutes."

Larissa bit her lower lip. "Okay, but don't shoot the messenger. Simone's here."

Sam's mind shut down. One second there was thought, then there was nothing. It took several seconds for his brain to begin re-booting.

"Here, as in . . ."

"In the foyer. Right now."

He was on his feet and moving before Larissa finished speaking. He sprinted down the hall, then consciously slowed as he rounded the corner.

Larissa had been telling the truth. His ex-wife stood looking at her cell phone, impatience pulling at every line in her body.

Sam came to a stop. She was older, but he couldn't see evidence of that on her face. She was still beautiful, still sexually appealing. She was five years older than him. Back when they'd met he'd been a relatively innocent twenty-two-year-old and she'd been far more experienced. Looking back he could see their courtship for what it was — a planned seduction with a specific outcome. But at the time, he'd been blown away by what he'd assumed was the woman of his dreams.

She was tall and thin. Large breasted. While they'd been married she replaced the implants she had with bigger ones. She'd also had her nose done. She was a blue-eyed blonde. Sassy, irreverent and, at her core, ruthlessly selfish. It had taken him five long years to figure out theirs wasn't a marriage. It was a platform from which Simone planned to launch the rest of her life. He'd been expecting love and a fifty-year marriage. She'd wanted exposure and a hook. In the end, she'd been the one to get what she wanted.

"Hello, Simone."

She glanced up at him and smiled. It was the same smile that had first caught his attention twelve years ago. Bright, perfect, welcoming. He'd been drawn in then. Intrigued. In a sea of groupies, she'd been a real woman with something to offer.

"Sam." She dropped her phone into her purse and walked toward him. "It's great to see you. You still look amazing."

She stopped in front of him and put her hand on his forearm before leaning in for a kiss. He let her, mostly out of curiosity. Her mouth brushed his and he felt nothing. Not revulsion, not anger. Just nothing.

Exactly what he'd wanted but it was nice to be sure. Their marriage had ended badly. But that had been a long time ago. Any feelings had long since died. Which made her return so interesting.

Before he could ask her what she wanted, he heard footsteps in the hall. Kenny, Jack and Taryn burst into the foyer and approached. Sam grinned as he saw them. They all looked pissed and protective. While he didn't need any help, it was nice to know they were there for him.

"Simone," Taryn said. "You're looking . . . older."

Simone stiffened. "I see you're still a bitch, Taryn."

"Yes, I am. I'm really glad you remember. Why are you here?"

Jack and Kenny flanked Sam. They were impressive but they would leave the talking to Taryn, Sam thought. Because neither of them had been raised to take on a woman. Still, there was strength in numbers.

"I want to talk to Sam," Simone said. "Not that it's any of your business."

Sam stepped between them. "Thank you," he said. "But I've got this." He motioned for Simone to follow him. His friends followed, stopping only when he and his ex entered his office.

Sam waited until she'd seated herself on the sofa in the corner. He took a chair opposite.

"This is nice," she began, glancing around

411

the office.

"Don't bother with small talk," he told her. "Get to the point."

She leaned toward him. "Oh, Sam, there was a time when you were thrilled to have me talk about anything. You loved the sound of my voice."

She'd had more work done, he thought as he studied her perfect face. Her blond hair tumbled perfectly over her shoulders. Her jeans clung to slender thighs. He remembered how his hands had shaken the first time he'd undressed her and how expertly she'd faked her orgasms. He'd only found out about the latter when he'd read her book. A how-to self-help bestseller on landing a professional athlete as a husband. Making him feel like he was a god in bed was her number-one tip. He still remembered most of the passage.

Don't worry if he can't get you off. This isn't about you — this is about making him feel that he's the king of the world. Get a decent vibrator and take care of yourself later. You're not in the relationship for sex. You're in it for the goal. Learn to fake it convincingly and you'll solve a lot of problems.

She'd detailed all the ways she'd faked it with Sam. And there had been many. The irony being how she'd apparently told his mother she missed him in bed.

"Sam?" she asked. "Are you listening to me?"

"No. Why are you here, Simone?"

She turned on the smile. "My publisher wants to reissue my book. A 2.0 version, if you will. I want to add some new material. I thought I could interview you, talk to your friends. That sort of thing."

Incredible. And yet not the least bit surprising.

"No."

She pouted. "Oh, Sam. Don't be like that. Why won't you help me?"

"Because your book violates every reasonable assumption of privacy a person can have in a marriage. You lay it all bare."

"It's a self-help book. I have to be honest so people believe me."

"When were you honest in our marriage?"

She sighed. "I should have known you would be difficult. I was hoping you'd changed in the past few years, but I guess that's too much to hope for."

"It is." He rose. "You need to leave."

She stood and moved toward him. "I can get what I want without your help."

"Then good luck with that."

Her pretty face hardened as she glared at him. "You were never there for me. Not once."

"Goodbye, Simone."

She stalked out of his office. He heard Jack in the hallway and knew his friend was escorting her out of the building.

Sam crossed to his desk and sat down, but he didn't return to work. Simone wasn't the type to give up easily. He had a bad feeling he wasn't going to like the rest of her plan.

CHAPTER NINETEEN

"When did you start throwing like a girl?" Justice called.

Ford glowered at the other man. "What did you say?"

Justice chuckled. "You heard me."

Sam used their momentary distraction to steal the ball. He bounced it once, twice, then jumped up and tossed it in for a clean basket. Kenny ran by and they exchanged a high five. From the sidelines came a shrill whistle. Eddie or Gladys was showing her approval.

The morning basketball game had become a fixture in all their days. Three times a week a group of them played hoops for an hour. It was a great workout and more fun than the treadmill. The small audience of two octogenarians was disconcerting, but the guys had all gotten used to them.

Justice took the ball out, passed it to Jack and the game was on again. It ended forty minutes later. Sam's team won by four points, something he would be mentioning most of the day. He shook hands with the other guys and reached for a towel from the stack Larissa dropped off every game day. His gaze caught unexpected movement. He turned and saw Simone sitting on the bench next to Gladys. She had a tape recorder in one hand and was nodding eagerly at whatever the old woman was saying.

Sam swore. If she couldn't get what she wanted directly, she would go around him. He wasn't surprised.

"Want me to take care of this?" Kenny asked.

"You gonna take on the old ladies, too?" Sam asked, then shook his head. "Leave it. She'll do whatever she'll do and I'll deal."

Kenny patted his shoulder. "It's hell to have an ex."

"You know it."

Close to one that afternoon, Sam headed for city hall. The mayor had asked him to join the business economic development council. He'd resisted, she'd insisted and here he was — going to his first meeting. He'd given himself extra time for the walk. He wanted to stop by Brew-haha and get a coffee. He had a feeling this wasn't going to be the most interesting meeting he'd attended this week.

But even as he mentally complained, he found himself looking forward to finding out what they had in mind. There were a lot of ways a community could support local business. Score's customer base was outside of the area, but most of the other companies were tied to the geography. He figured they could learn from one another.

He stood at the corner, across from Brewhaha. As he waited for the light to change, he looked in the windows of the coffee place. Most of the chairs were filled and there was a line. Some of the —

He retraced his visual steps and saw Simone sitting at a table with Dellina. Dellina spoke and Simone laughed. He saw the tape recorder between them.

Something hot and sharp hit him in the gut. Betrayal, he supposed. Given the circumstances, he almost couldn't blame Dellina. Simone could be charming when she wanted and there was no way Dellina would guess what she really was. But she had to know how he would feel about her talking about him. About them.

The light changed, but Sam ignored it. He turned and walked back the way he'd come. There was more than one way to get to city hall.

"I'm pretty sure I did this right," Dellina said as she pulled folders out of her tote. "I followed your instructions, which I know will make you happy."

She paused, waiting for Sam to make a comment. But although he nodded, he didn't seem that engaged in their conversation. He almost seemed . . . remote. As if he were holding himself apart, somehow. Which was really strange.

She'd brought the final invoice to the Score offices, as he'd requested. She'd also dragged along all the supporting invoices so they could go over them together. Now that she understood what she'd been doing wrong, she was pretty sure she could get the numbers to do their thing, but she appreciated Sam looking everything over for her — just in case.

Still, something wasn't right, she thought. She abandoned her tote and sat on the chair opposite his.

"Sam? What's going on?"

He looked at her. "What do you mean?"

"You're not yourself. Is something wrong? Or is this a bad time? We can reschedule the meeting."

His dark gaze was steady as he studied

her face. While she had no idea of the topic, she could practically *see* the wheels turning in his brain.

"What?" she demanded. "There's something."

"I saw you talking to Simone."

It took a second for the name to sink in. Because she didn't know any Simones. Only she'd met one today.

"Your ex? Yes. She wanted to have coffee." Dellina relaxed. "She's, um, interesting. She wants to do an updated version of her book and wanted me to help." She shook her head. "Can you believe it? As if I would give up any information. I told her that. I explained there was no way anyone in town would help her and that she was wasting her time."

Sam's wary expression never changed. "She was laughing."

"Okay," she said slowly. "I can be funny on occasion. Not that I'm ready for the stand-up circuit, but still." A knot formed in her stomach. "Sam, I didn't say anything about you. I wouldn't do that. Not only do I understand and respect your need for privacy, but I agree with you for a lot of reasons. She's out for what she can get for herself, the rest of the world be damned. I'm telling the truth about this. You have to know that."

She waited, hoping he would relax a little, but he didn't.

She searched for the right words, only there weren't any. She'd told him the truth. Now it was up to him to figure out if he believed her or not.

Love blended with fear and neither was especially comfortable. The logical side of her brain reminded her that without faith in each other, they were doomed. They could be doomed for a lot of other reasons, too, but this was a deal breaker.

She loved him, and because of that love, he had the power to hurt her emotionally. She didn't think he would be cruel on purpose, but he was determined and fairly rigid.

"Okay, then," she murmured, and began collecting her folders.

"You don't have to go," he told her.

"Yeah, I do. You don't believe me. After everything we've been through, you still think I could be the kind of person who would betray you to your ex-wife."

She shoved the folders back into the tote and started for the door.

"Dellina, wait."

She turned, trying not to hope.

His expression hadn't changed, she

thought. He wasn't moved by her words. Or, very possibly, by her.

"I want to help you with your invoices."

Words that cut to the bone. Or in her case, the heart. "Thanks, but I'll take my chances on getting them right myself."

She hesitated. She loved him. Despite this illustration of his biggest flaw, her feelings were unchanged. At some point she was going to have to suck it up and tell him, then accept the consequences. Just not today, she thought grimly. There had been enough emotional body blows already.

Sam took out his temper on the exercise equipment in the office gym. He ran eight miles, then did an entire circuit on the weight equipment. He finished with alternating single-arm push-ups, going until his strength gave out and he was lying gasping on the mat.

Sweat poured off him and burned his eyes, but the strange sense of everything being wrong hadn't gone away.

He got to his feet and staggered toward the showers. After washing up and dressing, he grabbed a bottle of water and downed it in a single gulp. He reached for a second and drank it more slowly.

Damn Simone for showing up, he thought.

She was like some marauding monster, wreaking havoc wherever she went. Worse, she'd gotten between him and Dellina. But even as he thought the words, a voice in his head pointed out he'd done that all on his own.

He swore and sat on a bench in the locker room. His gut said Dellina was telling the truth. She would never talk about him to anyone. She'd been the one to stand up to his mother.

But his head didn't agree. His head was wary and mistrustful. His head didn't believe. So he'd hurt her. She hadn't said anything, but he'd seen it in her eyes. He'd hurt her because when it came to a contest between what she said and what he'd seen, he went for the empirical evidence. Mostly because Simone always got what she wanted.

Kenny walked into the locker room. "There you are. Your car is still in the parking lot. I knew you had to be here somewhere. The bitch is back. Want me to throw her out?"

Sam stood. "No. I'll talk to her."

"She's in your office."

Going through his computer, he thought, following his friend out of the locker room.

Turned out he was wrong. Simone was

pacing, not rifling through drawers or logging on to his accounts. When he stepped into the room, she spun to face him.

"I get the girlfriend," she said, her voice shrill with anger, her gaze narrowed. "I don't like it, but sure. She's loyal. She thinks you're capable of a real relationship. She hasn't learned yet what an emotional tight ass you are. But the town? The whole damn town?"

He leaned against the door frame and crossed his arms over his chest. He didn't know what was going on, but if Simone wasn't happy, something good must have happened.

"You'll have to tell me what you're talking about," he said. "Because you're not making any sense."

She balled her hands into fists. "No one will talk to me. No one! Not those stupid old bitches watching you play basketball, not the woman at the coffee shop, not the weirdo at Jo's Bar. No one will discuss you beyond saying you're charming and a welcome addition to the community."

She stomped her foot. "Who do they think they're kidding? You a part of a town? You would never give up that much control." Her voice rose until she was practically screeching. "Damn you all to hell, Sam.

How could you do this to me?"

Dellina had told the truth, he thought, both relieved and ashamed. He should have believed her. He should have listened to his gut. Only it had been so long since he'd been in a position to trust a woman that he'd forgotten what it looked like. That wasn't only Simone's fault, he thought. There had been others who had fed that particular flame.

"Are you even listening to me?" Simone demanded.

"Not really." He motioned to the open door. "You'd probably like to get going on the drive back to L.A. It can be long."

She grabbed her purse and stalked past him. "You're a mean, selfish bastard, Sam Ridge. I hope you rot in hell."

He didn't bother to watch her go. Instead he crossed to his desk and picked up the phone. He tried Dellina's cell number, only she didn't pick up. That usually meant she was with a client. He would have to try her again in a half hour. Which seemed too long to wait.

Dellina accepted that one day she was going to have to enter the current century and put her calendar onto her computer. From there she could link it to her cell phone.

But for now, she was still old-fashioned and wrote down her appointments on paper.

She sipped her morning coffee and studied the schedule. There was a big Hendrix family party, a baby shower and the possibility of Taryn and Angel getting married. Or rather the question of what kind of wedding they were going to have. She was pretty sure Angel would get a ring on Taryn's finger one way or the other. But until they made up their minds about the kind of wedding they were going to have, not to mention when, she couldn't get them on her calendar.

"Clients," she murmured. "Can't live with them, can't tell them to jump in a lake."

Her house phone rang — something that rarely happened. She picked it up. "Hello?"

"You are *so* hard to track down. Do you have your cell phone off? It's Larissa, by the way."

"Oh, hi. My cell shouldn't be off." She checked it and, sure enough, it was on Mute. Her last meeting had been the previous day, so it had been off since then. "Sorry, I must have forgotten to turn it back on." She saw she had several messages, including one from Sam.

Seeing his name made her both happy and sad. If he was calling to say he'd been the biggest jerk this side of the Mississippi, then she was all for it. Otherwise, she had nothing to say to him. At least not for now.

"What's up?" she asked.

"I need help," Larissa told her. "This is bigger than my usual crisis. Jack is going to help because he always does, but it's bigger than Jack. Taryn said you'd be the one to know how to fix everything."

"That's a lot to expect of anyone," Dellina said, not sure if she would be pleased or give Taryn a stern talking-to. "What is the problem?"

"A cat rescue group in Sacramento needs help. There's a hoarding situation. An old lady has about fifty or sixty cats in a small house. The local shelters don't have capacity right now. So I need to find that many carriers and volunteers to caravan to Sacramento and pick them up. Then they have to be accessed, seen by a vet and fostered until they can be adopted."

Dellina blinked. "Okay, so this *is* big. Let me think. We can probably put, what, three carriers in each car. Maybe four. So we need about fifteen vehicles. Sixty carriers." She was already making notes.

"Give me ten minutes and I'll call you back."

"Thanks."

Dellina immediately called the local vet's office. Two minutes later Cameron Mc-Kenzie was on the phone. She explained what was happening.

"Sixty cats?" he said, sounding surprised. "That's a lot. I have a half dozen high school kids who get their volunteer credits working with the animals here. They can help with assessments and treatment. Hopefully not all the animals will be sick. I also know several families who will be willing to foster cats. You'll need carriers. I have ten you can borrow. Check with Max out at K9Rx. Some of the therapy dogs are small. You can probably borrow those carriers. I don't know where you'll get the rest."

"I'm calling the mayor's new assistant," Dellina told him. "And activating the phone tree. That will get us carriers and volunteers. I'll keep in touch, Cameron, and let you know when we're on our way back."

Dellina's next call was to Bailey, who took down the relevant information and promised to activate the phone tree. Dellina set up the rendezvous for two hours from now, in the convention center parking lot, then hung up and called Larissa back.

"Here's where we are," she said. "We'll be ready to go by eleven."

By ten-thirty, Dellina was forced to call in reinforcements. Not only were people bringing pet carriers, they were arriving with cat beds, food, toys and offers to foster. Larissa was collecting names and numbers of those willing to take in a cat or two until a permanent home could be found. Fayrene and Ryan arrived with his large truck. He loaded the food and other paraphernalia into the bed. Larissa said to take it all to Jack's house. She would sort it there, later. Dellina briefly wondered how Jack felt about that sort of thing, but decided that wasn't anything she could worry about now. Not when she had to distribute the growing number of carriers to the volunteers willing to go back and forth to Sacramento.

Taryn and Angel pulled up in his SUV. Taryn had exchanged her designer suit for designer jeans and a silk shirt. She walked over.

"Angel says we can take six crates by using the third-row seats," she said. "Kenny's coming, too. He drives a big Mercedes, so put him down for four. Larissa and Jack will take three, but she's probably already told you that."

"She has," Dellina said, noting the information, then waiting breathlessly for a report on how Sam would be helping.

What Taryn said instead was, "We can't believe how you're all jumping in to help her with one of her crazy projects. We're all used to it, but this is new for the town."

Dellina drew her eyebrows together. "Why wouldn't we help? We have pets in need. Of course we'll be there."

Taryn stunned her by pulling her into a hug. "I love this town so much," she said as she hung on. "It's magical."

Dellina hugged her back. "We have our issues, but usually it's not being afraid to do the right thing. And I wouldn't get too excited about it. Once we rescue these sixty cats, we have to find homes for them."

Taryn shuddered slightly. "You mean like take a cat? Don't they shed?"

Angel came up and put his arm around her. "That's my girl. Thinking with her closet."

"I wear a lot of suede. Do you know what cat hair would do to that?"

Larissa came up and grinned. "There are hairless cats. Maybe we'll find one of those."

Taryn looked doubtful. "Maybe. If it was really hairless."

Dellina left them discussing the issue. She

checked in more volunteers, and took temporary possession of additional carriers. By eleven, they had everything they needed.

There were fifteen vehicles in the caravan. Larissa had printed instructions on where they were going, along with various phone numbers. Everyone agreed to stop for lunch on the outskirts of Sacramento so, once they got the cats, they could drive straight back. Several people agreed to meet them back at the convention center parking lot for feline assessments and distribution.

Driving for nearly two hours with four cats meowing was not the most restful experience, Dellina thought as she pulled back into the convention center parking lot. While she understood the cats were scared, couldn't they express that a bit more quietly?

Larissa had phoned ahead to let people know they were on their way back. As Dellina parked, she saw several dozen people waiting to help with the cats, including Cameron and his nursing staff. She turned off the engine and unlocked her door, only to have it opened from the outside.

"You're a hard lady to track down."

Dellina stared up into Sam's dark eyes and braced herself for the inevitable thumpty-thump of her heart. Sure enough, the organ sighed while the rest of her body went on sexy-man alert.

He held out his hand. She put hers in his and let him draw her out of the car.

"I was helping Larissa," she told him. "With a cat rescue."

"That's Jack's job."

"This was bigger than Jack." She motioned to the cars pulling in beside hers. "There were fifty-seven cats in total. Some of them are okay, but several are obviously sick and a few act like they've never seen a human before."

She had more, but Sam didn't seem all that interested in the story. Instead he was drawing her away from the growing crowd. When they were by the front door of the convention center, he lightly kissed her.

"I'm sorry," he said. "About assuming the worst when it came to Simone. That was more about her powers of persuasion than you, but I was wrong to doubt you."

A weight she hadn't been aware of lifted. "I'm glad," she told him. "I would never have told her anything."

"I know that now and I promise to never doubt you again."

She smiled. "While I like the sound of

431

that, don't get too cocky with your promises."

"Are you going to let me down?"

"No."

"Then I don't see a problem."

He kissed her again, lingering this time. She kissed him back and wished they could be transported to her place or his place and practice whatever new technique his mother had emailed him.

He drew back. "You have cats," he said. "How can I help?"

"Foster a couple of them."

She expected him to recoil or explain why that wasn't possible. Instead he shrugged. "Sure. I don't know much about cats, so I'm going to need some instructions."

"Seriously? You'll take in cats?"

"Yes. Like I said, Larissa's causes are usually Jack's problem, but I don't mind being sucked in now and then."

"They shed," she told him.

"They have fur. I expect shedding."

She was still having trouble taking it all in. "Just like that?"

"I'm fostering them. This isn't a lifetime commitment. Yes, I'll take two cats."

First he'd apologized and now this. She'd loved Sam for a while now, but she hadn't expected him to be one of the good guys.

Emotion blossomed inside of her until speaking the words was inevitable. "I love you."

He froze. "What?"

She sighed happily. "I love you. You're a great guy and now you want to foster cats. How could I not?" She touched his hand. "I remember everything you told Fayrene, about being honest with Ryan. So I want to be honest with you. I love you."

Sam took a step back, then another. Before she could figure out what was happening, he'd turned his back on her and walked away.

CHAPTER TWENTY

Over the next couple of days Dellina learned that cats made pretty good roommates. The two she'd taken in to foster were quiet and clean. Best of all, they didn't seem to mind when she cried herself to sleep. The smaller of the two, a little short-haired marmalade, had even jumped onto the bed when her tears had turned into sobs. He'd cuddled close and tried to soothe her with his purr. Unfortunately cat support wasn't the same as being with the man she loved, but she was going to have to learn to make do.

After fixing her morning coffee, she carried a mug into her office. The cats were already fed and were now sitting in her east-facing kitchen window. Apparently daily grooming was best accomplished in sunlight.

She sat at her desk and turned on her computer. There were several emails from Larissa. The sick cats were still with Cameron while the rest had been sent to their foster homes. She was taking applications for permanent adoptions and would be setting up a booth at the upcoming Book Festival.

There were other emails from clients and a note from Fayrene, who wanted to set up a time to talk about her wedding. Dellina scrolled through the list again, but there was nothing from Sam. She'd already checked her phone and he hadn't left a message or sent her a text.

Not that she had expected he would. But it would have been nice to hear from him.

One of the cats rubbed against her leg. She bent down and petted him, scratching behind his ears.

She wasn't sorry for telling Sam the truth — despite the outcome. Mostly because she'd been brave. She'd put her feelings into words. She'd been honest and if he was too stupid to figure out she was a prize worth pursuing, then she was better off without him.

"Or not," she murmured. While she wouldn't take back telling him what she felt, she sure would have liked a better response. Something slightly more neutral than disappearing from her life.

She brushed away tears she hadn't realized were falling, then turned her attention to her email. She had a business to run and a life to live. She needed to get on with things. As for her broken heart . . . Well, that wasn't going away anytime soon, but she would figure a way to deal. She always had before.

Sam had done his best to figure out a way to avoid his second lecture on finances and small businesses. The last thing he'd wanted to do was have to face people who would be angry with him because of Dellina. He wasn't sure which was going to be worse. The accusations or the fact that so many people knew about what had happened.

But no one had said a word. The crowd was larger this time. He'd kept his lecture short and gone into the Q and A. Now nearly an hour into answering questions, he finally accepted that the reason no one was saying anything was that no one knew. Dellina hadn't told anyone.

"Yes, online banking is safe," he said. "Just make sure you follow all the protocols. Also, you want an extremely secure password. That means avoiding passwords that are your business name or your kid's birthday. Anything else?"

When no one asked another question, he

thanked them for coming and collected his notes.

The people attending stood and began talking to one another. He heard snippets of conversation about the cat rescue and the start of the upcoming Book Festival. But not a word about him and Dellina.

Hadn't she told her friends what had happened? Didn't she want to get drunk and call him names? Or say that she missed him? Except the latter was wishful thinking, he told himself. Just because he wanted to go see her, to explain, to . . .

To what? Ask her to put things back the way they had been before? It wasn't possible. The words had been said. She loved him.

Sam closed his briefcase and wished he could put a fist through the wall. She loved him. Dammit all to hell but he wanted to believe her. Wanted to think they could make it work. Because if there was anyone whom he could trust, it was her.

Except he knew what would happen. Oh, not the specifics, but the outcome. Something terrible would end things. Some disaster. It had always been that way. He had the scars to prove it. Dellina couldn't possibly be different. But he sure wanted her to be.

He started toward the door. Patience stopped him.

"My accountant is *thrilled* with my new financial literacy," she told him. "Thank you so much for doing this. I know it's a big-time suck for you and probably not very interesting, but it's helping so much." She wrinkled her nose. "I have a degree in business and put together a financial plan for Brew-haha, but none of that prepared me for real-world problems."

"I'm happy to help," he said. "Believe it or not, I like doing this."

"I'm glad. With your help, we're all going to do better."

A few more people spoke to him before he left. They were all pleasant and complimentary.

Rather than heading directly back to Score, Sam walked through town. He found himself nodding at people he didn't know and speaking to those he did. And he knew a lot. He couldn't go more than half a block without having to stop and talk to someone who wanted to know about the cat rescue or mention how nice his guests had been over that weekend.

Speaking of the cats, there were signs everywhere with pictures and a number to call. Apparently Larissa was going to host an adoption booth at the upcoming festival. Sam thought about his empty house. Because when he'd walked away, he hadn't bothered taking any cats with him. Nor had he thought to mention his willingness to foster with Larissa. From what he could tell — that didn't matter. She had plenty of help from the town.

Why was that? he wondered. Why would people who didn't really know her help? He thought about all the people who had shown up with carriers and food and offers to drive to pick up cats. It was this town, he thought. This same damn town that didn't talk to Simone and had made the entire Score family feel welcome.

He turned at the corner and walked to the office. When he got there, he went directly into Taryn's office and shut the door. She was on the phone but when she saw him she told her caller, "I need to get back to you. . . . Later today. . . . Yes, of course."

When she hung up, she motioned for the seat opposite her desk. "What's up?"

He put down his briefcase, but couldn't sit. He had to keep moving. "I don't know. This town."

"What about it?"

"Everyone's so nice."

She laughed. "Yes, I found that annoying at first, but now I go with it. It beats the alternative." She stood and crossed to him. "Sam, what's the real problem?"

She stared at him with her beautiful violet-blue eyes. She was lovely. Smart, bitchy, gorgeous. Why hadn't he fallen for her? He understood her. He trusted her. Only she'd been married to Jack once and there'd never been any chemistry and he knew in his gut he would be having the same doubt regardless of who the woman was. Because he was the problem.

"How did you know?" he asked.

He expected her to ask about what, but this was Taryn and she understood her "boys" better than anyone else.

"About Angel? I just did," she told him, taking his hands in hers. "It's a feeling in your gut and your heart. It's more than attraction and more than need. It's about connecting. It's about wanting to share everything for as long as you have on this earth."

Her words made him ache. Yes, he thought. He wanted that with Dellina. But how could he believe?

"Trust is hard," he said.

"It is." She led him to the sofa in her office and sat angled toward him. "We were all betrayed in different ways. The four of

440

us. We're so messed up. You with all your disasters. Kenny with, well, we know what happened there. Me with my father." She paused. "He used to hit me."

Sam hadn't known. "I'm sorry."

"It's okay. I got away and he's gone now. And Jack with his brother. Each one of us had been betrayed or hurt and that made us scared. Which means it comes down to a choice. What do you want, Sam? Do you want to be ruled by that fear? Or do you want to take a chance on a wonderful woman who's fallen madly in love with you?"

"She told you?"

"No. I could see it. We can all see it."

"I couldn't."

"You're an idiot." She spoke the words kindly. "I love you, Sam. You're my family. So I see the good and the bad in you. You're stubborn and set in your ways."

So much for expecting compliments. "Those sort of mean the same thing."

"Yeah, which is my point. Get that stick out of your ass and go tell her you love her back. Marry her and make beautiful babies together."

Was it as simple as that? Did he just *decide* to trust? Did he believe in Dellina be-cause . . . because . . .

"I'm in love with her."

Taryn rolled her eyes. "Hallelujah."

He stared at her. "You knew?"

"Yes. I knew. You escaped to her house when your parents were in town. You were upset when you missed the cat rescue and you've never cared much about Larissa's causes before. Dear God, Sam, you're helping local businesses *on purpose.* It's all Dellina." She patted his cheek. "Don't worry. Men are emotionally simple. You can't help it."

He grabbed her by her upper arms. "You don't understand. She told me she loved me and I walked away. How do I make that right? How do I fix it?"

Taryn sighed. "Wow. That was really stupid. You're going to have to go all out to make it up to her."

"Is it fixable?"

She smiled. "Of course it is. Angel did the same thing to me and I forgave him. Dellina loves you, you idiot. She's not going to lose you now. But we're going to need a plan."

Dellina smiled as she walked through the crowd. Faking normalcy wasn't too difficult. As long as she didn't think about Sam or missing him or how they were never going to be together, she could fake it pretty well.

She'd decided to make an appearance at the Book Festival so that no one would suspect she was breaking on the inside. Two hours, she'd told herself. Just two hours. Then she would retreat to her small house and sit with her cats and wait for her heart to stop hurting so much.

She crossed the street and headed for the park. There were booths everywhere — as there were at most festivals. Usually she indulged in something yummy, but these days she couldn't eat. Instead she concentrated on smiling and calling out greetings.

There were signs announcing various author signings all day today and tomorrow. She saw Larissa's booth right by the park. The big adopt a cat sign made the purpose clear. For those from out of town, an application with references was required. Even so, there was a line of people interested in talking about adopting one of the rescue kitties.

Dellina figured she was going to have to make a decision about her two. If she was keeping them, she needed to let Larissa know. Otherwise, they would be whisked away.

She saw Taryn and waved. The other woman walked over to her.

"How's it going?"

"Well," Dellina lied. "I have an actual Saturday off. It's exciting."

"I'll bet. Angel and I are going to have to decide what we want to do. I don't know. A big wedding sounds like a pain in the ass."

"Not if you let me handle it. Plus, think about the killer dress you could wear."

Taryn grinned. "I do love a killer dress." She glanced at her watch. "Come on. There's going to be a band onstage."

The stage in the park, Dellina thought, not really in the mood for music. "Thanks, but I need to be going."

"No, you don't. You're coming with me." Taryn sounded serious.

"Okay. Just for a few minutes." Because she could feel herself starting to fall apart. The last thing she wanted was to cry in front of Taryn. The other woman would want to know why and Dellina didn't want to tell her what had happened.

Taryn led the way to the stage and stopped right in front of it. "Wait here," she said.

"Wait for what?"

"You'll see."

A couple of minutes later, Mayor Marsha walked onto the stage.

"Welcome to our annual Book Festival," she said. "I hope you're all enjoying yourselves. We have an amazing lineup of authors with us this year."

People around them cheered.

"Good. Have a safe and happy weekend here in Fool's Gold. In case you haven't heard, we have a new town motto. The Destination for Romance. I have a few announcements before the afternoon program starts."

She went on to talk about the cats and the adoption booth. How there was no parking inside the festival zone and that the evening concert would start promptly at seven.

Dellina turned to Taryn. "You said there was a band this afternoon."

"Did I?" Taryn shrugged. "I must have been mistaken."

"My name is Sam Ridge."

Dellina spun back to face the stage and saw Sam had taken the microphone. Seeing him was the best and worst part of her day. She longed to feel his arms around her and, at the same time, wanted to run away and hide.

"What is he doing up there?" she asked.

"I guess we'll have to wait and find out."

"My business partners and I moved here last fall. We relocated our company, bought homes and settled into life here." His dark gaze scanned the crowd, then he found her.

"We made friends and some of us fell in love."

What? Did he mean him or her? Was he talking about himself? She found herself inching forward.

"A few weeks ago I was talking to a woman who had a great boyfriend. She wanted him to propose but rather than tell him that, she was trying to subtly show him what he should do."

"Men don't understand subtle," one woman yelled.

Sam smiled. "You're right. We don't. I told her that if she really loved the man in question, she had to be honest. Which is why I'm here today. To be honest with the woman I love."

Dellina froze in place. Her gaze locked with his. The need to run was gone. She wanted to stay exactly where she was. Only this was Sam and —

"You don't have to do this," she called out toward the stage. "Not publically. Sam, you'll hate it."

"I won't," he told her. "You deserve this." He returned his attention to the crowd. "I've had some bad luck with women in the past."

"We know," someone yelled. "We met your ex a couple of weeks ago."

Sam smiled. "Yeah, well, what can I say? I was young."

"And she was willing?"

"She was." His humor faded. "Unfortunately what I learned from her was not to trust. And that lesson was reinforced several times. So when I met a beautiful, bright, loving, giving woman, I wasn't prepared to trust her. I wasn't prepared for her to offer her heart." He looked down at her. "I was wrong, Dellina. About so many things. Mostly I was wrong not to recognize your love for the incredible gift it is."

She glanced to her right and saw stairs leading to the stage. She raced toward them, then ran up and joined him. He pulled her close.

"I love you," he said as he shoved the microphone back onto the stand. "I was a fool."

"It's okay. It's not like I changed my mind."

She stared into his eyes and saw the welcome there. He kissed her and she felt the promise on his lips. His arms were never going to let go.

"You still love me?" he asked.

"Yes. For always." She glanced at the people watching them. "But why like this? It's your nightmare — being so public."

"I figured you deserved witnesses." He cupped her face in his hands. "Will you marry me?"

She kissed him. "Of course. Oh, Sam." She straightened. "I have cats. At least, I think I do. Is that okay?"

He chuckled. "Sure. I could like cats."

"They're really nice."

"Hey," someone yelled. "What did she say?"

Sam reached for the microphone. "She said yes."

ABOUT THE AUTHOR

New York Times bestselling author **Susan Mallery** has entertained millions of readers with her witty and emotional stories about women and the relationships that move them. *Publishers Weekly* calls Susan's prose "luscious and provocative," and *Booklist* says, "Novels don't get much better than Mallery's expert blend of emotional nuance, humor and superb storytelling." While Susan appreciates the critical praise, she is most honored by the enthusiastic readers who write to tell her that her books made them laugh, made them cry, and made the world a happier place to live. Susan lives in Seattle with her husband and her tiny but intrepid toy poodle. She's there for the coffee, not the weather.